"Just saying thank you for everything you've done didn't seem quite enough."

Misty handed him a box of red velvet cupcakes. "These are just a token of my appreciation."

"You didn't have to go to all this trouble, but thank you." Leon was touched beyond words by her thoughtfulness. Misty wasn't the first woman to bring him baked goods, but unlike some of the others, she didn't have a hidden agenda.

"I am forever grateful, Leon."

He took a bite, then another. "Aunt Eleanor's right. You definitely know your way around a kitchen."

She laughed. "It's just a cupcake."

The look Misty gave him was so galvanizing it sent a tremor through him. The pounding of his heart quieted only once she disappeared outside.

Dear Reader,

I'm so excited to introduce my new series set on the fictional island of Polk Island, South Carolina, a small coastal town founded by Polk Rothchild in 1870. The lush green foliage, sandy beaches and well-maintained homes attract tourists from all over the world.

An unfortunate circumstance brings new resident Misty Brightwater into Leon Rothchild's life unexpectedly. Their initial meeting is tense, but eventually Leon and Misty discover they are destined to be a part of one another's lives.

This is a story of a love that was always meant to be, of new beginnings and finding the courage to take a second chance in love despite past experiences. I hope you will enjoy Leon and Misty's journey to their happily-ever-after. Thank you for your support, and I look forward to hearing from you.

Best,

Jacquelin Thomas

Facebook: Facebook.com/JacquelinWrites

Twitter: Twitter.com/JacquelinThomas

HEARTWARMING

A Family for the Firefighter

—

Jacquelin Thomas

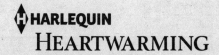

HARLEQUIN

HEARTWARMING

ISBN-13: 978-1-335-17988-3

A Family for the Firefighter

Recycling programs
for this product may
not exist in your area.

Jacquelin Thomas is an award-winning, bestselling author with more than fifty-five books in print. When not writing, she is busy catching up on her reading, attending sporting events and spoiling her grandchildren. Jacquelin and her family live in North Carolina.

Books by Jacquelin Thomas

Harlequin Kimani Romance

Five Star Attraction
Five Star Temptation
Legal Attraction
Five Star Romance
Five Star Seduction
Styles of Seduction
Wrangling Wes
Five Star Desire
Forever My Baby
Only for You
Return to Me
Another Chance with You

Visit the Author Profile page
at Harlequin.com for more titles.

CHAPTER ONE

TIRED AND HUNGRY, Leon Rothchild parked in the driveway of his aunt's home in the Victorian district of Polk Island a few minutes past 8:00 a.m. He'd just finished a twenty-four-hour shift at the local fire department. Whistling softly, he got out of the truck and walked past neatly trimmed rosebushes in pink, red and white to the steps of the wraparound porch. Perched on each side of the front door were Eleanor Rothchild Pittman's beloved Boston ferns. He paused in his tracks when he spied her keys still in the lock.

Aunt Eleanor forgot to take her keys inside... They'd probably been out here all night. He grabbed them and entered the house that he had grown up in.

"Hey... It's just me, Auntie." Leon always felt a sense of security whenever he visited his childhood home.

"C'mon to the kitchen, son," she called out in response. "You're just in time for breakfast."

He'd been fighting hunger pangs all morning, so her words were music to his ears.

The sound of bacon sizzling in the pan on the stove, the smell of fresh coffee and the stack of pancakes made Leon's mouth water.

Eleanor assessed him as he strolled into the kitchen. "Son, you look like you're losing weight. I don't know what they feed you at that station, but you need to come by here or the café every day to pick up a plate of food."

Laughter spilled from his lips as Leon embraced her. "Aunt Eleanor, I'm fine. You don't have to worry about me." Dangling her keys, he said, "But you're going to have me worrying about you. You really need to be more careful. We get a lot of strangers on the island."

"Oh, my goodness," she murmured. "I would've been running myself ragged looking for them." Eleanor took the keys and hung them on a hook beside the refrigerator.

When his parents died in a car accident twenty years ago, Eleanor and her husband, Walter, stepped up to care for Leon and his younger brother. He was ten years old at the time and Trey was eight. Four years later, Walter passed away. Bonded by blood and their grief, Eleanor and the boys clung tight to one another.

Leon picked up a plate and placed two slices of bacon and a small stack of pancakes on it.

"I'm glad you finally hired somebody for the bakery. You've been working some pretty long hours for the past couple of months." Leon poured himself a cup of coffee, then strode over to the table in the breakfast nook and sat down.

"Me, too," Eleanor stated. "She started earlier this week. She moved to Polk Island from Charleston. She's very dependable and the girl can *bake*..."

"Sounds like she's perfect for the job, then."

Eleanor pressed both hands over her eyes as if they burned with weariness. "It's perfect timing too with June right around the corner. I already have five contracts for wedding cakes. This month and the next are gwine be busy months. Polk Island, South Carolina, is becoming a popular spot for weddings. There was even a nice article in one of the bridal magazines about our little island."

The ringing of the telephone cut into their conversation.

"Hey, sugar... Your ears must've been burning. I was just talking about you..." Eleanor's left eyebrow rose a fraction. "Whoa... Slow down... I'm having trouble understanding you."

Leon blessed his food, but before he could take a bite, the change in Eleanor's tone caught his attention. When she hung up, he asked, "Everything okay?"

Worry colored her expression. "I'm not sure. I need to go to the shop, son. My new employee has a family emergency. Silas isn't coming in until noon. Josh can't handle the morning rush alone. Finish eating your breakfast." Eleanor picked up her purse and keys. "Just put everything in the dishwasher when you're done."

"You're finally using it?" Leon asked in amazement. She'd put up a fuss when he first purchased it for her nearly two years ago. His aunt had insisted it could never clean her dishes as well as she could.

Eleanor broke into a grin. "I've seen the light."

He chuckled.

She planted a kiss on his cheek. "Love you, son."

"I love you too, Auntie."

Leon returned his attention to the food on his plate.

TEARS BLINDING HER eyes and choking her voice, Misty Brightwater rushed into the day care. "How could you just let my ex-husband walk in here and take my daughter? I should've been notified the moment he arrived." She struggled to keep her voice at a normal volume to avoid upsetting any of the children.

The woman working the front desk uttered, "I had no idea… I'm so sorry."

"I made it clear to the director that John didn't have permission to ever take Talei from here. He has *supervised* visitation only." Misty put a hand to her mouth to keep from screaming as her heart pounded rapidly. After a moment, she said, "I've called the police. They should be here any minute."

"I'm so sorry, Miss Brightwater. I didn't know."

"Where's Mrs. Washington?" Misty asked. She grappled to keep the panic she felt from her voice. She was working at Polk Island Bakery & Café when John called to let her know he had their daughter and was going to disappear. "I wouldn't have known a thing if my ex-husband hadn't called me."

"Mrs. Washington left to pick up some supplies, but she should be back soon. I really am sorry. There wasn't a note in the system."

"Well, there should've been," Misty stated.

The thought of Talei being with John terrified Misty. His actions of late had caused her to take certain precautions to avoid exactly what just happened.

Twenty-six years old, Misty had moved to Polk Island three weeks ago to build a new life for her and her three-year-old daughter, Talei.

When she and John were first married, Misty used to ride with him in his delivery truck to different towns, including Polk Island. She fell in love with the small-town charm of the place. After their divorce was final, she decided to put down roots here. It was the perfect place to raise Talei.

At least she thought so at the time.

LEON LOCKED UP his aunt's house and climbed into his car. He was so tired his nerves throbbed. The May air blowing hot through the open windows of his truck did nothing to stop the sweat dampening his neck and chest. Leon made a mental note to take his truck to the shop to have the air conditioner checked out before the hot weather took over. He considered stopping by his mechanic right now, but he really wasn't up for it.

Leon was exhausted. He never slept well whenever he had to stay at the station. At the moment, he was looking forward to a shower and his bed. A couple of hours of sleep would do him a world of good.

A cow darted out into the middle of the road just as a car was speeding up the road. Stomach churning, Leon watched the events unfold as if in slow motion.

The Mercedes Benz GLS 580 connected full

force with the animal before it careened off the road and smashed into a huge oak tree, stopping the car.

Leon quickly pulled off the road and parked. His heart fluttered hard against his ribs. He took a deep breath, then exhaled to calm himself. Certified as an EMT, he called 9-1-1 as he rushed over to the vehicle to check on the occupants inside.

"There's been an accident on Highway 171," Leon said when someone answered. "I have a male unconscious. Massive head trauma, extrication necessary... John..." he uttered, recognizing his friend. For a moment, he forgot to breathe. "Thirty-year-old male."

The sound of a child screaming hysterically commandeered his attention.

Leon's gaze swept to the back seat. A little girl strapped in a car seat sobbed and trembled with fear. He worked swiftly to get to her. "It's gonna be okay, little one," he murmured. Faced with the choice of whom to care for first, Leon chose to remove the child. John's injuries were life-threatening, which made performing triage in the field impossible.

Talei... John's daughter...

"There's a toddler in the vehicle, as well," he told the operator who was on speaker.

He laid the phone on top of the vehicle to free

the little girl from the restraints of the car seat and checked for visible injuries. "She's scared but looks okay otherwise."

Leon's emotions were all over the place when she stopped crying and clung to him for dear life. "We're gonna get your daddy some help," he whispered while keeping John out of his daughter's view.

"Daddee..." she said, her eyes bright with un-shed tears. "I w-want Da... Daddy. I...s-scared."

Leon's heart broke at the stark fear he saw in her eyes. "You're safe, Talei. I promise."

Teary-eyed, she looked up at him.

"My name is Leon. I'm a friend of your daddy."

"Eon," she said in a trembling voice. "I scared."

He took her tiny hand in his. "You don't have to be afraid."

Leon glanced over his shoulder at his friend and prayed help would arrive soon. He released a short sigh when he heard sirens. "Hang in there, buddy. Paramedics are coming. I have your little girl and she's fine. Hang in there." He could see the fire engine moving swiftly to-ward them. He knew an ambulance would be close behind.

The paramedics arrived seconds later, fol-lowed by a police car.

Leon gestured for a female coworker to come over. He was more than a little relieved to hand over the little girl to someone else. Had his own daughter lived, she would've been the same age. It was too much of a painful reminder.

"This is my friend Lizzie. She's going to stay with you so I can help your daddy."

"Help D-Daddy."

"Hey, sweetie. I have this little guy for you." Lizzie gave Talei a teddy bear wearing a T-shirt with the fire station logo emblazoned on it. "He's gonna be right here with you, and so am I."

His coworker Charles asked, "You know the driver?"

"Yep. He's the friend I told you about. His name is John Hayes."

Leon and John had been roommates in college until John was forced to withdraw from school to help his father with the family trucking business in Orangeburg, South Carolina. He was shocked seeing John and wondered when he'd arrived on the island. Normally, his friend would notify him whenever he was coming to the area.

Leon walked with Charles to the damaged vehicle, where they were in the process of extricating John.

"This doesn't look good," he mouthed under his breath.

Charles placed a comforting hand on his shoulder. While he stood there, random thoughts circulated in his mind. Leon recalled the moment when John asked him to be Talei's godfather. He couldn't accept at the time because it was too soon after the death of his own wife and child. Leon wasn't able to attend John's wedding because he'd just started training with the fire department, so he never had the opportunity to meet his ex-wife.

In recent months, John often confided his struggles and frustration in wanting to get his family back together. He'd shared with Leon that his marriage had been a tumultuous one. He blamed his ex-wife for being selfish and thinking only of herself.

Once John was extricated, paramedics transported both him and his little girl to the hospital. Talei put up a fuss when they put her in the ambulance, but she calmed eventually when Lizzie promised to ride to the hospital with her. They decided it was best to transport John in a separate ambulance.

Leon gave the police an overview of what happened, then he was free to leave.

Exhausted and emotionally drained, Leon headed in the direction of his home but turned around abruptly and drove to the hospital instead. There was no point in going home when his thoughts were of John and Talei.

A notification came across his phone. It was an Amber Alert for Talei Hayes.

"John, what did you do?" Leon whispered, bewildered. "They're acting like you kidnapped your daughter."

At the hospital, he spoke briefly with a nurse who informed him that his friend was taken to the trauma center.

His stomach in knots, Leon dialed the number to Hayes Trucking. "Hello… I need to speak with Elroy regarding his son. Tell him it's Leon Rothchild calling."

Elroy came on the phone a minute later. "Hey, it's good to hear from you…"

"John's been in an accident," Leon quickly interjected. "He's at Polk Island Hospital."

"What happened?"

"A cow ran into the middle of the road… His daughter was with him."

"Is Talei…" Elroy's voice broke.

"No… She's fine," Leon quickly assured Elroy. "She's scared, as you can imagine, but no injuries. But John's in serious condition."

"Clara and I will be heading your way within the hour. Keep me posted on my son, Leon, until we arrive."

"I will."

Leon hung up and placed another call. "Aunt Eleanor, I'm at the hospital. John was in an accident. He's in bad shape."

"Oh, honey, I'm gonna pray for him."

"They're saying he kidnapped his daughter. I need to speak with the sheriff. It has to be a misunderstanding."

"Lawd, noo," Eleanor moaned.

"What's wrong?" Leon inquired.

"Misty's little girl was taken by her daddy. That's why I rushed over here to the shop."

He was stunned. "Is her name Talei?"

"Yes."

Leon couldn't believe it. There had to be an explanation. "John wouldn't do something like this, Auntie. I've known him a long time."

"The man Misty described sure doesn't sound like the one I got to know and love," Eleanor said. "I had no idea that she was even married to John Hayes. She never mentioned his name."

"I called his parents. He's in surgery right now, but I thought they should know what happened."

"Of course they should," Eleanor agreed. "Sugar, how are you doing?"

"I don't know what to do with all this," Leon confessed. "When I last saw John, he mentioned taking his daughter on a trip. I knew he and his ex were fighting for custody, but he led me to believe that they had worked everything out."

"I can't believe he'd just take his daughter like that," Eleanor said. "John must've felt pretty desperate."

"There are two sides to this story—that's for sure," Leon stated.

"When Silas comes to work, I'll come to the hospital to sit with you."

"Thanks, Auntie."

Leon heard Talei crying for her mother. He walked in quick strides toward her room.

As soon as the little girl saw him, she reached for him.

Leon hesitated a moment, unsure whether he should pick her up, but the fear on her face propelled him into action. He took her into his arms. "Talei, hey. It's alright. You're safe. This nurse just wants to make sure you're okay. Her name is Amy."

Sniffling, Talei eyed him as a lone tear rolled down her cheek.

"Leon, how does she know you?"

"Her father is my friend. Were you able to make contact with her mother?"

"She's on the way," Amy responded. "Do you think you can stay with this little princess while I check her out?"

He nodded.

"I want M-Mommy," Talei whimpered.

"She will be here soon," Leon said. Stark fear glimmered in Talei's eyes. He just wanted to make her feel safe.

"Daddy...c-car..."

"The doctor's taking good care of him," Amy told her. "Can you tell me who this is on your dress?"

"Minty M-Mouse."

"I love Minnie Mouse." Smiling, Amy continued to check Talei's vitals. "I love Mickey Mouse, too."

"Mickey and Minty on TV."

"Yes, they are. Would you like to watch some television?"

Talei nodded.

Amy turned to the Disney Channel. "Here you go, cutie."

"Wado," she whispered when the nurse left the room.

Wado. Leon recalled a conversation he'd had with John. His friend had boasted about his daughter learning the Cherokee language and traditions. He'd also confided that his father was against it—Elroy Hayes thought it disgraceful that his daughter-in-law had dismissed her Black heritage by choosing to live as a Native.

Leon sat on the bed with Talei on his lap. Mickey and Minnie Mouse danced across the screen, but the little girl remained strangely quiet. Every now and then she would jump at the sound of a loud noise.

"I scared," she mumbled.

"I'm not gonna let anything hurt you," Leon assured her. "Your mom will be here soon, but until she gets here, I'm not gonna leave you, little one."

She turned to look at him. "Eon… I want Daddy."

"He would be here with you, but he got hurt, so the doctor has to take care of him."

"Doctor make him better?"

"Yes. The doctor's going to take care of him."

Amy entered the room.

"Leon…" She placed her hand on his shoulder. "I'm sorry."

He felt the familiar stirrings of sadness. He knew John's condition was serious, but still he'd hoped and prayed for a positive outcome.

"He didn't make it," Amy said softly.

Leon fought back tears. "Thanks for letting me know." A raw and primitive grief overwhelmed him.

He glanced down at Talei, who looked to be falling asleep. When Leon tried to lay her down in the hospital bed, she began crying again.

"I'm here, sweetie. I'm not going anywhere.

I just wanted to make you comfortable. You look sleepy."

Talei clung to him, her dark curly puffs of hair tickling his neck.

"Okay, little one." Leon held her close to his heart.

Talei's eyelids grew heavy. She fought her exhaustion, but eventually drifted off to sleep.

Leon swallowed hard as he rocked gently back and forth.

John was dead. His friend was gone.

Anguish threatened to overwhelm him. His heart hadn't fully healed from the deaths of Vera and his own child. It was still broken into so many fragments, he wasn't sure it could handle another loss.

CHAPTER TWO

FEAR AND ANGER knotting inside her, Misty parked in the first available spot she could find near the emergency room. She nearly lost her footing when rushing out of the car, but she didn't let that stop her from running.

At the main registration desk, she demanded, "*Where's my daughter?* Her name is Talei Hayes."

The woman directed her to room 230.

When she neared the nurses' station, a doctor approached. "Are you John Hayes's next of kin?"

"Yes."

They found a quiet place to talk. "We did all we could, but John passed away while we were performing surgery. I'm very sorry."

"Where's my daughter?" Misty asked a second time, her voice rising an octave. "I want to see my little girl."

"Mrs. Hayes…"

"My last name is Brightwater. John and I are divorced." Misty eyed the doctor, shifting indignantly from foot to foot. "Look, I can't deal with his death right now. I just need to be with my child. She's probably terrified, and I need to be with her."

At the moment, she didn't care what anyone thought of her actions. Her focus was only on reuniting with Talei. Misty was devastated at the news of John's death, but she couldn't think about that now. He'd made her life miserable.

SHE WALKED BRISKLY toward the room, resisting the urge to break into a run. She burst in without knocking and was shocked to see a man holding and comforting her daughter. "Hello," she greeted. "Who are you?"

"I'm Leon Rothchild. I witnessed the accident."

She gave him a wry appraisal. "You're John's friend. You went to college together."

"Yeah, I am," he confirmed. "I just found out that you work with my aunt at the bakery. I called her earlier to tell her about John."

"Miss Eleanor was kind enough to give me a job when I needed one." Misty took her sleeping child out of his arms without preamble.

"She fell asleep about ten minutes ago."

They stared at each other.

His face was bronzed by long hours in the sun. Dark compelling eyes framed his handsome square face—Leon held his head high with pride. Misty noted how his long, muscled legs filled out the dark jeans, and the navy T-shirt with the fire department logo emblazoned across it pulled taut over his broad torso. His profile spoke of power and strength, but she was drawn by the sadness of his face.

As the silence stretched out, Misty grew more and more uncomfortable. She chewed on her bottom lip, while Leon stood so still, she could barely make out the slight rise and fall of his chest as he breathed.

After a moment, Misty said, "You said that you were there when the accident happened."

"Yeah. A cow ran out into the road. All John could do was swerve to keep from hitting the animal. I didn't know it was him at the time. I was the first person on the scene."

"It's fortunate that you of all people were there." Misty gestured to his shirt. "Being a firefighter and all."

"Yeah," Leon responded. "I just wish I could've done more."

"They told me when I got here that John died on the operating table." Holding her daughter close, she said, "I wanted to see Talei. I needed to be sure she was okay."

He leaned forward in his chair, and in a controlled voice, stated, "The police are saying he kidnapped her."

Misty eyed him as if trying to read his expression. "It's true. John took her from day care without my permission."

His eyes flickered a little. "I don't understand."

"John was upset over the judge's decision. I was given sole physical custody and he had supervised visitation."

Leon shook his head in dismay. "I know that John never would've hurt that little girl," he responded. "He loved his daughter."

"You don't really know the kind of man he was…"

Leon rose in one fluid motion. "I'll leave you to spend time with your daughter."

The tense lines on her face relaxed. "Thank you for everything."

"I'm just sorry things didn't turn out better for John. His parents are on the way here. I don't know whether to call and tell them that he's gone or just wait until they get here."

"It won't matter," Misty said. "It's not going to go well at all. They just lost their son."

LEON HADN'T EXPECTED to be struck by Misty's beauty or her generous mouth, which he found incredibly inviting. She had a curvy build, and her black hair flowed past her shoulders in soft waves. Her coppery-brown skin glowed from the sheen of perspiration. She wore a pair of faded jeans and a loose, floral-printed top.

That awareness of Misty; even the unfamiliar compulsion Leon had to stare at her was unlike him. It unsettled him in her presence. "I guess I'll go make that call."

He walked briskly out of the room just as his aunt was fast approaching.

"I came as quickly as I could," Eleanor said. She took a moment to catch her breath before asking, "How is Talei?"

"The doctor says she's fine physically. She fell asleep when I was holding her." Leon glanced over his shoulder toward the room. "Her mother's in there with Talei now."

Eleanor looked visibly relieved by the news. "How's John?"

"He didn't make it, Auntie. I'm about to call his parents now." Leon's stomach clenched tight. This was not a call he ever wanted to make, but he had to be the one to do it—he owed John that much.

Tears welled in Eleanor's eyes. "Nooo…" she moaned softly.

"Talei and her mom are in room 230. I'll be right back after I make this call."

Leon found a quiet area near the waiting

room where he could inform John's parents of the sad news.

After the difficult call, he walked back to the hospital room and peeked inside.

Eleanor and Misty appeared to be in deep conversation, so he decided to give them some privacy.

He wandered to the waiting room and sat down to wait for John's parents to arrive. The muscles of his forearm hardened as he clenched his hand so fiercely that his nails dug into his palm.

Leon sat there silently for a long time. He hated hospitals. He had been in this one too many times, and all of the memories were tragic. He became a firefighter to save people. It pained him that when it came to those he loved, he wasn't able to help any of them.

"HIS PARENTS NEVER thought I was good enough for John," Misty told Eleanor as they sat in the room waiting for Talei to wake up. They were careful to keep their voices down. "I'm not sure why. I've never done anything to them."

"From all you've told me, it seems like it's more your father-in-law who has something against you. Not Clara," Eleanor responded.

"Elroy is a mean-spirited, controlling jerk who thinks the best way to deal with people is by being abusive. I once asked John if his father was abused growing up because that would explain why he acted the way he did... Miss Eleanor, he got so angry with me."

"I can't believe John could do something like this."

Misty nodded as she tried to sheath her inner feelings. "That's why I divorced him. I grew up in an abusive home, and there's no way I was going to allow my daughter to go through that." She paused a moment before confessing, "I'm so angry with John right now for taking Talei, but I never wanted him to die."

"Sugar, I'm so sorry."

"I was so in love with John—from the moment I met him. I thought he was the perfect man for me, Miss Eleanor. But then I realized John wasn't happy," Misty said. "I used to tell him that he needed to get some professional help, but John would become furious with me. I really wanted our marriage to work. However, the verbal abuse was nonnegotiable for me."

"I'd have to say I would've done the same thing."

Misty gently stroked her daughter's cheek. "I'm so grateful to your nephew for being there when the accident happened."

"Leon is a good man and he's always been the type of person to help others," Eleanor said.

"As a child he would recue animals, assist the elderly. His degree is in criminal justice, so I thought he'd be in law enforcement, but I wasn't surprised when he decided to become a fire-fighter."

"John told me that Leon lost his wife and a child."

"Yeah, losing Vera and baby Selena nearly took him out of this world. Leon shut down, and even now he's still not the man he used to be. He works hard. That's all he does. *Work.* I think he does it to keep from thinking about all he's lost."

An image of Leon's handsome face swam before Misty anew, along with the unexpected impact of his sad, dark eyes. Despite everything she'd gone through, she was still a woman who appreciated a gorgeous man.

He was a grieving widower, she reminded herself. Definitely not her type.

Two hours later, Elroy Hayes burst through the doors of the emergency room pulling his wife, Clara, along behind him.

Leon approached, walking swiftly. He gestured for the doctor to join him.

"Where's my son?" Elroy asked. "I want to see him now."

The physician standing beside Leon went on

to explain, "We did everything we could to save your son… "

Leon had to put some distance between him and the doctor's words. He couldn't bear to hear it a second time. He waited near the nurses' station for John's parents.

Her slender frame seemed fragile as Clara walked over to him with shoulders slumped, arms folded across her chest and tears glistening on her heart-shaped face. "Where's my granddaughter?"

"She's sleeping right now," Leon stated. "Her mother is with her."

When Elroy joined them, he led them toward Talei's room.

"Misty is the reason John is dead," Elroy uttered as they stood in the hallway. His angry eyes were wet with unshed tears.

"I had nothing to do with your son's death," Misty said, her voice thick. She strode up to them with Eleanor. "John took my daughter without permission and had an accident. Elroy, whether you believe me or not, I hate that he's gone. I was hoping we'd find a way to co-parent Talei."

"I don't believe that for a minute," Elroy shot back, sending Misty a sharp glare. He stood in front of her, his stance intended to be intimidating. "You wanted John out of that child's life—that's why you took him to court and took away his rights. I warned him about marrying you in the first place. John should've just listened to me."

Misty didn't flinch. She boldly met his gaze, saying, "I'm sorry for the pain you're going through, but I'm not going to stand here while you badmouth me. When you can control your anger, then you're more than welcome to see your granddaughter." Not wanting to cause a scene, she turned to walk away, but paused long enough to say to Clara, "I'm really sorry for your loss."

Misty went back into Talei's hospital room.

Shocked by Elroy's behavior, Leon placed a hand on his shoulder. "I know you're hurting right now, but she's not responsible for what happened to John. It was a tragic accident." He knew grief was causing Elroy to strike out like that. Unfortunately, Misty was the closest target.

"If she'd just let John have his daughter, none of this would've happened. I told him to let the attorney handle everything."

Eleanor eyed Leon but remained silent. He could tell by the expression on her face that she was struggling to keep silent. She had a low tolerance for people like Elroy. After a moment of tense silence, she uttered, "I'm gwine check on Misty."

She walked with purpose into room 230.

Leon had known John's parents for a long time. Elroy was always belligerent and controlling, but he was stunned by the man's treatment of Misty.

Looking about ready to explode, Elroy stalked off to speak with someone at the nurses' station.

"Leon, my husband's in a lot of pain," Clara said. She gulped hard, hot tears slipping down her cheeks. "We're both in such agony. Our son is gone."

"I understand that, but it doesn't give him the right to talk to Misty that way. John was the one in the wrong here."

Leon caught a flash of hurt in her eyes.

"She gave my son no choice. You understand? I don't know how well you know Misty, but she's just as stubborn as John. Sure, he made mistakes as a husband, but I know for a fact that she wouldn't let him forget his shortcomings."

"She's the mother of your granddaughter," Leon said. "You don't want to alienate Misty."

Clara shrugged. "I know, but Elroy can't stand the girl. It won't be easy to change his mind about Misty after all that's happened." Swiping at a lone tear, she said, "I love Talei and I'm not gonna let anyone stop me from being in my granddaughter's life, even if it means going against my husband."

CHAPTER THREE

LEON CHECKED ON Talei while Elroy and Clara went to say a final goodbye to John. He had to escape the heart-wrenching sobs coming from the grieving mother.

He knocked on the door of Talei's room.

"Come in."

Misty was sitting beside the bed where her daughter lay sleeping. Eleanor sat in the chair near the window.

"How are you holding up?" Leon inquired.

"I'm numb right now," Misty responded. "I feel terrible for Clara, but Elroy—that hateful man makes it so hard for me to feel anything but disdain for him."

"This is a sad situation all around…"

"One that I'd rather not talk about." Misty picked up the teddy bear. "Tell me, Leon. What made you become a firefighter?" Although Eleanor had given her some insight, she wanted to hear directly from him.

"My dad," Leon responded. "I'm second generation. I used to love going to the station with my father, but it wasn't until I was in college that I realized I wanted to be a firefighter."

"My dad was a volunteer firefighter," Eleanor said. "I don't know if I ever told you that, Leon. I just remember him helping when that fire nearly destroyed the house two doors down from the old church."

"Are you talking about the Praise House?" Misty inquired. "I've heard a couple of people mention it."

Eleanor nodded.

Just then Talei woke up and saw her mother. "Mommy…"

"Hey, baby…"

Talei's gaze slid to where Leon stood. She smiled, then reached for him.

Leon felt a warm glow flow through him at her response to him and picked her up.

"I told you I'd keep you safe, little one."

She held up the teddy bear for him to see. "Eon."

Rising to her feet, Eleanor said, "I'm gwine to the cafeteria to get something to drink. Y'all want anything?"

"I'm fine," Misty responded.

"*Fench* fries," Talei interjected before reaching for her mother.

Leon chuckled as he put her down and pulled out his wallet. "Would you get the little one some French fries, Auntie?"

Misty opened her purse, but he stopped her. "I got it. It's my treat."

"Thank you."

"I'll be right back, sweetie." Eleanor walked out into the hall.

"John enjoyed being a dad," said Leon when they were alone in the room.

"Did he tell you that?" Misty inquired.

"He didn't have to tell me," Leon stated, "I could hear it in his voice whenever he talked about Talei."

"You look a lot like your father," Misty said, changing the subject. She didn't want to become emotional while talking about John. His death was beginning to have an effect on her. "Miss Eleanor has a picture of your parents in her office."

"She and my dad were very close. I know she misses him as much as I do. My whole family is pretty close-knit." Leon met her gaze. "What's it like to be the new star of the Polk Island Bakery & Café?"

She smiled. "I don't know about all that, but I do love my job."

They continued their small talk until Eleanor returned with a drink, French fries and a juice box.

Talei clapped her hands in glee. "*Wado*, Miss Ellie."

"It's Tsalagi… Cherokee for *thank you*," Misty explained. Her expression suddenly became tense when she heard Elroy's voice outside the room.

Seconds later, Clara stuck her head inside. "Is it okay if we come in to see Talei?"

"Yes, of course," Misty responded.

Talei seemed thrilled to see her grandparents. "Granma… Paw Paw…"

"I'm going to head on home," Leon told Misty. "I'm glad Talei is fine and I'm sorry for your loss."

"I really appreciate everything you did today."

He smiled. "It's nice to finally meet you, Misty. I'm sorry it was under these conditions."

"Same here. I'm sure it won't be the last time I see you. The island's not that big."

Leon smiled. "No, it's not."

He hugged Eleanor, then Clara, before leaving the room.

Leon strode toward the hospital exit with purpose. His body ached with weariness; he just wanted to go home, shower and relax. He needed to process everything that had happened today.

MISTY AND ELEANOR sat in a small waiting area to give Elroy and Clara some time with Talei.

"I hope the doctor releases her soon. I'm so ready to take my baby home and get her settled." Misty sighed. "To be honest, I'd like to go back to bed and start this day all over again."

Eleanor chuckled. "If only it was that easy."

"Thank you for coming to support me. I'm not sure I would've gotten through all this without you."

"It's my pleasure, Misty." Eleanor stood up. "I'm gwine go relieve Josh at the shop. You take tomorrow off and spend it with Talei. Make sure she's okay."

The two women embraced.

Just as Eleanor was about to leave, Elroy and his wife walked out of Talei's hospital room. "Maybe I'll hang around a lil longer," she told Misty.

"Talei was asking for her daddy. Isn't that right, Clara?"

His wife nodded. "I didn't know what to say to her."

"She's too young to really understand," Misty said. John's parents were heartbroken and grieving, so, she was careful with her words. "Talei knows about heaven, so I guess we can just say he's up there."

"We wouldn't have to have this discussion at

all," Elroy said, "if you hadn't run away with Talei."

"I didn't run away. I moved here to start a new life in peace," Misty stated. "*Something I didn't have in Orangeburg*. Miss Eleanor offered me a chance to do what I've always loved doing and I accepted the job."

"You knew taking Talei from John would destroy my son," Elroy hissed. "You're selfish and you never cared about what he wanted. You humiliated my son."

"That was *you*," Misty responded, struggling to keep her temper in check. "It was your controlling ways that destroyed your son."

"Emotions are running high right now," Eleanor interjected. "Misty, I think I hear Talei calling for you. Why don't you go check on your daughter?"

She gave Eleanor a grateful nod, then walked into her daughter's room.

"Did I hear correctly that she works for you?" Elroy asked, his brow pulled into an affronted frown.

"She does."

A muscle flickered angrily at his jaw. "You might want to watch her—she can't be trusted."

Eleanor eyed Clara and asked, "Is there anything I can do for you?"

Elroy wasn't going to be ignored. "Can you bring John back?"

"You shouldn't talk to Eleanor this way," Clara said. "None of this is her fault."

He sent his wife a sharp glare.

"It's fine," Eleanor stated. "I understand grief and the many ways it can affect a person. We're all sad about losing John, but right now we need to try to come together for Talei. The last thing she needs is to see what's left of her family fussing and carryin' on like this. That little girl needs every one of y'all. Try to remember that."

Elroy eyed her.

She stared back until he looked away.

"Please tell me they're gone," Misty said when Eleanor returned to the room. "The doctor released Talei and I just want to take her home."

"They left." Eleanor shook her head in dismay. "That man… He started to get on my last nerve. I don't know how Clara puts up with him. I've never seen anyone so embittered and angry with the world."

"He's always like that, which makes everyone uneasy around him," Misty said. "The strangest thing is that he's a completely different man with Talei. He adores his granddaughter—that's about the only good thing I can say about him."

Misty picked up her purse. "C'mon, sweetie…

Let's get you home. We've both had a very long day."

In the parking lot, she said, "Thanks so much for being here for me."

Eleanor embraced her. "It's my pleasure. You sure you're okay?"

She nodded. "I called my mother and she's coming to the island to spend a couple of days with us. I'll be fine."

Deep down, Misty wasn't as confident as she wanted Eleanor to believe. She was faced with having to raise her daughter alone. Although she and John had been at odds, she never thought he wouldn't be around to be a father to Talei.

AT HOME, LEON wandered from room to room. He felt restless, unsettled and his mood heavy.

He recalled the day he and Vera moved into this house. John had come up with his truck to help with the move. Leon leaned in the doorway of the master bedroom.

"This is the room where the Rothchild legacy will continue," John had proclaimed that day. "Make lots of beautiful babies."

Shaking his head sadly, Leon walked down the stairs to the first level.

He spent the rest of the evening going through his college photo album. It was still difficult for him to believe that John had gone as far as to kidnap his daughter. He sat down on the sofa, his thoughts traveling back to one of the many conversations he'd had with his friend.

"It was thoughtless of me to ask you to be my daughter's godfather in light of all you had to deal with. I should've realized that you were still grieving the passing of Vera and little Selena, but I want you to know my offer still stands. Whenever you're ready. If something ever happens to me, I want you to be there for Talei."

"I'll do what I can, John."

"Is it getting any better for you?"

"I still wake up expecting to see Vee." Leon picked up the napkin and wiped his mouth. *"I still haven't packed up her stuff or the baby's room."*

"I can come over to help you," John offered.

Leon shook his head. *"You need to spend every moment you have working on your relationship with your wife and being a father to that little girl of yours. Life is fleeting."*

"Sometimes I think that getting married was a mistake, Leon," John blurted. *"I don't think either of us was ready."*

"Why do you say that?"

"I proposed three months after we started dating and we got married eight weeks later. We should've spent more time getting to know

*one another. We rushed into this whole mar-
riage thing."*

*"Marriage is hard work, John. Now that
you're divorced, I think it's an even bigger challenge to have a positive relationship with your
ex-wife."*

The sound of the telephone ringing cut into
his thoughts.

"Hello."

"Hey, sugar. I'm just leaving the hospital."

"Is Talei okay?"

"Yes," Eleanor said. "They released her, so
Misty's taking her home right now."

He settled back against the cushions, trying
to get comfortable. "And John's parents? Are
they still there?"

"They left," Eleanor said. "Son, that Elroy…"

"He's not an easy man by any means, but he
loves his family." Leon had no idea why he kept
making excuses for Elroy's behavior. Maybe it
was because he felt bad for the man.

"I have to tell you. I can't stand the way he
treats Misty. It ain't right by no means."

Still trying to stay neutral, Leon said, "We
don't know their history. Maybe there's a reason he responds to her like that."

"You and I see things very different on this
situation."

"I don't agree with his actions, Auntie. I'm

just taking into consideration that Elroy lost his son. I think we should give him some slack."

"I would agree with you, but the same should go for Misty. She lost the father of her child."

"There are no winning sides," Leon stated. "If I could've talked to John, I'm sure I could've gotten him to return Talei to her mother. If only that cow hadn't run out into the road, things would be different right now."

"We can't change what happened, son. No matter how much we may want to, we just can't."

Leon released a long sigh. "Auntie, I know that from personal experience. Like I said, nobody wins."

CHAPTER FOUR

AFTER A BUBBLE BATH, Talei climbed into her mother's bed and was asleep within minutes. Misty decided to let her stay there in case she had a bad dream. She knew her daughter would experience some depth of trauma after such a frightening experience.

Now that she was in a quiet place of peace, Misty could take a moment to allow her emotions free rein.

She sat down on the padded window seat in her bedroom and stared outside. Stars were carefully sprinkled across the sky so as not to upstage the moon as it shone brightly against the blanket of darkness.

Pen in hand, Misty reached for the journal that lay open. There was so much she wanted to say, but she didn't know where to start.

Her stomach churned with nervous energy. Talei was safe, but John was gone. Misty thought about the way she'd responded to his death at the hospital and felt a thread of guilt snake down her spine.

Teary-eyed, she began to write:

Today I lost the man I once thought I'd spend the rest of my life with. John had a lot of problems, but I always hoped he'd overcome them. All we ever really wanted to do was love each other—instead we ended up hurting one another. My heart is sad that John is no longer here; that he won't get to see his little girl grow up. He won't see her graduate high school or college; he won't be here to walk her down the aisle on her wedding day.

I was so angry with him for taking our daughter—I didn't want to care that he'd gotten hurt in the accident. In a way, I felt justified, but it lasted not even a minute. It was more of a passing thought. What lingered in my mind is whether or not John would be able to rest eternally knowing what he'd done.

John acted out of desperation, and in part I feel responsible. My intentions were to protect my daughter at all costs, giving no thought as to how it would affect him. Now I have to live with the question of whether I made the right choice in seeking supervised visitation. I know he didn't want me to leave Orangeburg, but that place gave me no peace—the environment was too toxic. I wanted to be away from his parents, more so that father of his. I wanted to get away from John because I got tired of him just show-

*ing up whenever he wanted to my home. I also
wanted to be closer to my mother because she
made me feel safe.*

Was this a selfish decision?

Is John's death my fault?

MISTY THOUGHT ABOUT her father and how he
never once tried to reach out to her or her
mother, Oma, after they left Atlanta. He didn't
contest the divorce. It was as if he had washed
his hands of the two of them.

She was glad he was no longer a part of their
lives, but she felt the sting of his abandonment.
It was clear he didn't love her enough to try to
change for the better. He didn't love her mother
enough to fight for the marriage.

There were times when she heard her mom
crying over the breakup of her marriage. Misty
had even overheard Oma confiding her heartache to her own mother. She'd loved Michael
Taylor and once believed he was the love of
her life.

After the divorce, Oma had both her and
Misty's surname changed legally to her maiden
name. She was done with Michael and wanted
a fresh start.

Over the years, there were no interactions
with his family. When Oma called her former mother-in-law, she was told that Michael

didn't want his family communicating with her. Misty's grandmother thought it was best to appease her son by forsaking her granddaughter.

She shrugged, trying to shake off the hurtful jabs of rejection piercing her heart.

"Talei and I are fine," she whispered.

We don't need them. I have my mom and my daughter, and they have me. This is enough.

The doorbell sounded.

Misty rushed down the staircase to open the door for her mother.

"I'm so glad you're here," she said, falling into Oma's embrace.

"Why didn't you call me earlier? I would've come straight away."

"So much was happening at the time, Mama."

Oma sat down her tote. "I'm going to make you some tea to help you relax. Where's Talei?"

"She's in my bed sleeping."

They walked to the kitchen.

Oma washed her hands. "I'm sorry about John."

"Mama, he's gone, and I don't know how to explain to my daughter that he's never coming back." Tears fell from her eyes.

Her mother embraced her a second time. "I'm so sorry."

Misty gave in to the sobs that had been threatening to consume her.

Two days later, Leon walked into the Polk Island Bakery & Café for breakfast, where he was greeted by the aroma of coffee, baked goods and an assortment of meats. He was always assaulted with a sense of nostalgia whenever he came here—the shop that had been in his family for a couple of generations. He'd spent a lot of time in this place over the years with friends and family, eating, talking and laughing. He'd brought past girlfriends here on date nights. He and Vera used to come here often.

The shop was the setting for people looking to find ways to make their lives better. It was a place where solutions to problems were discovered; a place to enjoy company. For Leon, it was a fragment of heaven.

A line had already formed to order coffee and herbal tea drinks. He sat at an empty table in the center facing the door on the right and the kitchen on the left.

He glanced around looking for his aunt. He glimpsed Misty in the kitchen and waved in greeting. The plastic cap on her head, no makeup and the apron she was wearing did nothing to diminish her natural beauty. He could tell that she wasn't a slave to fashion, but he had no doubt Misty cleaned up well. Her job required comfortable, functional clothing and shoes.

Waving back, Misty rewarded him a tentative smile.

"I didn't expect to see you here today," he said when Misty came to his table a few minutes later.

"I couldn't just sit home another day. I need to keep busy," she responded. "It takes my mind off things."

"I've been there for sure." Leon glanced around. "Is my aunt here?"

"Not yet. Miss Eleanor called five minutes ago to say she was on the way. She should be here at any moment."

"How is your daughter doing? I know the accident was very traumatic for her."

"Talei isn't sleeping well. She wakes up screaming and she's been a bit clingy," Misty said. "There's a part of me that's so angry with John for doing this to my baby. He never should've taken her from day care."

Leon's face went grim. "It's not as if John intended to have an accident."

Arms folded across her chest; Misty frowned with cold fury. "You're actually defending his actions?"

"He made an error in judgment," Leon said. "All he wanted was his family back."

"Then he should've been a much better husband," Misty said sharply. She tossed her hair and eyed him with cold triumph.

"What are you talking about?"

"There was a side of John that you didn't know about. He had a temper and like his father was verbally abusive. The one time it almost turned physical, I ended the marriage."

Leon shook his head in disbelief. "I know John had his issues, but he wouldn't harm a woman."

She glared at Leon. "I don't have any reason to lie about his treatment of me."

Her words had taken him by complete surprise.

"Leon, I should've figured you'd be here," Eleanor said, interrupting his conversation with Misty.

He smiled. "I'm not about to miss the fish and grits."

Eleanor chuckled. "You can always count on Leon to show up bright and early on Friday for the breakfast special. Leon loves seafood." Her gaze traveled from him to Misty. "What's going on?"

"Your nephew seems to think I'm a liar." Misty's lips thinned with irritation. She lifted her chin, meeting his gaze straight on.

"That's not what I said," Leon stated.

"Oh, the implication was clear," she countered. "The fact of the matter is I don't really care what you think of me. Nothing will change the truth. John kidnapped our daughter and threatened to do it earlier. That was the reason his visits had to be supervised."

He didn't respond.

When Misty walked away, Eleanor sat down across from her nephew. "She's been through a lot, Leon."

"I'm sure it wasn't a cake walk for John either. All he ever talked about was trying to get his family back."

"I know how much you love your friend, but John was abusive."

Leon shook his head in disbelief. "I guess that's why John didn't fight the divorce," Leon said almost to himself. "That's what he meant when he said Misty didn't give him any choice but to sign off on the petition."

"She did what she had to do—I would've done the same thing," Eleanor said. "I don't blame her at all."

Leon studied Misty as she moved about the restaurant. She seemed nice enough. Misty was fiercely protective of Talei—as any mother would be under the circumstances. He thought back to his last conversation with John.

"I love Misty and I'm working hard to get her back, Leon."

"Does she still love you?"

John finished his drink. *"I think so, but she wants me to leave the company. As much as I want to quit, I can't do that. My dad needs me. We've been having a lot of employee turnover."*

"I thought you wanted to leave, as well."

"It's not about what I want, Leon. It's what I have to do. I keep trying to get Misty to understand this, but she's only focused on what she wants."

"How is the co-parenting going?"

John shrugged. *"Fine, I guess. Only I don't get enough time with my daughter. My ex is doing a good job teaching Talei about Native American culture and traditions. My dad is against it, of course."*

"Why?"

"He feels that it will complicate Talei's life and he doesn't want her confused. He wants her to identify as Black—not Native. He thinks that Misty denies her Black side." John shrugged. *"It doesn't make sense to me. I want my daughter to experience both cultures."*

"Did you tell Elroy that?"

John signaled for another drink. *"Leon, you know my dad. You can't tell him anything. I just let him talk. It doesn't matter, though. I'm doing what I can to get along with Misty, and it's working out great. She's finally agreed to let me spend more time with Talei. I've been thinking of taking her on a trip somewhere out of the country. I could definitely use a vacation."*

"Is Misty okay with this?"

John nodded. "Yeah, things are so much better between us right now."

Silas brought Leon's meal.

"Thanks," he said.

While he ate, Leon replayed his final conversation with John repeatedly in his head. Each time brought him back to the same troubling conclusion.

When Eleanor came to check on him, he said, "Auntie, I was just at Rusty's store and he mentioned that you'd made a couple of pies for him. I told him I'd pick them up. I have to go back by there to pick up my order."

"He installed a couple of ceiling fans for me. He wouldn't accept payment, so I told him I'd make him a key lime and his favorite, a chocolate peanut butter pie." Smiling, Eleanor said, "I knew he wouldn't turn them down."

Leon laughed. "You know Rusty is in love with you."

"Rusty Stanley and I have been friends since we were in middle school. He took me to my junior prom and when it was over, he didn't even attempt to kiss me. He's never even flirted with me."

"He also never married."

"That's probably because he hadn't met the right person or maybe he enjoys being one of the island's eligible bachelors," Eleanor suggested. "Regardless, I consider him one of my dearest friends, but that's all we have between us."

Leon shook his head. "I don't know about that, Auntie. Whenever you talk about him, I see something in your eyes."

Eleanor laughed. "Boy, you need to worry about your own love life. Speaking of which... Don't you think it's time for you to get back out there?"

Leon regarded her with amusement. "I'm fine."

"You're too young to live life alone."

"I'm not alone. I have you, Auntie."

MISTY WALKED OUT of the kitchen carrying a tray of fudge. She was keenly aware of Leon's scrutiny. It bothered her that he thought so little of her. He didn't even give her the benefit of the doubt—just believed everything John had told him about her.

"Try not to be so hard on my nephew, Misty," Eleanor said as she wiped down the counter.

"Maybe he shouldn't be so judgmental."

"Leon considered John a friend. I know they kept in contact."

She wiped her hands on her apron. "Oh, I had no idea."

"John came to the funeral when Leon's wife and child died. He definitely helped Leon get through that day."

"Really? He never told me." Misty was surprised to hear how her ex-husband could be so supportive to Leon, but extremely selfish when it came to his own family.

"Yes. They were closer than you know. I know that Leon encouraged John to fight for his marriage." She poured herself a cup of tea. "When my brother and his wife died, Leon and his brother..." Eleanor paused for a moment, then continued. "Oh, Misty, they were so heartbroken. I never thought they'd ever get over losing their parents. Then Leon met Vera in college. I hadn't seen him that happy since they were children. Just when he'd found happiness with his wife and the impending birth of their little girl, tragedy struck a second time. Vera developed what they said was an amniotic fluid embolism. Somehow the fluid entered Vera's bloodstream. Losing both Vera and Selena—it was almost too much to bear for all of us."

Her gaze traveled to Leon. "I can't imagine going through something like that."

"I was terribly worried about him during that time. He shut completely down—it was John who was finally able to get through to Leon and get him out of his shell."

"Miss Eleanor, excuse the interruption, but we're almost out of eggs and sugar," Silas said.

She frowned. "Silas, we should have plenty. A delivery came yesterday."

"There were no deliveries, Miss Eleanor."

Her eyes widened in alarm. "They come every Wednesday."

"Yes ma'am, I know. I just checked with Josh and he said we didn't have one yesterday."

Misty made a quick phone call. She hung up a few minutes later, saying, "They had no record of an order, but don't worry—I placed it and they're rushing it through. They should be here in about fifteen to twenty minutes."

Eleanor released an audible sigh of relief. "I can't believe I forgot to order supplies. I need to do a quick inventory to make sure we have everything we need."

"There was a lot going on," Misty said. "If you hadn't been there for me and Talei, you probably wouldn't have forgotten."

"It was a busy day." Eleanor shrugged. "I thought for sure I'd placed that order."

"It was an easy fix," she reassured her.

Leon pushed away from the table, stepping in Misty's path. "I need to ask you something."

"What is it?"

He captured her eyes with his. "During my last conversation with John, he told me that you'd agreed to let him spend more time with Talei," Leon said. "He mentioned that he was planning to go on vacation out of the country and take her with him. Is any of that true?"

"No, it's not. There's no way I'd let Talei go without me."

He took a deep breath. "He was planning to run away with her. Misty, I want to apologize to you," Leon said. "I know there are two sides to every story and I only know John's side. I should've kept my mouth shut."

"Leon, I appreciate the apology. I get that John was your friend, but he was troubled more than you knew."

"I see that now." Distracted, Leon glanced over at his aunt.

"Is Aunt Eleanor okay? She looks upset about something."

"Yes," Misty said. "She forgot to place an order, but it's been taken care of—no worries."

"I keep telling her that she needs to slow down. She feels like she has to be here every day."

"Miss Eleanor loves this place."

Leon smiled. "Yeah, she does. I can't even think of this shop without my aunt's presence. Aunt Eleanor did all of the baking back then."

He glanced around the room. "I have a lot of wonderful memories in this place."

"I'm sure," Misty murmured. "I hear that a lot from the locals. A few of them have told me that their families have been coming to the shop for generations. The other half say they're related to your family. One of the things I love about Polk Island is the history."

He smiled. "I'll have to give you the five-dollar tour one day."

"I'd like that," she responded.

She cautioned herself not to get too involved with Leon. The last thing the handsome widower needed in his life was someone who was more broken than him.

CHAPTER FIVE

THE NEXT MORNING, Leon reported to the station house for work.

Charles greeted him when he entered the day room. "Hey, Leon, how you doin'? I know you have to be pretty broken up about your friend."

"It doesn't really seem real to me yet." He walked with Charles to the dorm area. "I have to tell you... I don't know what or how to feel. Grief seems to be a permanent fixture in my life."

There they were joined by another coworker. "I heard that it was your friend who died in the accident. The truck driver."

"Yeah," Leon responded, ignoring the stab of pain in his heart. He stuffed his backpack into one of the metal lockers.

"Did he really kidnap his daughter?" one of the other coworkers questioned.

"Hey, don't ask the man something stupid like that," Charles interjected. "He just lost his friend."

"I honestly didn't mean anything by it, Leon."

"Joe, I know you didn't. Look, John just wanted to spend time with his little girl. He wasn't a bad person, but he handled this situation wrong and it cost him his life."

"I'm sorry for your loss."

"If I were married to Misty Brightwater, I'd do everything I could to get my family back, too," Leon overheard another one of the guys say. "She's stunning."

His coworker was right. Misty was a beautiful young woman, but there was a side to her that Leon perceived as unsympathetic. When she first learned of John's death, she wasn't overcome with emotion. He knew she was more concerned about Talei, yet it bothered him that she hadn't displayed any outward signs that John's passing upset her.

John had once told him that she could be cold. He said she had the ability to just turn her emotions on and off. Leon had witnessed this himself.

Misty was the type of woman he would never give a second thought. She could break a heart with just the flick of a switch.

IT WAS THE hottest day in May so far this year. A perfect day for spending time at the Sterling Village community pool. Misty laughed in pure delight as a giggling Talei dipped her tiny toes in the wading pool while enjoying the momentary cool breeze swirling around them.

"Mommy…"

"Yes, baby?" she prompted.

Pointing to the Olympic-sized pool on the other side of the gate, she said, "I wanna get in wata…"

"We have to stay on this side, sweetie. It's too many people over there." Misty led her toward the middle of the children's pool. She sat down with Talei beside her. "This feels good, doesn't it?"

Her daughter nodded. "Daddy love wata."

"Yes, he does." She ran her fingers through Talei's curly puffs. "He did love the water."

Looking up at Misty, the little girl asked, "Daddy coming?"

She shook her head regretfully. "No, sweetie. He can't come."

"He hurt," Talei said softly.

"Yes, your daddy was really hurt from the car accident." She released a short sigh. "Do you remember where heaven is?"

Talei pointed upward. "Daddy go to heaven?"

Fighting back tears, Misty said, "Yes."

"Daddy get better in heaven."

She planted a kiss on her daughter's forehead. "Yes, my beautiful little girl. Your daddy is in a much better place. He is going to watch over you always."

Talei chuckled when she put her duck in the water. She watched it float, then went after it.

Misty loved the sound of her daughter's laughter. It signaled that she was feeling safe and secure, but she missed her father.

The best thing she had done was move here, Misty thought. She loved living on picturesque Polk Island. The beaches, the oaks draped in Spanish moss and the awesome beauty of the island were the main reason she'd come to the area. Historical landmarks citing the rich Rothchild history were prevalent around the island. This was the perfect place to raise Talei, especially now.

She left work early to spend quality time with Talei, and also to note if her daughter might be experiencing any trauma. Her mother left for Charleston when Misty arrived home earlier. It had been wonderful having her with them.

Misty glanced down at her as she played in the water. "Five more minutes, then we're going home."

"Okaay."

When time was up, Misty said, "We have to leave now."

Batting her long eyelashes, Talei responded, "Five minutes, pleeze."

Misty eyed her daughter in amusement. "Okay, but after that we have to go home so I can make dinner."

Talei continued splashing around in the pool, happily.

Misty checked her phone, then stood. "Time's up. We have to get out of the pool."

Talei didn't protest, provoking a soft sigh of relief from Misty.

She wrapped a towel around her daughter, then placed one around herself, as well. Misty picked up her tote. "So, what are we gonna cook?" She held Talei's hand as they walked along the tree-lined sidewalk to her condo.

"Hot dawg and *fench* fries."

She bit back a smile, then offered a suggestion. "How about grilled chicken nuggets, broccoli and—"

"Macarooni," Talei interjected.

"We can do that." Misty stifled her chuckle.

Five minutes later, they walked inside their home, a two-bedroom condominium with a picturesque view of the ocean from the patio and the balcony. It was this stunning view that sold her on the property. Her condo wasn't a large place, but it provided just enough space for her and Talei, and her alimony payments covered the rent and utilities. Now that John was gone, Misty considered that she might have to take on a second job. It didn't matter. She would do whatever was necessary to make ends meet.

"Let's get our baths out of the way."

Talei patted her damp swimsuit. "Mommy, I don't need bath. I clean."

Misty chuckled. "We still need to bathe after we get in the pool, sweetie."

Talei sighed. "Okay, Mommy."

They entered Talei's bedroom, a yellow-and-white haven stocked with stuffed animals, dolls and a closet filled with everything from everyday clothing to Native American fringed dresses, and a feather headdress designed by Misty's mother, Oma.

She opened a drawer to retrieve a pair of pajamas.

In the bathroom across the hall, Misty gave Talei a bath, dried her off and then dressed her in pink-and-white-polka-dotted pajamas.

Talei followed her into the master bedroom. "Sweetie, you can watch television in my room while I take my shower."

Misty left the bathroom door ajar.

She came out dressed in a pair of black yoga pants and an oversize black-and-white T-shirt. Talei was sitting cross-legged in the middle of the king-size bed playing with Pooh Bear and the one she called Eon. She looked up and said, "I hungry."

"Dinner will be ready soon, sweetie."

Thirty minutes later, they sat down to a quiet dinner.

"Mommy, we call Daddy?" Talei asked.

Misty wiped her mouth with a napkin. "I'm afraid we can't, sweetie. Daddy's not able to talk to us."

Talei nodded, and then turned her attention to the bear she'd brought to the table. Normally, Misty wouldn't allow it, but this bear was a gift from John and her daughter kept it close.

"How is Pooh Bear feeling today?" Misty inquired.

"Sad," Talei responded. "Her miss Daddy."

She got up and went around the table to her daughter. "I know you miss your daddy. I want you to know that he loves you. He will always love you, sweetie." She knew that Talei was too young to fully comprehend the reason for John's absence.

Misty cleaned the kitchen afterward while her daughter watched television.

With Talei settled in for the evening, Misty retrieved a box of photos from her closet—photos of her with bruises on her arms, neck and face. Leon had no idea the chameleon John was; he could be charming and loving one minute, and then transform into a malicious, abusive tyrant in another. She decided there was no need to keep the pictures any longer, so she ripped them up and threw them in the trash. She didn't want Talei to ever see them. Misty didn't want to taint her daughter's memory of her father.

LEON LEFT WORK and met up with John's parents at the funeral home. They were making the arrangements to transport his body home to Orangeburg. The magnitude of their despair was almost overwhelming.

"Thank you so much for coming," Elroy said, shaking Leon's hand. "I don't know how we're going to get through this. I never thought I'd outlive my own son."

"I understand."

They were seated in the lobby area when Misty walked in, surprising them all.

"What are you doing here?" Elroy demanded, rushing to his feet. "You're not John's wife anymore. You have no right to be here. This is family business."

"I'm still the mother of his daughter," Misty responded. "I came to be a source of support. Not to fight with you."

It was clear to Leon that she refused to let herself be intimidated by this brute. He watched her in amazement.

Pulling on his sleeve, Clara pleaded, "Elroy, please don't make a scene."

"Just go home, Misty. We don't want you here or at the funeral."

Leon glimpsed the hurt in her eyes. They were all in pain and it bothered him that John's death still couldn't bring them together as a family. This was not the time for fighting.

She swallowed hard before saying, "So, you will deny your granddaughter a chance to say goodbye to her father?"

"No," Clara quickly interjected. "Misty, you must attend the service. John would want you there." She met her husband's enraged gaze. "He would want her at his funeral, and you know it."

"Your wife is right," Leon said.

"Y'all think you know *my* son better than I did. I'm telling you that woman over there ruined his life."

Leon decided not to remain silent. "This has gotten way out of hand, Elroy. I know you're grieving, but I'm not going to let you attack Misty like this—she was the love of John's life."

"You don't have to protect me, Leon," Misty stated. "I'm leaving."

"Elroy, you're making a scene."

He glared at his wife. "Stay out of this." Turning his attention back to Misty, he said, "We're gonna sue for custody of Talei."

Misty kept her voice low. "Give it your best shot. Once my attorney sees the police report, you'll be lucky if you get visitation because trust me, I intend to let the judge know about your history of physical abuse, as well."

Her words rendered Elroy speechless.

She glanced at Leon before leaving.

"You see what a hateful woman she is," Elroy stated. "Misty is nothing but a selfish woman looking to take advantage of the kindness of others. She tried to get my son to leave the family business."

Leon knew that John was not happy as a truck driver but didn't have the courage to stand up to his father. "Misty was John's wife," he stated. "She is the mother of his child. I'll say it again. She should be allowed to attend the funeral."

"I don't agree."

"I want my granddaughter there to say goodbye to her father," Clara said. If Misty can't come, she won't allow Talei to attend. Let's just keep the peace for John's homecoming service." Tears slipped from her eyes. "I'm tired of all this fighting. That poor girl hadn't done nothing to you. She and John had their issues, but none of that matters now."

Leon embraced her. "Everything is going to work out, Clara."

"I've lost my son, Elroy. Isn't that *enough*?" She broke down into sobs.

Having witnessed Elroy's venom, Leon had

a much better understanding of what Misty and John had to deal with through the course of their relationship and marriage.

A wave of disappointment flowed through him. Elroy had verbally attacked Misty and it was unwarranted. If he didn't work through his anger, he would end up missing out on a relationship with his granddaughter.

Leon knew Misty would fight them with her all—even if it meant keeping Talei away from Elroy and Clara. She was determined to protect her daughter from a toxic environment.

He prayed it wouldn't come to that.

"I DIDN'T EXPECT you back here so soon," Eleanor said when Misty walked into the shop.

"Elroy started acting a fool when I showed up," she responded. "He didn't want me there, so I left."

Disgusted, Eleanor shook her head. "That man needs to be ashamed of himself."

Misty shrugged in nonchalance. "It's fine. He's probably right. I have no right to be there. I'm no longer married to John."

"You're still the mother of his child," Eleanor countered.

"Your nephew was there, and he stepped up to defend me. I felt bad for him. He was so uncomfortable." She pasted on a smile. "Leon is the nicest man I've ever met."

"He's one of the good ones for sure," Eleanor said. "He and Trey never gave me an ounce of trouble. Don't get me wrong. They did the normal kid stuff, but that's about it."

"It's a testament to you."

"I did my best to give them what they needed."

Misty nodded in understanding. "That's all I want to do for Talei."

"Don't trouble your mind, sugar. You're doing a good job with that little girl." Eleanor frowned. "I can't remember if I ordered the meat for the box lunches. They have to be ready by Friday."

Misty slipped on her apron. "I can do a quick check."

"Thank you. If not, we need to do it right away."

This was the second time Eleanor had forgotten to restock the kitchen. Misty knew she had a lot on her mind these days. Maybe it was becoming more of a challenge to run both the bakery and the café.

"We're good on meat," Misty told Eleanor. "The only thing we need is more condiments. We have enough to put in the boxes, but we're going to be wiped out pretty much after that."

"Thank the Lawd."

"Miss Eleanor, would it be easier if I focused

on working the bakery? This would leave you to manage the café."

"I like that idea."

"Really? Please don't think I'm trying to tell you how to run your business."

"This is why I hired you, Misty. It made good business sense."

"Thank you for your faith in me, Miss Eleanor."

Misty spent most of her day in the kitchen, preparing baked goods for the next day.

"We just got an order for your key lime layer cake," Eleanor said. "They want to pick it up by noon tomorrow."

"I can do that." Misty stirred the ingredients in the bowl to make frosting for the carrot cake baking in the oven.

At three o'clock, she left to pick up Talei from day care. From there, they drove home.

Their daily routine was pretty low-key, Misty thought. Home, dinner, bath, bedtime story, sleep, then do it all over again the next day. However, she wouldn't trade the simplistic and peaceful life they led for anything in the world.

She made spaghetti for dinner, a choice that thrilled Talei.

Misty quietly observed her daughter as they ate their meals. Her heart was saddened at not being able to say a final goodbye to John. She wanted a sense of closure.

Later that night as she prepared for bed, the telephone rang. She looked at the caller ID and debated whether or not to answer. She didn't want to deal with any more drama.

"Hello."

"This is Clara…"

"What can I do for you?" Misty worked to keep her tone neutral and devoid of any emotion.

"I would like for you and Talei to attend John's funeral and sit with the family."

"Elroy made it clear that he doesn't want me there. I really don't want to be humiliated in front of your family and friends."

"This is my decision. Elroy's not thrilled about it, but he won't make a scene, Misty."

"I know how he feels about me, Clara," she responded. "I'm sorry but this feels like a setup."

"It's not. I give you my word."

"You and I both know that you can't control your husband."

"I promise you Elroy will be on his best behavior. My family will be here. *All* my brothers are coming. Trust me… With my family present, my husband will be on his best behavior."

CHAPTER SIX

ON THE DAY of John's funeral, Leon got up early to drive to Orangeburg. He was not particularly looking forward to saying goodbye to yet another person he cared about. In truth, he was tired of grieving, having lived with it for so long. Despite his feelings, Leon felt it was his duty to attend.

When he arrived at the church, Leon was surrounded by somber-faced mourners dressed in black. He accepted a program one of the ushers handed him.

Leon was standing near the door to the sanctuary when he spied Misty and Talei entering the church. He had never seen a simple black dress look so stunning on a woman. Her hair was pulled back into a sleek ponytail. Talei's white dress was trimmed with a black-and-white-striped ribbon around the collar and the waist.

The little girl saw him, smiled and waved. Grinning, he waved back.

Leon bent down to speak to her as they approached him. "Do you remember my name?"

Talei looked up at her mother.

"This is Leon, remember? He was your daddy's friend," Misty said.

"Eon."

He glanced up at Misty. "I'm glad to see you."

"I had no intentions of coming, but Clara called me last night and insisted that we attend the service."

Leon responded. "You have as much right to be here as any of these other folks."

"I don't know about that." She glanced over her shoulder, then back at Leon. "Elroy has done a pretty good job of poisoning almost everyone's thoughts about me. You see how people are staring and whispering."

Leon shrugged with nonchalance. "Don't let it bother you."

"I'm not. I'm just here for my daughter." Misty pulled gingerly at the collar of her dress. I'm also here out of respect for John."

"Eon," Talei patted his hand.

He kneeled down so he could better hear her.

"Daddy in heaven. He get better."

Leon didn't know how to respond so he remained silent. She was so young and seemingly unaffected by her father's death.

"I didn't know what else to tell her," Misty said.

Standing up, he nodded in understanding. "I can imagine it's difficult."

"She thinks he can come back. Talei keeps looking for him, Leon."

The funeral director signaled for the family to line up for the processional.

Inside the sanctuary, Misty sat beside Clara in the front row while he sat on the opposite side of the sanctuary on the second row.

Leon could tell by Elroy's body language that he wasn't happy about Misty being there, but he didn't make a scene.

When it was time for him to speak, Leon walked up to the podium. His gaze traveled and settled briefly on Misty.

"I met John when we attended Clemson University. He was my roommate. It didn't take us long to realize that we had a lot in common. We were instant friends. One of my memories of John was his boundless enthusiasm. He and I had a lot of fun and laughed a lot. When his daughter, Talei, was born, it was clear that she had stolen his heart. John was beside himself with happiness."

His eyes watered. Leon inhaled deeply and released the breath slowly before he continued. "I had dinner with John the day after Mother's

Day. Ten days later, he was gone, and to be honest, I'm still trying to wrap my mind around it. Instead of celebrating his birthday with him at his favorite restaurant in Charleston like we planned, I'm here to say a final farewell. There are no words to explain the hole he's left in my life—in all of our lives." Looking upward, he said, "We're going to really miss you. Rest in heaven, John."

He could feel Misty's eyes on him. Leon felt uncomfortable showing his vulnerability in her presence. He preferred to be seen as a pillar of strength.

CLARA EMBRACED HER during the repast. "Thank you so much for coming, Misty."

"I wanted to be here...to say goodbye to John."

"I hope he can finally have peace," Clara murmured. "Losing you and Talei broke his heart, Misty. He truly loved you. I hope you know that."

She gave a slight nod. "I believe that he loved me. He just didn't know how to show it."

Careful to keep her voice low, Clara said, "You should know that you're the sole beneficiary on John's life insurance."

She handed Misty a business card. "You need to call and give them your information."

Misty was stunned. "I had no idea about this."

"He wanted to make sure you and Talei were taken care of in case…"

"Clara, we need to speak with Pastor Reynolds before he leaves," Elroy muttered, taking her by the arm and whisking her away.

Misty saw Leon standing by a window. She walked up to him saying, "What you said about John—it was really nice. He would've loved it."

"Thank you."

They joined the buffet line to get something to eat.

"Talei seems to be having a great time with Elroy," Leon observed. It thrilled him to see the little girl in such a happy mood despite the somber surroundings.

"He's always been very good with her."

They got their plates and found a table with empty chairs.

Misty discovered she didn't have much of an appetite.

"Are you okay?" Leon inquired; his expression filled with concern.

"I'm not really hungry right now."

"I always thought John and I would grow to be two old men…" Leon's voice trailed off momentarily. "He was looking forward to scaring the boys away from Talei. He always said she was going to be stunning like you."

Misty's eyes became bright. "We shouldn't be here in this place. John should be alive and well."

Leon nodded in agreement.

She scanned the room, her gaze landing briefly on Elroy. He was seated across the room glaring at her.

When Leon prepared to leave, Misty asked, "Do you mind if I follow you back to the island?"

"Are you ready to go?"

"Yes," Misty responded. "I'll get Talei and meet you outside."

She stayed behind Leon's truck the whole way back to Polk Island. He'd called her a couple of times to make sure she was fine.

"Do you want to grab a bite to eat before we cross the bridge?" he asked. "You didn't touch your food earlier."

"I'd like that." Misty was grateful Leon couldn't hear her stomach growling.

They stopped at a fast-food restaurant and sat in a corner booth.

"You love French fries, don't you, Talei?" Leon chuckled when their food arrived. "I love them, too."

Turning up her smile a notch, Talei nodded. "Fench fries and hot dawg." She pointed to his plate. "Shilli dawg."

Misty and Leon laughed.

"She's a sweetheart."

Misty placed an arm around her daughter. "I love her more than my own life. She's such a beautiful blessing."

She looked at him, noting the pain etched in his expression. "I'm sorry. It must be so hard for you."

"It's not as bad as it was," Leon responded. "I couldn't be around children for a while. To be honest, Talei is the first child I've held since my daughter died."

"Oh, wow… I had no idea."

"I want to be here for you and Talei as her godfather," Leon stated. "It's what John would have wanted. I hope it's fine with you."

"It's definitely okay with me," Misty said. Pointing to Leon, she stated, "Talei, this is your godfather."

"Gawfather…"

He burst into laughter when Talei scrunched up her face at him. "Is that a happy face or a sad face?"

"Funny face," she said before bursting into giggles.

Misty and Leon cracked up laughing.

"She can be a little silly at times."

"I love it," he responded. It was nice to be

able to laugh after such an emotional day that started in sadness.

Encouraged, Talei continued to make faces and Leon responded in laughter and light banter.

When they finished eating, Leon walked them to their car. "I'm sure it's been a long day for you both. I'll check in with you tomorrow."

"I'll talk to you then." Misty unlocked her car door and helped Talei into her seat. Once her daughter was all buckled in, she climbed into the driver's seat. "As soon as we cross the bridge, we'll be back on the island, sweetie. Almost home."

"Almost home," Talei repeated. "Eon in car."

"Yes, he's in his car. He's in front of us."

Two hours after they arrived home, Misty put Talei to bed, then went down to the kitchen to work on a new recipe that had been floating around in her mind for days.

She opened the refrigerator and retrieved the carton of eggs. Next, she went to the pantry and took out a bag of flour. Minutes later, Misty had all the ingredients she needed to make what she called a buttery cinnamon cake. Baking was a way to relieve her stress. At the moment, she was feeling very stressed. By midnight, she had baked a cake, a dozen cupcakes and peanut butter cookies.

THE NEXT DAY, Leon woke up with his brother, Trey, weighing heavy on his mind. They texted often but he hadn't had a real conversation in over a month.

He picked up his phone and punched in a number.

"Hey, big brother."

Leon exhaled a long sigh of contentment. "Trey, it's so good to hear your voice. I miss you, man."

"Same here," Trey responded. "How's Aunt Eleanor?"

Leon sat up in bed, propped against a stack of pillows. "She's fine. Hey, you remember John Hayes?"

"Yeah. How is he?"

"We buried him yesterday."

"What?" Trey gasped in surprise. "What happened?"

"He had a bad car accident here on the island." Leon decided not to tell his brother about Misty and Talei over the phone. There would be time for that later.

"Man, I'm sorry to hear that," Trey said.

"How are things with you?" Leon inquired.

"Things are actually good for me. I have leave coming up, so I'll be home the twenty-second of June until the day after the Fourth of July. I can't wait to see everyone."

Leon couldn't be happier at the news. "That's great. Can I tell Aunt Eleanor?"

Trey laughed. "Yeah. That's fine. The last time I tried to surprise her, she almost had a heart attack."

"Man, I can't wait to see you."

"Same here," Trey said. "Well… Duty calls, big brother. I'll call you and Aunt Eleanor some-time next week."

When he arrived at work, Leon phoned his aunt while still in the car. "Guess who's com-ing home in a couple of weeks."

"Trey," she responded. "Is my baby boy com-ing back to the island?"

He laughed. "Yes, ma'am."

Leon talked to his aunt a few minutes more, then said, "I'm at work. It's time to get my day started."

He ended the call and got out of his truck.

Leon saw Lizzie as she was leaving the sta-tion house and threw up his hand in greeting.

He navigated to the dorms, put his backpack away, then headed to the bay where the fire en-gines were stored.

"Leon… Where are you?" Charles called out.

"Over here. I'm washing engine two."

"You have visitors. They're waiting for you in the lobby."

"Me?" Leon walked from the back of the truck. "Who is it?"

"Go up there and see for yourself."

He washed and dried his hands, then walked into the station. Leon's heart turned over when he saw Misty and Talei. He felt a ripple of excitement.

"*Oseeyo*, Eon," the little girl said and rushed over to him. She gave him the bag containing peanut butter cookies.

"*Osiyo*," Misty clarified. "It means *hello*."

"I figured it was something like that."

"Just saying thank you for everything you've done didn't seem quite enough." Misty handed him a box of red velvet cupcakes. "These are just a token of my appreciation."

"You didn't have to go to all this trouble but thank you." Leon was touched beyond words by her thoughtfulness. Misty wasn't the first woman to bring him baked goods, but unlike some of the others, she didn't have a hidden agenda.

"I am forever grateful, Leon. I'm also glad you want to be her godfather."

Leon picked up the toddler. "We already have a bond, don't we?"

Talei nodded, then pointed to a stuffed Dalmatian puppy on the desk behind him.

"Dawggie."

Misty laughed. "My child can spot a stuffed animal anywhere. It's like she has a sixth sense or something."

"Here you go," Leon said. "It's my gift to you, little one."

"What do you say, Talei?"

"Wado."

"Is it okay if she shares a cupcake with me?"

Misty nodded. "Sure."

Leon escorted them to the dining area. He sliced a cupcake in two and gave a half to Talei while he kept the other.

He took a bite, then another. "Aunt Eleanor's right. You definitely know your way around a kitchen." Misty's nearness made his senses spin.

She laughed. "It's just a cupcake."

"You should've met the guy you replaced. I don't know if he started having issues with his vision but even on his best day, not one of his baked goods were as good as this cupcake."

Misty smiled and took Talei out of his arms and set her on the floor. "We need to let Leon get back to work, sweetie."

"Bye, Eon," Talei said, wrapping her arms around his legs.

"Thank you again for the goodies," Leon said.

The look Misty gave him was so galvanizing it sent a tremor through him. The pounding of his heart quieted only once they disappeared outside.

CHAPTER SEVEN

AFTER MISTY AND Talei left, Leon's coworkers tossed a bunch of questions at him.

"Hey, you're gonna share those, right? Those cupcakes look pretty delicious."

"You and Miss Brightwater sure seem pretty close."

"We're friends," Leon said. "That's all y'all need to know." He felt an unfamiliar shiver of awareness. There was something more than a mild interest where Misty was concerned. An undeniable magnetism was building between them. He had to wrench himself away from his ridiculous preoccupation. He and Misty could only be friends.

Nothing more.

"So, what about those cupcakes and cookies?" Charles interjected. "You sharing your bounty?"

Amused, Leon nodded. "Sure."

He placed the snacks on the table just as the alarm sounded, prompting the team to rush and gather equipment.

"Engine one," Charles called out.

Leon grabbed his gear and jumped into the truck.

"It sure is good to see you smile again," Charles told him. "That little girl seems to have taken a strong liking to you."

"John asked me to be her godfather, but I couldn't accept it until now. I'm going to be there for her since her dad can't."

"Your friend will be able to rest easy," Charles said.

Leon leaned back against the seat. They were on their way to the site of a car accident.

"You okay?" Charles asked.

"Yeah, I'm good," Leon said as he stared out the window and tried to keep his mind focused on the job.

They arrived at the accident location.

It was quickly determined that they weren't needed, much to Leon's relief.

"Now we can pick up where we left off," Charles said with a chuckle once they'd returned to the station. "I can't wait to get my hands on one of those red velvet cupcakes."

Leon laughed, then headed to his bunk. Now that he had some downtime, he couldn't escape the thoughts of Misty that plagued him. Fate had ushered her into his life, blindsiding him plain and simple. The chemistry between them shook Leon down to his bones. Misty and Talei had stormed into his life like a tornado, turning his world inside out. He was unprepared for the emotions that were suddenly running rampant and rattling him to the core.

Leon lay down on his bunk and closed his eyes. *What do I do now?*

MISTY DROVE TO the shop so that Talei could spend some time with Eleanor.

"She's been asking to see you."

Smiling, Eleanor hugged Talei. "Hey, sugar. I'm so glad you came to visit me."

"Where Mr. Josh?" the little girl asked.

"He's in the kitchen. I'll let him know you're here."

Misty guided her daughter into a booth, then sat down beside her. Leon was at the forefront of her mind. She had no ulterior motives in taking the cupcakes and cookies to the station, but there was something different in her interaction with him—something new. She'd felt an eager affection coming from him earlier. It was as if something intense flared between them, not to mention the tingling in the pit of her stomach—the way her heart lurched, and her pulse pounded whenever she was around Leon.

Eleanor walked to the entrance of the kitchen and said, "Talei wants to say hello to you."

Josh appeared, wiping his hands on his apron. "Hey, little Princess."

Grinning, Talei waved, then said, "You got fench fries?"

"I sure do," Josh said. "Would you like a grilled cheese sandwich to go with them?"

"Yes, pleeze."

Misty kissed the top of her daughter's head. "I love you so much, munchkin."

"Love you, Mommy."

Eleanor walked over a few minutes later carrying Talei's lunch. She sat down across from Misty and watched as the little girl dived into her food.

Gesturing to the stuffed animal on the table, she said, "Did you go by the station?"

"I did," Misty responded. "I dropped off some cupcakes and peanut butter cookies to Leon. I wanted to thank him for what he did—from the accident to the funeral. He's really been a great help to me."

"I'm sure he appreciated the treats. My nephew has a sweet tooth."

"He even offered to be Talei's godfather. It's what John always wanted."

"I'm so glad to hear this," Eleanor said. "It means that he's finally ready to move past his own pain and grief. I actually think you have something to do with this change in him."

"I have a meeting with Brittany in an hour, so we'd better head home," she announced, checking her watch. "I'll see you in the morning."

"Thanks for bringing this little lady to see me," Eleanor said. "She really made my day."

One thing Misty hadn't counted on—her emotions where Leon was concerned. Unnerved by the intensity of her response to Eleanor's comment, she forced herself to shut out all thoughts of him.

MISTY WAS ON the planning committee for the upcoming Children's Festival taking place the first weekend in August. She'd missed the last meeting because of John's funeral, so her friend Brittany had graciously offered to come by the house to update her and had also emailed her the notes.

She designated the dining room table as a workspace for them.

Talei was in her bedroom watching a Disney movie when Brittany arrived.

Opening her tote, Brittany said, "I brought the pictures from the festival last year. We had people come from the mainland attend—it was great. Ours is a smaller version of the one they have every year in Charleston."

"I'm super excited to be a part of this event," Misty responded. "I read the notes from the last meeting. Looks like it was a very productive one."

"It was," Brittany said. "I wanted to stop by because I have more great news. Annie Bell Watts contacted me about doing a workshop on quilting. She's even supplying all of the materials."

"That's wonderful," Misty murmured as she made some notes of her own. "The island is known for the beautiful quilts sold in the boutiques. I think the craft should appeal to the teens."

Misty updated Brittany on the tasks she'd completed. "All of the sponsorship packets have been sent out and we've gotten some great responses. I've just emailed you an updated list of the donors for this year."

They spent forty-five minutes going over more details. Misty made a couple of phone calls regarding the venue.

"Everything's confirmed," she said after the last call.

"That's everything on the festival," Brittany stated. "How did things go in Orangeburg?"

"John's father was his usually angry self. I'm so glad Leon was there—I didn't want to deal with that man alone."

"I take it things are going well with Leon, then."

"He's really nice, Britt. I'm hopeful that we're going to be great friends." Misty was careful to keep any emotion out of her voice.

Brittany gave her a sidelong glance. "Friends… That's all you want with that gorgeous man? A *friendship*?"

"Yeah. After John, I realized I make terrible choices with men. I think I'm better alone."

"Do you really believe that?"

"Britt, you have no idea the emotional abuse I endured with my father. I had a string of bad relationships, and when I met John, I thought all that changed, but it was more of the same. Trust me, Britt… I'm better off alone."

Shaking her head, Brittany said, "You just haven't met the right man. *Until now.*"

LEON EXITED THROUGH the gym doors, wiping his brow with a towel as he made his way to his car.

"I'm beginning to see you everywhere."

His heart jolted at the sound of her voice. "It's bound to happen every now and then," Leon said smoothly. "We live on an island."

Pointing to his gym bag, Misty inquired, "On your way to a workout?"

"Actually, I finished up not too long ago." Misty's nearness made his senses spin, and he couldn't ignore the smoldering flame in her eyes. Without thinking about the consequences, he said, "I was about to grab some lunch. Would you like to join me?"

"You're stepping out on your aunt," Misty said when they walked through the door of Tony's Italian Bistro. "Shame."

"Every now and then I come over here for the Italian sandwich."

"I have to confess that I love Tony's sandwiches, as well."

Leon swallowed tightly as he dropped down next to her. It made him feel good to be around Misty.

"What's on your agenda for the weekend?" Leon inquired once their food arrived.

"My mom's here," Misty said. "We're going to enjoy some girl time with Talei."

"I hope y'all have a great visit."

"What are your plans?" Misty asked. She took a bite of her sandwich.

"I'm working."

She gave him a tiny smile. "I hope that it will be a quiet weekend for you, then."

"Thank you. I'm taking vacation for a week. I need to do some much-needed work and repairs around my house. My brother is coming toward the end of June for a visit."

"How wonderful for you and Miss Eleanor. She misses him a great deal."

"I know." Leon bit into his sandwich. He

swallowed, then said, "I'm really glad you decided to attend John's service."

"He was my ex-husband. I wanted to say goodbye," Misty responded. "I debated whether to bring Talei. My mom didn't think it was a good idea, but in the end, I felt like she needed to be there."

"How is Talei doing?"

"She still talks about her dad. She woke up a couple of times saying he was hurt in the car. This morning she picked up my tablet and said she wanted to see him. John used to FaceTime with her."

"I know this isn't easy for either of you."

"It's not," Misty said. "It's heartbreaking to watch my little girl yearn for her daddy and there's nothing I can do to help her."

"You're doing all the right things," Leon assured her. "I'm curious. What does her name mean?"

"*Talei* means *Precious One*," she responded.

"It fits her." He finished the last of his sandwich and considered a moment before speaking. "For the record, I never knew about John's treatment of you."

"I'm not surprised," Misty said. "He didn't want that getting out to anyone. Growing up with a man like his father, John didn't know how to stand up to him. Drinking was the way he dealt with it; only it made him just like the man he despised."

Leon took a sip of his water. "John could never really handle his alcohol. After a couple of drinks, I'd have to practically carry him back to our dorm room."

Misty smiled. "He told me how you always looked out for him."

Leon agreed. "Yeah."

"I love your aunt," Misty said, changing the subject.

"Everybody loves her. Aunt Eleanor used to tell me that she was called to be of service to others. If you didn't have any money you could still eat in the café. She just asked that you come talk to her first. Each year, elementary school students tour the bakery. Aunt Eleanor always makes sure there are cookies, even gluten-free options, for the children."

"I saw all the thank-you cards in her office from the different schools," Misty said.

"John never mentioned that you were a baker," Leon stated.

"He didn't want me to work while we were married. This is my first real job in a while. I came to Polk Island to see some property and had lunch at the café. Miss Eleanor and I got to talking. I went back to Charleston with a condo and a job. It seemed like the perfect choice."

CHAPTER EIGHT

"I'm back, Mama," Misty said when she arrived home. "I ran into a friend. We had lunch together." She laid her purse on the counter. "Where's Talei?"

Oma came out of the kitchen carrying a bottle of water. "She's taking a nap. She's been down for about fifteen minutes. I made some fried squash bread and Cherokee casserole for dinner."

"Thanks, Mama. You know how much I love your squash bread."

They sat down in the living room.

Misty freed her hair from its ponytail. "Was she still asking for John? She had a tantrum this morning because she couldn't FaceTime him."

"A couple of times. What's an *eon*?"

"She means Leon. He was the first person there when the accident happened and again at the hospital. He's the person I had lunch with earlier."

"Is he a firefighter?"

"Yes, he is. Why?"

"Talei has a bear with a Polk Island Fire Department T-shirt in bed with her. She would give it to me and say *eon*. I didn't know what the child was talking about."

"I think he gave it to her the day of the accident. Leon and John were friends. He's known him since college."

Oma looked surprised. "Really?"

Misty nodded. "I didn't know they still kept in touch."

"What do you think of this man?"

"He's nice," she said. "Leon is a caring person—he looks out for his aunt and all the people he cares about. He's been here for me and Talei. He's friendly and funny. A little old-fashioned in some of his ways, but I like it."

"Is he married?"

"He lost his wife and child three years ago."

"How tragic," Oma murmured.

"Very much so," Misty said. "He would've made a great father. You should see him with Talei."

"She was talking to that bear as if it were him. Now, when did he become her godfather? I never heard mention of it before."

"John named Leon her godfather. He couldn't accept initially because of what he was dealing with, but he wants to be there for Talei now."

"That's nice of him."

Misty agreed.

Her eyes strayed to a bag containing a colorful quilt. "Who is that for?"

Oma smiled. "It's for you. I thought it might look nice on your bed."

Misty pulled the quilt from the bag. "Mama, it's gorgeous. I love it."

"I also bought some new moccasins for Talei. The others look like they're too small for her feet."

"*Wado*, Mama."

"*Hawa.*"

"Have you heard from Aunt Lois?"

"I haven't spoken to her in years. Your father doesn't want any members of his family communicating with me, so they don't. They never wanted to be in the middle."

Misty's eyes grew wet. "I guess he divorced me when you divorced him."

"I'm so sorry," Oma said.

"It's not your fault, Mama. There's no way we could've stayed with him. He was an alcoholic and a cheater. You deserved better than that."

"When I found out he had a baby on the way, I knew the marriage was forever broken."

"It's just really sad that he cut his whole family off from me. I would love to have gotten to know them. I have siblings I've never met. I don't even know their names. There was a time when I didn't care to meet them, but I feel differently now."

"Misty, you can reach out to your family—you don't have to wait for them to contact you."

"I know that, Mama. You've never tried to keep me from them. When I was younger, I felt like they should be the one to contact me since I was a child. The truth is that my grandmother has been on my mind a lot lately. She's the one I'd like to see."

"Then you should give her a call, Misty. I don't know if the number I have for her is still good, but it's a start."

Misty embraced her mother. "I'll try to contact her tomorrow."

She could purposely ignore the feeling of abandonment that flowed through her, but it was always there, taunting her. Misty hadn't forgiven her dad for disrespecting her mother by parading his girlfriend around their friends and even bringing her to one of Misty's school events. He was intent on embarrassing Oma. When her mother left him, he never attempted to reach out to her. He simply moved on with his new family.

Misty blamed him for all the dysfunctional relationships in her life. She blamed him for the hole that was left in her heart because of his absence. She faulted him for not loving her enough to at least try to be a better father.

THE NEXT DAY, Misty did what she'd told Oma she would—she keyed in the phone number, hoping her grandmother would answer on the other end.

"Hello."

"Is this Waverly Taylor?" she asked.

"Yeah. Who is this?"

"This is Misty…your granddaughter."

"Misty? Mike's daughter?"

"Yes, ma'am. Oma is my mother."

"I haven't heard from your mama in years. I didn't know if y'all was dead or alive. If you lookin' for your daddy, he ain't here. He lives in New York now."

"No, ma'am, I'm not calling about him. You've been on my mind a lot," Misty said. "That's why I called."

"Baby, I'm so glad to hear from you. I know Mike didn't do right by you and your mama. I want you to know I didn't raise him to be that way."

"I don't need a father," Misty said. "I have a beautiful little girl and we're fine. My mother is good. Like I said, you've been on my mind for a while and I decided to just reach out. There's no need to live in the past."

"Sounds like you're a right smart young woman. Are y'all still in South Carolina?"

"Yes. My mom is in Charleston, but I live on Polk Island."

"I would certainly love to see you and my great-granddaughter before I go home to glory."

Misty smiled. "I would love to see you, too."

"I'm gonna tell you this. I'm sorry for letting Mike keep you away from us. I hope you and Oma can forgive me. I was trying to keep the peace in my family back then, but it was wrong. I should've spoke up."

"It's okay, Grandmother. I know how my dad can get. Besides, I allowed him to keep me away as well, but I won't let him do it again."

"I won't either," Waverly promised. "I'm gonna do better by you, Misty."

When they hung up, Misty found her mother and gave her a quick recap.

"Sounds like you and your grandmother had a good conversation."

"We did, Mama. She wants to see me and Talei."

"That's wonderful news. The creator will work things out and his timing is always perfect."

"I'm glad I called her. I won't have to spend any more time wondering what would happen or if she ever thought about me."

"I'm happy for you."

Misty scanned her mother's face. "Are you really happy, Mama? You don't feel like I'm betraying you or anything? I want you to tell me."

"You should know me better than that," Oma responded. "I've always wished for you to have a relationship with Michael's family."

"I'm so lucky to have you as a mother."

"And I've been blessed to have you as my daughter. I want you to have the life you've always dreamed of—it's still possible."

Misty settled back against the cushions. "I thought I had it with John, but I was never so wrong."

"That's all in the past now."

"You're right. Time to live in the present."

LEON DROVE TO Charleston to pick Trey up from the airport. "I'm so glad you're home."

The two men embraced.

"Big brother, I'm so happy to be here. You know the first place I want to go is to the café. I need some of Aunt Eleanor's chocolate cake in my life."

"She has a new employee named Misty helping her with the baking. Man… She truly has a gift. She's been at the bakery since May and business has increased, according to Aunt Eleanor. They had several wedding cakes for this month already and more for July."

"Really?"

Leon nodded. "In fact, she was married to John."

Trey's eyes grew wide in his surprise. *"John Hayes?"*

"Yeah. It's a small world..."

"How did John's wife end up working for Aunt Eleanor?"

"When Misty came to the island to find a place to live, they connected."

"Wow, it really is a small world," Trey said. "I can't wait to meet her."

Grinning, Leon glanced at his brother. "Auntie is gonna be beside herself when she sees you. She really misses you."

"I miss her, too."

"We're here," Leon said as he pulled into a vacant parking space in front of the café.

Eleanor was standing in the doorway. "Trey, I'm so glad to see you," she said, embracing her nephew.

Trey kissed her cheek. "It's great being back on the island."

Misty walked out of the kitchen. When she spotted Leon, she gave a tiny wave.

He gestured for her to join them. "Trey, this is the lady I was telling you about."

Trey shook her hand. "Leon was actually talking about your cakes."

She smiled. "Okay…"

Eleanor made the introductions. "This is Misty. Leon's right. Her cakes sell out fast. We've had wedding cake orders every weekend this month. Birthday cakes, too."

Rubbing his hands together, Trey said, "I have to try this chocolate cake right here."

"I'll cut you a slice." Smiling, Misty glanced over at Leon. "You want anything?"

"No, I'm good."

Leon and Trey sat down with Eleanor at one of the tables near the kitchen.

"How have you been?" Trey grabbed the menu and perused it. He glanced up at Eleanor.

"I'm doing fine. I've been a lil forgetful from time to time. I guess it comes with getting old."

"Auntie, I've told you that you're not old," Leon interjected. "You need to stop saying that."

"Leon's right. You're nowhere near old."

"In my mind I feel twenty-five years old, but my body constantly reminds me that I'm fifty-five."

One of the servers brought a plate laden with a huge slice of chocolate cake. She placed it in front of Trey.

Leon's eyes kept traveling to the kitchen for glimpses of Misty. As much as he tried to fight the emotions threatening to escape from behind the wall, he'd carefully erected to protect what was left of his heart, she was still able to infiltrate somehow. Leon found himself looking forward just to seeing that beautiful smile of hers.

He tried to deny the pulsing knot that had formed in his stomach when Misty walked out of the kitchen.

"She's beautiful," Trey said.

Leon nodded in argument. "Yes, she is."

"Well, if I were in your shoes, I'd do something about it."

His words gave Leon something to consider.

MISTY STOLE A peek into the café area. Leon and Eleanor looked to be having a wonderful reunion with Trey. She enjoyed seeing him so happy. A visit from his brother was like medicine for him.

She gave herself a mental shake, then went back to decorating the cake she'd been working on before Leon and his brother showed up.

Eleanor appeared in the doorway. "Sugar, when you get a free minute, come join us."

"I will," Misty said. "Give me five minutes."

She did a quick check in the mirror to make sure she didn't have any flour on her face. Eying her reflection, Misty removed the cap and freed her curly tresses.

Leon moved over to make room for her. She could feel the heat emanating from his body and drank in the comfort of his nearness.

"Looks like they're keeping you pretty busy today," he said.

Misty nodded. "I have to have a birthday cake done for pickup later today. I spent most of my morning helping out in the café."

"Trey, this lady here is a godsend," Eleanor stated. "She can practically run this shop all by herself."

"I wouldn't say that," Misty responded. "I just do what I can to help out around here."

"Hey, Aunt Eleanor isn't one to give meaningless compliments." Trey picked up his water glass. "She's really needed someone new. The last time I was home that other guy wasn't that good."

Eleanor chuckled. "He was fine, but after his heart attack, nothing was the same."

"I'm with Trey on this one," Leon said. "Aunt Eleanor had to make all of the specialty cakes."

"Y'all leave Augustus alone. He done retired."

"Thank goodness," Trey said.

"Why don't we have a cookout or something for the Fourth of July?" Eleanor suggested.

"Sounds good to me," Trey responded.

"That's the perfect way to end my vacation. I love the day after."

Leon agreed, then looked over at Misty. "You're invited, too."

Smiling, she said, "I'd love to come. Can I bring anything?"

"Cake," Leon and Trey said in unison, sparking laughter all around the table.

CHAPTER NINE

"I CAN TELL that you really like Misty," Trey stated when they walked out of the shop. "I saw the way you were looking at her."

Leon gave his brother a sidelong glance. "What are you talking about?" He wasn't ready to admit his attraction to anyone—not even himself.

"Man… You know you like that woman. Hey, I can't blame you. She's gorgeous."

"She was married to my friend."

"From the sound of it, John wasn't the man we thought he was," Trey responded. "Sounds like he didn't deserve a woman like her. I think she'd be good for you, Leon."

"I haven't gotten over losing Vera. It wouldn't be fair to her when I still have feelings for my late wife."

"A part of you never will never stop loving Vee, but life isn't over for you, big brother. It's time for you to get back out there, Leon."

"That's what everybody keeps telling me, but

it's just not that easy. I can't erase my feelings for Vee. I miss her more and more every day."

"Leon, I get that."

"I don't want to meet someone and mislead them. I'm not ready to date."

"Okay," Trey murmured. "I'm not gonna push you."

"I wish I could get Aunt Eleanor to stop."

"You know she means well."

"Yeah."

"I think I'd like to walk around the town for a bit," Trey said. "It's been a while and I miss the island."

"Is that your way of making sure the ladies know you're back?" Leon teased.

Trey burst into laughter. "Hey, I just want to say hello to a few people. What are you about to get into?"

"I'm going home," Leon said. "I think it's time I redecorated my room."

"Why don't you ask Misty to help you?"

"I'm sure I can manage," Leon responded. "I'm just getting new bedding. Something to match that new quilt Aunt Eleanor made for me last Christmas."

He unlocked the door to his truck. "You want me to drop you off anywhere?"

"I'm good," Trey responded.

"Think you'll be around for dinner?"

"Yeah. I'll be there."

Five hours later, the doorbell rang just as Leon was about to make dinner. He left the pack of hamburger sitting on the kitchen counter and went to answer the door.

He opened it quickly, expecting a package delivery or one of his neighbors bringing misdelivered mail, but instead he found Trey standing there, holding two boxes of pizza.

"No offense, brother, but you're not a cook, so I thought I'd spare you by getting dinner tonight."

Leon took the pizza boxes from him. "Nothing like a night of pizza, beer and brotherly conversation."

They sat down at the dining room table, eating and talking.

"I'm really glad you're here," Leon said. "I know Auntie feels the same way."

"Have you noticed that she's starting to repeat some things? She mentioned being forgetful. Anything we should be worried about?"

"I don't think so, Trey. I can be forgetful at times."

After several slices of pepperoni and sausage pizza, they watched a movie before Leon marched upstairs, calling it a night. "Come by the station if you run out of things to do or people to see."

Carrying the paper plates to the trash, Trey laughed. "I'll do that."

Leon showered, then slipped on a pair of pajama pants and a T-shirt.

He climbed into a king-size bed. Most times, he slept in the guest room, which had a full-size bed. It didn't make him feel quite as lonely as he did in the one he'd shared with Vera. With Trey there, he had no choice but to sleep in the master bedroom. The third bedroom had been converted into a home office.

Three hours later, Leon punched his pillow with his fist. Plagued with thoughts of Misty, he was having a tough time sleeping. His mind warred between his attraction for a woman who wasn't his late wife and his guilt for feeling that way. Although he no longer wore his wedding ring, Leon was still bound by his vow to Vera.

She's gone, he told himself. The promises made on their wedding day remained in force only until the day she died. However, Leon chose to continue to remain faithful as a way to honor Vera. She'd meant the world to him and he wasn't going to dismiss her so easily.

He had not expected to develop feelings for Misty beyond friendship. After all, she was John's ex-wife.

Although Misty tried to keep her expression neutral, Leon knew that their attraction was mutual. He was rusty when it came to this sort of thing, but he was sure that he'd caught glimpses of interest in her eyes whenever they were in the same room.

Groaning, Leon turned from his left side to the right. He was scheduled to be at the station at 8:00 a.m. to start his shift.

Why was it so hard to get this woman out of his head?

Why couldn't he stay away from her?

THE NEXT MORNING, Misty followed her usual routine of dropping Talei off to day care at 6:00 a.m., then heading down Main Street to the shop to start the morning baking.

As she waited for the lemon blueberry muffins to come out of the oven, she worked on carrot cake muffins next, all the while trying to keep her mind off Leon.

She was failing miserably.

If Leon hadn't been so blatant in his attraction to her, Misty could've easily dismissed his actions as simply the thoughtful gestures of a nice guy.

Initially, Misty had been certain he kept his distance because she was John's ex-wife. But now she felt his reservations were less about whom she'd been married to and more about his grief. In his present state of mind, Misty represented a risk to his broken heart. His daughter would be around Talei's age now—how often did being around her remind him how much he missed her? If her daughter got too attached to Leon… It worked both ways. Misty ran the same risk.

She was so conflicted. It seemed wrong to feel any sort of attraction or desire for a man grieving his late wife and child.

She had worked hard so far to keep a polite distance, but the truth was the damage had already been done.

LEON ACCEPTED THE cup of coffee from Trey. "Thanks, man. You don't know how much I need this." He wasn't really a coffee drinker, but after a night with no sleep, he needed the caffeine.

"Actually, I do. I heard you moving around in your room. I knew you had trouble sleeping."

"I suffer from a little insomnia," Leon said. "Since Vee died. I thought changing the bedcovers and stuff would help, but it didn't."

"Maybe you need to say goodbye," Trey suggested. "A real goodbye."

Leon looked at his brother. "I know."

"You can't move forward until you stop being Vee's husband. She's gone and she's not coming back."

Leon didn't respond.

"I made breakfast," Trey announced. "Nothing special. Just scrambled eggs, bacon and toast."

"That's probably all you can cook," Leon said with a chuckle.

"Neither one of us inherited Aunt Eleanor's cooking skills." Trey handed a plate to his brother.

"You're right about that."

They sat down to eat.

"Thanks for this," Leon said. "I appreciate it."

After they finished eating, Leon cleaned the kitchen before heading out to work.

Leon's day at the firehouse started with an exchange of information from the previous day. When the meeting ended, he spent the latter half of the morning checking his fire apparatus and protective gear.

He helped his team clean up around the property before leaving to do fire hydrant maintenance.

The tasks complete, Leon returned to the station house. It was his turn to make dinner for the crew.

Leon made spaghetti for the evening meal while Charles prepared a large bowl of salad to go with the entrée.

An image of Misty formed in his mind as he

stirred the pasta in the hot boiling water. There was a part of him that wanted to be with her and Talei. In fact, it took everything in him to not pick up the phone and call her.

The timer on the oven went off.

With a sigh, Leon tried to forget the woman who stayed on his mind night and day.

CHAPTER TEN

MISTY WAS LOOKING forward to spending the holiday with Eleanor and Leon. Otherwise, she and Talei would've spent it on the beach or at home. Her mother had gone to visit her sister in Florida, and her friend Brittany was vacationing with her fiancé.

"Happy Fourth of July," Trey greeted when he opened the front door. "Leon's out back with Aunt Eleanor."

Bending down, he said, "This pretty girl must be Talei. Hey, cutie."

"Oseeyo," she said, grinning.

"My name is Trey. Leon is my brother."

"Trey," she repeated, then peeked around him. "Where Eon?"

"He's back here." Trey led Talei and Misty to the patio.

"Eon… *Oseeyo.*" Talei ran up to him. "Gawfather."

Trey looked at Leon. "Did she just call you godfather?"

He nodded.

"Cool."

Trey moved on to greet other guests.

Leon sat down beside Misty. "I know we told you to bring cake, but I heard about your shrimp and crab deviled eggs from Eleanor and hope you brought some."

"I did," she confirmed. Lowering her voice, she whispered, "And I bought an extra tray just for you."

"And a cake?"

Smiling, she nodded. "Yes, I brought cake, too."

Leon broke into a grin. "You know you just made my day, right?"

Misty laughed.

There was something in Leon's manner that soothed her, making her feel safe and secure.

Misty wasn't able to shut out any awareness of him, so she embraced it instead. He wasn't like the other men she'd dated, and he had no hidden motives. She could call him *friend* and it was true by any definition of the word. Misty had never believed in the label "perfect gentleman," but that's exactly what Leon was—a perfect gentleman.

THE FOURTH OF July cookout was in full swing.

Misty heard a giggle near the rosebushes in

the backyard. She crept through the grass to find Talei hiding near them.

"What are you doing, sweetie? Remember, don't touch Miss Eleanor's roses."

"I hiding from Trey. He tickle monster. He wanna get me."

She felt the presence of someone behind her and glanced over her shoulder.

"Where is the little princess?" Trey questioned. "When I find her, I'm gonna tickle her."

Talei burst into giggles, leading him straight to her hiding place.

Trey swooped past Misty to pick up Talei.

"Who's gonna save the princess now?" he asked.

"Eon," Talei called out.

"I'm coming to the rescue, little one," Leon responded.

Eleanor was standing beside Misty. "Both my boys are gwine make great daddies."

Misty nodded. "I believe you're right."

Talei was a bubble of pure joy being the center of attention. When she wasn't following behind Leon, she was with Trey. However, when other children began arriving, Talei abandoned them both. It didn't last long. One of the boys found a worm, which sent her running back to Leon.

Misty and Eleanor shared a look of amusement.

"She's definitely my daughter. I hate bugs and worms—all forms of insects."

"I'd better go tell them kids to stop scaring her," Eleanor said.

Misty coaxed Talei into playing with another little girl who was about the same age.

"I need to finish the pasta salad," she told Leon. "Do you mind keeping an eye on her? I shouldn't be gone long."

"Take your time," he responded. "She'll be fine."

Fifteen minutes later, the food was ready to be served.

Misty and Eleanor made plates for the children first.

She was one of the last people to eat. Misty sat down beside Leon, who seemed to be enjoying his burger.

"Thanks for fixing a plate for me," she said.

He responded, "You were so busy looking out for everybody else. I didn't want you to miss out." Lowering his voice to a whisper, he added, "Aunt Eleanor's friend Rusty is nice, but his relatives like to pack up food to take home."

"Oh, I see."

Misty loved the way Leon's lips parted when he laughed that deep, throaty laugh. Being this close to him made her very aware that it had been a long time since a man had made her feel special. She was not a woman who needed a man in her life, but that didn't mean she wanted to be alone either. She had always wanted to share her life with someone—a man who was family-oriented, had a strong work ethic, great sense of humor—a man who would love her and value her with his whole heart.

Misty just wasn't sure a man like that existed.

After they finished eating, Trey hooked up a speaker to his iPhone to play an old-school music playlist.

She swayed to the music. Talei ran up to her and began dancing with her.

"That's right, baby, I like your moves," Misty told her daughter.

Trey swooped in, picking up Talei and swinging her around. "Dance with me, Princess."

"Having fun?" Leon asked when she joined him by the chest containing the drinks. He handed a soda to her.

"I am," Misty said. "I'm going to have to run ten miles to lose the extra pounds I gained from eating all this food. Everything was delicious. In fact, I might have to have one more hamburger."

"I've never seen you eat this much," Leon said. "You normally eat like a bird."

"Really? That's what you think?"

"Maybe I shouldn't have said it like that. All

I'm saying is that I've never seen you finish a meal—you normally take half of it home."

Misty smiled. "That's intentional, Leon. A girl has to watch her figure."

A group of people started a line dance.

She grabbed Leon by the hand and led him to join in.

"I'm not good with this," he said.

"Just follow me," Misty encouraged. She was having the time of her life.

At six thirty, everyone walked down to the park to watch the fireworks.

Misty noted the set of earphones in Leon's hand. "Who are those for?"

"For Talei," he responded. "Some children don't like the noise. It scares them."

She gave him a gentle nudge. "You're so sweet and thoughtful."

When it was time for the fireworks to begin, Leon found a great area for them to sit to watch the display.

The fiery sparks burst through the night like brilliant colors on a canvas of stars. The explosive sounds startled Talei, but she was fine once he placed the headphones over her ears.

Misty thought the soaring golden yellow, red, green and blue flares resembled flowers exploding in the air.

"Pretty…" Talei murmured, pointing upward. "Look, Mommy."

Leon reached over and took Misty's hand in his own.

Misty felt the electricity of his touch. It made her feel good, and she was glad to be with him.

IN SPITE OF the dreary weather, and Trey's leaving to return to Camp Pendleton, Leon was in a great mood as he drove his brother to the airport. He had thoroughly enjoyed their time together.

Leon was sad to see Trey go but grateful for the time they'd had. This brief visit was exactly what he'd needed—to reconnect with his brother.

"I hope you're finally gonna go after Misty," Trey said. "You're good together."

He stole a glance at his brother. "You really think so?"

"Yeah," Trey responded. "So does Aunt Eleanor and probably the whole town."

Leon burst into laughter.

Trey pointed to the console. "I've been meaning to ask… You have this state-of-the-art satellite-navigation system in your truck. Have you ever used it? Do you even leave the island?"

"I'm not a hermit, Trey. I get out," he said as

they drove across the bridge to Charleston. "In fact, I plan on getting out a lot more."

"I'm happy to hear this. Hopefully you'll be taking Misty with you. It's time for you to jump back into the dating pool. You deserve to have that family you always wanted."

Leon grinned. "I hear you, little brother, and I'll consider your advice."

He pulled curbside to the airport. "Here we are…"

Trey nodded. "Back to California. Next time, you gotta come out to see me. You'd love Oceanside."

"I'll do that."

Leon got out to embrace his brother. "Stay safe and thank you for your service."

CHAPTER ELEVEN

"So, I met Trey," Misty told Brittany when they got together for dinner and a movie. "He's such a sweetheart."

"Yeah…he is… I had fun with him when we dated. I hate I missed seeing him while he was in town."

"Well, you were vacationing with your bae," Misty said. "Did you have a good time?"

Brittany held up her left hand to display an engagement ring. "I had a wonderful time."

Misty gasped. "Congratulations, Britt. Oh, my goodness! You're getting married."

"Girl, it's about time," Brittany uttered. "Rick and I have been together for five years. We've been talking about marriage forever. Even though I was already saying he was my fiance… it's official now."

"You spoke it into existence."

"I sure did."

Misty laughed. "I'm happy for you, Britt."

The waitress arrived with their meals.

"How are things between you and Leon?" Brittany inquired while they ate.

Misty wiped her mouth on a napkin. "What do you mean? There's nothing going on with us."

Brittany picked up her wineglass. "Girl, pleeze…"

"You're wrong about this. Leon is a nice guy but it's obvious that he's still grieving the loss of his wife."

"I saw you two at the barbecue. Y'all are good together. I think you're just what Leon needs to move on with living. *You and Talei.*"

"My daughter loves him, Britt. She lights up every time she sees Leon. He's her godfather so I don't want to mess things up between us. But… I can't stop thinking about him."

"Take it one day at a time," Brittany advised. "And enjoy the journey."

They finished dinner, paid the bill and walked across the street to the movie theater.

Two and a half hours later, they exited through the glass doors and headed to their cars.

"I was hesitant initially about taking Talei to meet my dad's mother," Misty announced, "but after seeing this movie, I'm going to do it."

"*Really?* You talked to her?"

Misty nodded. "We've had a couple of conversations and they've been very positive. I'm looking forward to seeing her again. It's been a long time."

"What about your father?"

"I've made it clear that I'm not ready to see him. He's moved on with his new family—that doesn't have to change."

The two women embraced.

"I'm really happy for you," Brittany said before getting into her car.

Misty climbed into her vehicle and locked the door. She followed her friend out of the parking lot and then turned in the opposite direction. She had to pick up Talei from Eleanor's house.

"GOOD MORNING, MISS ELEANOR," Misty greeted. "Thanks again for watching Talei for me."

"Great morning to you. It was my pleasure." Eleanor slipped on an apron. "What are you working on?"

"Pastries and doughnuts," Misty replied. "We had a pretty busy morning. The raspberry cream cheese muffins sold out quick."

"Really? I think we should add them to the regular menu."

Eleanor washed her hands, then began working across the table from Misty. "I need to make some more grits." She placed a towel next to the burner as she talked. "How are you feeling now that things are settling down?"

"I hate that John's gone…that he won't get to see Talei grow up. Our marriage ended before it really began. His father had a lot to do with that."

"That Elroy is a piece of work."

"That he is," Misty responded as she kneaded the dough. "When I put these in the oven, I'll change the daily specials on the sign outside."

"Okay. Josh just left to pick up some napkins and other stuff. I'm going to get everything ready for lunchtime."

Misty grabbed the signs once the pastries were baking and headed outside.

Humming softly, Eleanor moved about the kitchen retrieving ingredients for items on the lunch menu. Next, she seized the broom and walked out of the shop.

"Hello, Eleanor," someone greeted.

"Mamie, I haven't seen you in a while."

"I was in Philadelphia taking care of my mother. I'm so glad to be back here on the island. I've missed my morning ritual of your fresh-baked muffins."

"This is Misty Brightwater," Eleanor said. "She's the new baker. Wait until you taste her baked goods."

They stood there with Mamie in deep conversation for the next twenty minutes.

"Eleanor, I think there's a fire in your kitchen," Mamie cried suddenly.

They rushed inside the shop to see timbers charring and blackening, a smoke haze coating the room and paint bubbling as the full blaze threatened to get out of hand quickly.

Misty tried but couldn't get to the fire extinguisher through the billowing flames.

Eleanor called the fire department.

The cackle of the fire had Misty's attention, but it was the woof and hissing sounds that concerned her. "We need to get out of here," Misty said. "C'mon, Miss Eleanor."

Outside a crowd was gathering.

Josh ran over to them. "I was worried when I didn't see y'all. What happened?"

"I think I left my towel on the stove," Eleanor said and shuddered.

Misty embraced her. "Here comes the fire truck."

Eleanor's eyes teared up and she started to cough from the thick smoke and ash.

Leon rushed to her side. "Auntie, are you okay?"

"I'm fine. We all got out. The s-shop…"

"I need to get in there."

Eleanor wiped away her tears. "Be careful, Leon."

"Don't worry. They're going to do what they

can to save the shop," Misty said. "Looks like most of the damage will be in the kitchen."

Rusty walked up. "I heard about the fire and wanted to make sure everyone was safe."

"We're fine," Eleanor said. "Devastated and heartbroken, but fine."

LEON AND THE other firefighters worked furiously as the blaze moved quickly, leaving behind a trail of damage. They were able to contain it there, but the rest of the shop couldn't escape the flood of water that was everywhere.

Eleanor placed a call to her insurance company. "I need to file a claim for fire and water damage." She gave them the policy number.

"Mrs. Pittman, I'm afraid that policy lapsed a month ago for nonpayment."

"That can't be right," Eleanor said indignantly. "I paid the premium and y'all gwine do your part. I'ma check my records and give you a call back with the proof."

She covered her face with trembling hands and gave vent to the agony of her loss.

What if she'd messed up? She had been so forgetful lately.

Leon and Charles walked over to discuss the damage in full. She gave them her full attention.

When everyone left, she sat down in the café area with her laptop.

"What in the world..." Stunned, Eleanor stared at her bank account. She had no memory of some of the transactions or the cash withdrawals. Worse, she couldn't find proof of payments that were made to the insurance company. Eleanor had been told that her policy had lapsed, but as far as she was concerned, they were wrong.

"Why didn't I make the payments?" she whispered.

Eleanor knew that she'd been a little forgetful, but mostly small things. Thankfully there was no mortgage on the bakery or on her house. However, if her insurance had truly lapsed, how was she going to pay for the repairs on the bakery?

She looked back at the computer monitor. Could someone be stealing from her? Eleanor wasn't ready to accept that her memory issues were greater than she had assumed.

"Miss Eleanor..."

She glanced up to find Misty standing there. "C'mon in, sugar."

"Are you okay? Is there anything I can do for you?"

Eleanor checked her watch, then glanced around. "We need to get moving. The lunch crowd will be arriving within the hour."

Misty eyed her. "I put a sign on the door."

"Why?"

"The fire… Miss Eleanor, the kitchen is a disaster."

She looked confused. "It is?"

"Yes, ma'am."

Eleanor stood up and went to the kitchen. "Oh, Lawd, there's so much damage…" she uttered. Tears sprang into her eyes once more. "Noooo."

Misty embraced her. "There's damage but Leon feels like it can easily be repaired. He said it looks worse than it really is—it's going to be okay."

Eleanor nodded. "You're right. I just need to call the insurance company."

"Josh and I will start cleaning up the debris. Silas said he'd come by when he returned from Charleston."

"I guess there's nothing for me to do but go home, but I might need your help, Misty. I need to find the insurance paperwork."

"Let me finish here and make sure Josh is okay. I'll be there shortly."

"Thanks, sugar." Right now, Eleanor was filled with nothing more than nervous energy.

Polk Island Bakery & Café was her baby— her lifeblood. The thought that it had nearly been destroyed by fire brought tears to her eyes.

CHAPTER TWELVE

MISTY RANG THE doorbell and waited for Eleanor to open the door. Her eyes landed on the large Boston ferns framing the entry. They were a vivid green, luscious and full. Eleanor's yard was a beautiful landscape of rosebushes in red, pink and white blooms. Misty wished she possessed a green thumb. She didn't have a gift for taking care of plants or flowers, which was why all the arrangements in her house were artificial.

Eleanor opened the door and released a sigh of relief. "I'm so glad you're here. I need to find my insurance documents. Maybe you can help me."

"Sure." Misty noted how Eleanor was repeating herself. Maybe it was because she was still upset over the fire. That was enough to stress anyone.

She found the insurance cancellation notice amid the stack of paperwork on Eleanor's desk. Bewildered, Misty knew Eleanor was too responsible to just let the policy lapse for nonpayment. Something was definitely going on with her.

"Did you find anything?" Eleanor asked.

"Just a letter of cancellation."

The spark of hope in the older woman's gaze was quickly extinguished. "I've really made a mess of things."

"Miss Eleanor, you don't need to blame yourself," Misty said. "It was just an accident."

Tears filled her eyes. "I can't understand how I let things get so out of control. I've always been good about paying my bills. I'm never late on them."

"I know that."

"I really can't figure out how I missed paying the insurance company, but they're telling me that's what happened. I know I've been forgetful…"

"Miss Eleanor, I'd like to help with the repairs," Misty offered. "We were both outside talking and weren't paying attention to what was going on in the kitchen. I feel just as responsible."

"Sugar, you don't have to worry about this. I'll figure something out."

"Have you considered seeing a doctor?" Misty asked. "I've noticed that you seem a bit more forgetful lately, but it's not just that. A couple of times you had some confusion at the cash register. I know you've had a lot on your mind, so it might just be that, but it won't hurt to get checked out by a doctor."

"I'm just getting older," Eleanor stated. "Just wait and see… It will happen to you eventually."

"I'm not trying to upset you. You've been so good to me and my daughter. I'm just worried about you."

"There are times when I do feel confused," Eleanor confessed. "I forget to take my keys out of the door… One time, I even left my car door open after I got out. Someone could've stolen it. The more I talk about this… Misty, you might be right. This isn't me and I'm scared."

"You don't have to be afraid, Miss Eleanor. I'm here for you and so is Leon."

"I don't want Leon to know anything about this. He doesn't need to worry about me." Eleanor paused a moment, then said, "Please don't tell him about the insurance."

"Let me help you," she insisted.

"I can't take your money, Misty. I have some money saved. This is all my fault, so I'll have to deal with the fallout."

"Miss Eleanor," she pleaded, "when I needed help, you came to my aid. We will keep this between us. No one has to know."

"You are such a dear. Thank you, Misty, but it'll be fine. I'll take care of everything somehow."

"Is my aunt here?" Leon asked the next morning. He left the station and went straight to the shop to check on her. He knew Eleanor was upset. He also wanted to make sure that an insurance claim had been filed. The sooner they received payment, the sooner the bakery and café would be back up and running.

Misty shook her head. "She's at home. I told her I'd come in and help Josh and Silas with moving some stuff around."

A timeless moment stretched while she stared at him, absorbing the warmth of his gaze above smooth high cheekbones, appreciating the fullness of his mouth. A pulse of uneasy heat flickered in the pit of her stomach. Misty cleared her throat noisily.

Leon pointed to the mop in the corner. "You need some help?"

Misty snatched in a quick breath to regain her flustered wits.

"Oh, no… We got it covered, Leon. Thank you, but I think it's best you go check on your aunt. Miss Eleanor tried to hide it, but I could tell she was really shaken by the fire. It took a lot for me to convince her to go home."

Leon was instantly concerned. "I'll head over there now."

"Call me if she needs anything."

He smiled. "I will."

Misty stood at the window watching Leon as he strode to his truck. He climbed inside, turned the ignition and drove away.

She found it strange that she already missed him.

LEON BROKE INTO a grin when Eleanor opened the front door. "I see you finally took some time off."

"I was actually ordered to stay home by my staff," she responded. "They told me they would take care of everything. I decided to let them."

"It was a good call," Leon said. "I went by there. They have everything under control. Now all we need to do is let the insurance company do their part. I came by to see if you need any help with filling out the claims paperwork."

"Oh, you don't have to worry about that," Eleanor stated. "Everything's done."

The doorbell sounded.

Leon followed Eleanor to the foyer.

She broke into a smile when she opened the door. "Rusty, hello. C'mon in. I guess everybody's checking on me today. I'm a lucky woman."

"That's because we love you," he said, closing the door behind him.

"Rusty's right," Leon interjected. "You're loved by this community."

"I feel it and I'm grateful." Making her way into the living room, she said, "We might as well make ourselves comfortable."

Leon chose the love seat while Rusty sat down beside Eleanor on the floral-printed sofa.

"How long do you think the shop will have to be closed?"

"I stopped by there before I came here," Rusty said. "I'd say you're going to be closed two weeks to a month. Shouldn't be any longer than that. Josh and Silas can work at my store in the meantime. I doubt Misty will have any interest in building supplies."

Eleanor smiled. "That's so sweet of you, Rusty. Josh and Silas will appreciate that. Misty, I think, will be all right."

"Don't worry, Auntie. We're going to have the shop back up and running as quickly as we can. We have the whole community behind us." Leon rose to his feet. "I need to leave but I'll give you a call later."

"Thanks for coming by, son," Eleanor stated.

She waited until Leon walked out of the house and said, "Rusty, thank you for coming by. I was planning to call you. I need to talk to you about something."

"Sounds important."

"Hopefully, it's nothing." Eleanor didn't know quite how to begin, so she opened up with, "We've been friends for a long time, Rusty."

He nodded. "We have."

"I've always been able to count on you. Right now, I need to unburden myself." Eleanor got up and stood in front of the fireplace.

"What's wrong, Ladybug?"

"I let my insurance lapse. It was not intentional. I just don't know what happened. I've been forgetting a lot of stuff lately. I'm getting scared because I'm missing important things like locking my car, leaving the keys in the front door and not paying my insurance premium."

Rusty stood up, walked over and embraced her. "I think that comes with age. I walk into a room, then forget why I went in there the first place."

"That's what I thought at first, but now… I think something might be wrong with me."

"One way to find out for sure," he responded. "If you want, I'll go with you to see your doctor. I think you should get a professional opinion."

Eleanor smiled. "I knew I could count on you. But I need you to keep this just between you and me, Rusty. I don't want to worry Leon."

"I'll do whatever you want."

"Thank you, Rusty." Eleanor picked up her phone. "I'd better call the doctor now while it's on my mind."

CHAPTER THIRTEEN

RUSTY DROVE ELEANOR to her doctor's appointment.

While seated in the waiting area, she confided, "I have to admit that I'm scared. What if I have a tumor on my brain or cancer?"

He reached over and gave her hand a light squeeze. "Don't be afraid, Ladybug. It's gonna be alright. I feel it in my spirit."

She smiled. "You're just saying that."

"Is it working?" Rusty teased.

His words had the desired effect. Eleanor chuckled. "You're right. I have to remain positive."

"That's my girl."

"Thank you so much for coming with me."

Eleanor was called to the back where the examination rooms were located while Rusty stayed in the waiting room.

After seeing the doctor, she walked out and said, "Dr. Brown wants me to have an MRI done. They took some blood work. He mentioned Alzheimer's disease." Eleanor glanced at Rusty. "What if he's right and I have that disease? What will happen to the café? Or to me if I lose my memory?"

"Whoa… Let's not worry until we have a reason to do so, Ladybug."

She couldn't stop herself from pondering aloud, "But what if that's what is wrong with me, Rusty?"

"You won't be alone. I'll be here to take care of you, and you have your family."

"I don't want to be a burden."

"You won't be—none of us would ever consider you a burden."

Eleanor met his gaze. "There's something I want to know. Why didn't you ever get married?"

"Because the only woman I ever loved chose someone else to spend her life with."

"You're talking about me," Eleanor said with complete clarity.

"I am," he confirmed. "You have owned my heart since I saw you walk into the classroom when we were in first grade in the red-and-black polka-dot dress. You reminded me of a ladybug."

"Rusty, you never said anything in all these years. Why are you telling me now?"

"This is the first time I ever thought you'd

take me seriously." He took her hand in his own. "Eleanor, I love you and I want to marry you."

She gasped in surprise.

"We've known each other a long time. We have no idea what the future holds, but we can face it together."

"I used to have the biggest crush on you, Rusty, but I never thought you were interested."

"I didn't think I was good enough for you," he confessed. "You're a Rothchild. I don't feel that way anymore. I need to know how you feel about me."

Eleanor placed a hand to his face. "I've always cared for you—you know that. You're a very dear friend and if I were to marry again, you would be the man I'd choose."

"So, you're turning down my proposal?"

"No, I'm not. I'd just like to take some time to think about it," Eleanor responded. "Until this moment, I honestly never considered marrying anyone. To be honest, I thought that part of my life was over."

"I'm tired of being alone. Aren't you?" Rusty asked. "I want to share whatever life I have left with the only woman I've ever loved."

She nodded. "I get lonely."

"Then consider spending the rest of your life with me as my wife, my best friend and my ladybug."

"I will," Eleanor said. "I'm going to give it a lot of serious thought."

"I hope you do," Rusty responded. "Because I want you to marry me."

MISTY HELPED TALEI out of the vehicle. She stood there surveying the charming one-level brick house. They had come to Atlanta for a visit with Waverly Taylor, the grandmother she hadn't seen in years. A wave of apprehension washed over her, but she pushed through it. She had come too far. There was no turning back now.

Talei grabbed her hand. "Mommy, I scared."

"Sweetie, there's no reason to be afraid," Misty assured her. "We're just visiting my grandmother."

"Ganmother."

"That's right." Misty rang the doorbell.

She swallowed her nervousness as she waited for someone to answer the door. She took Talei's hand with her right. In her left, Misty carried a box.

Her grandmother suddenly appeared in the doorway. Misty's gaze swept over the woman's sturdy frame, her hair a stunning platinum-gray color and pulled back into a bun at the nape of her neck. Her beautiful cocoa-tinted complexion bore few wrinkles—it was as if time had stood still for Waverly Taylor. She looked just as Misty remembered.

"Oh, my goodness, I'm so happy to see y'all." Waverly glimpsed Talei and exclaimed, "Look at this little angel right here. She's downright gorgeous, Misty."

She ushered them inside.

The inside looked nothing like Misty remembered. The main living area boasted high ceilings with a skylight. A crystal chandelier in the living room doubled as a fan.

"Grandmother, the house is beautiful."

"Thank you. Mike had it completely renovated last year for my birthday. He put this luxury tile in the kitchen. I got granite countertops, stainless-steel appliances and all new carpet in the bedrooms."

"That was really nice of him." Misty swallowed the sour taste of bitterness that threatened to rise up. She remembered the huge argument her parents had when her mother wanted a new washing machine. Misty reminded herself that he was supposed to be a different man now. And Waverly was his mother and not his wife.

"How was the drive?"

"Not too bad," Misty responded. "Talei slept most of the trip."

"I'm so glad you decided to come. I really wanted to see you and the baby." Waverly paused a moment, then said, "I have to confess that I told your daddy about our phone conversation."

Misty shrugged in nonchalance. "It's fine, Grandmother. I don't care if he knows."

"I'm glad to hear you say that. I don't want no secrets. I just want my family to come together. I don't know how many more days I have on this earth—we're blood, and we need to start acting like it."

She led them to the family room at the back of the house. Waverly eased down in an olive-green recliner while Misty and Talei sat down on a matching sofa.

"I'm not ready for a conversation with Mike. I hope you'll respect my decision."

Waverly nodded. "I hope one day you'll change your mind about that."

Misty didn't respond.

Waverly didn't push her. "How is your mother doing, Misty?"

"She's good. Mama's always on the go—she travels, volunteers…anything to keep busy."

"Good for her," Waverly said. "Does she still sew? She used to make the most beautiful blankets and quilts."

"She still does," Misty responded. "She designs clothing, as well."

Waverly settled back in her chair. "I've always liked your mother."

"She says the same thing about you."

"I feel terrible over everything that happened. I surely do."

"Grandmother, it's okay," Misty told her. "I'm just glad to have you in my life now."

"I keep looking at the box you brought in here. What's in it?"

"I made you some banana bread. I remembered that it was your favorite, only this one is gluten-free."

Waverly broke into a wide grin. "You did? I haven't had no banana bread in such a long time. Well, since they told me I had a gluten allergy. I can't tell you how much I've missed it. I bought a gluten-free one and it tasted horrible."

Misty chuckled. "Well, I hope you'll find this one to your liking."

Waverly sampled a piece. "Oh, this is delicious, Misty. You have to tell me how you made it."

"I just replaced all-purpose flour with wheat-free, gluten-free, dairy-free, one-to-one baking flour. You can turn any recipe into a gluten-free one easily."

"I'ma have to get me some of that."

They exchanged recipes for the next thirty minutes.

"I think you might have inherited your love for baking from me," Waverly said. "I hadn't done much of it lately because of this gluten-free diet the doctor put me on."

"I'm so happy we've reconnected, Grandmother. There's so much I want to know about this side of my family."

"Your aunt Lois and your cousins are coming to the house around lunch. They're all very excited to meet you. Boo Boo—her name is Christina but we call her Boo Boo—has a little girl the same age as Talei. Your aunt Marsha will be here in a few."

"I can't wait to meet them."

"Mike and his family live in New York. I made it clear no one was to say anything to him about your visit just yet."

"Thank you, Grandmother. I know that I have to have a conversation with him—I just want do it on my terms."

"I respect that, but I have to tell you that I don't like keeping secrets."

"I understand."

By the end of the day, Misty had met two aunts, three first cousins and five second cousins. She'd also met a great-aunt Lucy, who was Waverly's sister. Her dad's brother lived in Virginia, but she was able to speak with him via FaceTime.

Mike's youngest sister, Marsha, offered to call Mike, but Misty politely declined the offer.

"I only want to enjoy this day with all of you," she explained.

Talei rushed over to her from the back of the house. "Mommy, I have fun."

"Me, too."

"Where's her dad?" Marsha inquired.

"He passed away in May," Misty stated.

"Oh, I had no idea. I heard her mention him when the kids were eating lunch."

"Oh, if you hear her say anything about an Eon, she's talking about her godfather. His name is Leon."

"I did hear her say that a few times. I didn't know what she meant. I thought it might be Cherokee or something. She must be pretty close to him."

"He's been a great comfort for her since losing her father."

Marsha embraced her. "I hope life has been good to you, Misty."

"It's been *life*. Some good some bad, but I'm grateful for all of it. I've learned a lot about me."

"Well, you look beautiful and very well-adjusted. I'm really glad you reached out to Mama. We wanted so much to contact you, but…"

"I'm sure Mike didn't want that. It's okay."

"No, it really isn't," Marsha stated. "I'm sure you know my brother wasn't no joke back in the day. He did some terrible things, but now he's a different man. He's really turned his life around."

"He truly has," Lois said. She sat down beside Misty on the sofa. "My brother is a different man."

"I'm glad to hear that," Misty said. "All I can remember about him is that he was really mean."

The room was enveloped in silence.

After a moment, Marsha changed the subject. They three women discussed the adventures of motherhood.

That evening, Waverly showed Misty to the room she and Talei would sleep in.

Talei was out by the time her head hit the pillow.

Misty went back to the front of the house to help her grandmother straighten up.

"I know you got to be tired. Go on to bed," Waverly said.

"I'm good," Misty responded. "Grandmother, thank you for today."

"Thank you for giving us another chance. You didn't have to because of your father."

"You're not Mike," she stated. "He is solely responsible for his actions."

"I been praying for the day he'll come to you and make things right," Waverly said.

Misty bagged up the trash. "I'll put this outside."

When she returned, Waverly said, "Now you go on to bed. I know you plan on leaving early to get back home. I'm very happy you came."

The two women embraced.

"Grandmother, I love you. I'm beyond thrilled to have you back in my life."

"Don't hold on to that anger and unforgiveness forever."

"I hear you, Grandmother. It's just going to take time. I didn't just get here overnight."

SHOES IN HAND, Leon walked along the sandy beach, enjoying the solitude of his late afternoon stroll and watching the squadrons of brown pelicans fly into an endless horizon. The sand dunes held stories and secrets of those who had lived on the island and were long buried.

He found a spot on a grassy knoll and sat down to reflect on his life. Three years had passed since the death of Vera and his daughter. There was a moment in time when Leon didn't think he would survive a day without them. His throat still tightened at the thought that she was truly gone from his life forever.

Leon heard laughter and turned his attention

to a woman and small child walking along the beach. As they neared, he recognized them.

Misty looked beautiful dressed in a pair of denim shorts and tank top, her black hair tumbling down past her shoulders. She seemed free from any worries and her smile flashed frequently as she and Talei walked to the water's edge. He was by no means blind to her attractiveness, as much as he tried to ignore it.

Leon had always wanted a beautiful wife and children—he wanted a family. And this sweet, loving pair seemed to fit right into his heart. He had to remind himself that this wasn't his life and never would be. The only thing he could offer Misty was friendship.

He stood up and made his way down to the beach.

Talei saw him first and waved animatedly. "Eon… Eon… Mommy, look."

"Hey, little one," Leon greeted as he picked her up and swung her around.

Her laughter filled the air.

Leon smiled at Misty. "I see we had the same idea this Sunday afternoon."

"Yeah, we did. I wanted to come and enjoy this beautiful view."

Still in his arms, Talei touched Leon's cheek. "I like ocean."

"So do I," he told her.

"I wanna play in ocean."

"Not today, sweetie," Misty said. "I'll take you to the pool when I get off work tomorrow."

Talei pursed her lips into a pout.

"You're going to have so much fun at the pool," Leon said. "I'm jealous. I'll be at the station working."

"I gonna have fun."

"Have some fun for me, too."

Talei nodded.

"I drove back from Atlanta this morning. We went to meet my dad's side of the family."

"Did you enjoy your visit?"

Smiling, Misty said, "Very much. I hadn't seen my grandmother since I was a child. My grandmother is a hoot. It was nice meeting my aunts and their children, too. Talei has quite a few little cousins."

"I love family get-togethers, too."

"How are the repairs going at the shop?" Misty inquired. "How is Miss Eleanor holding up?"

"Some of the men in the community have agreed to help with the repairs of the café," Leon announced. "Hopefully, we can have everything done in a month or two at the latest. My aunt's doing okay when she's not beating herself up over this."

"I told her it could've happened to any of us," Misty said.

"That place means everything to my aunt. Actually, to the community as a whole. It's been a part of my family's history for many years."

"I read somewhere that it was your great-great-great-grandfather who founded the island."

"In 1870, Polk Rothchild left Darien, Georgia, with his family to start a new life in New York. His wife, Agnes, became ill and died during the journey. She always loved the water, so he buried her here. Polk couldn't bear to leave his beloved wife behind, so instead of continuing on to New York, he settled on this island to raise his family. His brother Hoss soon joined him. They decided to carve the uninhabited patch of swampy land into suburban plots. Hoss had a passion for farming, so he planted indigo, cotton and rice."

"I've heard that indigo was a valuable export back then."

Leon nodded. "It was pretty profitable for Polk and Hoss because of the demands for the dye product in the textile industry. Hoss eventually opened a fabric store. He wasn't just a farmer. He could sew. I'm told he designed several suits for the Rockefeller and other wealthy families. They would stop here whenever they journeyed to Sea Island, Georgia. Hoss's shop was where the café stands now. My grandparents converted it after he died. His sons worked with him, but they left the island for New York after his death."

"I know this island is known for the beautiful quilts made by residents. There are some very talented quilters on this island," Misty said.

"If you're not in a rush to get home, I can give you a quick tour of my family's land and our history.

"I'll get Talei a snack and we're good to go."

Misty followed him in her car to a property on the other side of the island.

When they got out of their cars, Leon said, "There was a time when Polk Island was only accessible by ferry. The original houses were built from a mixture of lime, shells and water. This is the house that Polk built for his family. Next door is the church. That's our family cemetery in the back. Polk, his wife and all but one of their children are buried there. His son Abraham is buried in Savannah. Hoss and his wife are buried back there, but the rest of the family is buried in Forest Lawn across town."

Misty read the sign over the door. "Polk Island Praise House... Wow, what a wonderful remnant of history. So, Polk was also a minister?"

Leon nodded. "Yeah. So was his son Ezra. He's my great-great-great-grandfather." Pointing, he said, "This is what's left of the house where Ezra and my great-great-grandfather Eli were born," Leon said. "It was destroyed when a tropical cyclone touched down on the island in 1893. It struck this island, Hilton Head, Daufuskie, Parris, with some of the smaller islands getting the worst of it. The storm killed more than two thousand people along the coast—it was one of the worst storms to hit until Hurricane Hugo in 1989."

"The Praise House doesn't appear to have suffered any damage," Misty said.

"I know," Leon responded. "My family considered it a miracle that practically everything on this street was destroyed, but the church wasn't touched."

"I'm curious… Why didn't they rebuild?" Misty inquired.

"They did. Just not on this side of the island. Aunt Eleanor said they always intended to rebuild this area—it just never happened. They built a house on the land where my aunt lives. Her grandfather built the house she's in now when the one before that was damaged by fire."

Leon had a captive audience in Misty. She loved hearing about his family and the history of the island.

"Did Polk ever leave the island?" she asked.

"Only once and that was to find a mother

for his ten children," Leon said. "His new wife brought her family with her. When Polk died in 1940, at the age of one hundred, the island had grown to a population of nine hundred. Seven generations of the Rothchild family has lived here."

"And now it's one of South Carolina's most popular areas."

"I know," Leon replied. "It's a good thing, but there are times when I wish we didn't have so many tourists coming here. Especially during spring break. That's when we have problems with crime—nothing big, but it's still a nuisance."

"I can imagine it gets pretty wild."

"Yes, it does," Leon agreed.

He bent down and plucked a handful of leaves from a prickly ash tree. "Put one in your mouth and chew it."

Misty did as he instructed. Within a few seconds she experienced a numbing sensation.

"We call this the toothache tree."

"I'll have to remember this whenever Talei has one."

Leon pointed to the Spanish moss. "Stuffing some of that in your shoes will relieve you of aches and pains. People here had to come up with their own first aid treatments at that time."

"Wow."

He chuckled. "They don't do that anymore—
we simply call 9-1-1."

"I do know about this one," Misty said as fingered a yellowed flowered plant. "Life everlasting. My mother uses it as a tea and an essential
oil for inflammation and stomach issues. She
says that it has anti-aging properties."

"I have peppermint, aloe and life everlasting plants in my yard," Leon announced. "Vera
never liked taking medicine—she would always
seek out alternative solutions."

"She and I have that in common."

Talei began jumping up and down on a piece
of wood.

Leon figured she was getting bored, so he
said, "This ends this part of our tour. I'll take
y'all around the island on another day."

Smiling, Misty responded, "Looking forward
to it. Thank you for sharing your family history
with me."

CHAPTER FOURTEEN

TALEI CLIMBED OUT of the car asking, "Mommy... where Eon?"

"He had to go home, sweetie. We'll see him again another day."

Inside the house, Talei ran over to the couch to get her teddy bears.

Misty noticed that her daughter kept Pooh Bear and the teddy in the fire department shirt with her most of the time. She would've taken them to the beach with her, but Misty had her leave them home.

While Talei played on the carpet with her bears, Misty stretched out on the couch with a novel she was determined to finish before going to bed.

She was able to read through five chapters before her daughter commanded her attention.

"I want Eon."

Misty swung her legs off the couch and sat up. "Sweetie, he's at his house."

Talei pointed to the tablet on the coffee table.

Misty sat up. "You want to FaceTime Leon?"

"Yes, Mommy."

"Let me see if he's busy." Misty sent him a quick text.

Seconds later, he called her via FaceTime.

Talei lit up when she saw Leon on camera. *"Oseeyo..."*

"I heard you wanted to talk to me, little one."

"Yes," she responded.

"I was happy to see you today."

"I happy, too." Talei proceeded to tell him about her stuffed animals and what was on the television.

Leon was an animated listener as he engaged her daughter in conversation.

"You can call me anytime you want to talk, okay?" Leon said.

"What you doing?" Talei inquired.

"I'm just sitting over here watching some television."

"You want talk to Mommy?"

"Sure."

Talei handed the tablet to Misty.

"Clearly she's done with me," Leon said with a chuckle.

"I think whatever is on television just caught her attention," Misty responded. "Thank you for doing this."

"Anytime. I'm always here for you both."

There was something in Leon's manner that soothed her. He made her feel safe.

Misty knew their attraction was mutual, but she resolved to keep her emotions grounded and in check. She wasn't really looking for a relationship. Her most important priority right now was to make sure Talei was adjusting well to their move to the island and the sudden loss of her father.

"HAS THE ADJUSTER come by here yet?" Leon asked. "It's been about a week and a half."

Eleanor picked up some papers off her desk and pretended to be reading them. She was still trying to figure out what to tell her nephew.

"Do you want me to give the insurance company a call? It shouldn't take this long to have someone come out for an inspection."

"Uh gwine gone dey tomorruh," she uttered as she turned her back to him.

Leon eyed her. His aunt spoke the Gullah language only whenever she was nervous or troubled about something. "What's going on, Auntie? What aren't you telling me?"

"Actually, I'm not gwine file a claim," she stated, turning to face him. "I'm just gwine pay out of pocket for the repairs."

Frowning, Leon inquired, "Why would you do that?"

"I don't want to go through the fuss of all that."

"But that's the reason you're paying for insurance, Auntie."

"And I decided not to use it."

Shaking his head, Leon said, "This doesn't make sense to me."

"Son, don't worry. I have everything taken care of. Rusty told me he's gonna come by with you on Saturday to get started on the repairs. I really appreciate y'all helping me."

"You know we don't mind, Auntie." Leon paused a moment, then said, "You really should file the claim."

Eleanor sighed heavily. "Seeing that you ain't gwine let this go… I might as well tell you the truth."

"The truth about what?"

"The insurance company ain't gwine pay nothing. I let it lapse. I didn't do it on purpose. Somehow I missed a payment."

"How?"

Shrugging, Eleanor replied, "I don't know."

"I showed you how to put everything in Bill Pay."

"I know, but I must have forgotten about it, Leon. I'm just devastated. I have so much going on in my head all the time… I feel like I'm running around in a million different directions."

"You probably just need to slow down, Auntie." Leon poured himself a cup of coffee. "We need to go over your finances just to make sure everything is good."

Eleanor agreed. "Yeah, we need to do that. The older I get, the more forgetful I become."

"I'll get the materials we need for the repairs."

"Son, I don't want you to go through all that expense. Besides, Rusty already said he'd donate the materials we need."

Rusty's family owned Stanley Building Materials & Construction. The Stanley and Rothchild families had been friends for generations. Leon believed that Rusty had feelings for Eleanor, but she would dismiss his claim with a chuckle and a wave of her hand.

Leon took a sip of coffee. "If you need help with *anything*, I want you to come to me."

"You have your own life."

"Don't do this, Auntie. You were there when Trey and I needed you most. I'm here for you, as well. Never doubt that."

"I know and I love you for it."

"Some of my coworkers and others in the community have offered to help with the repairs," Leon announced.

"That's so sweet," Eleanor said. "I love the way we all come together to help one another. This is what Polk and Hoss envisioned all those years ago."

MISTY LAID DOWN her cell phone. "Brittany, I'm sorry. I needed to check on Talei. She wasn't feeling well this morning. Now, where were we?" She picked up her iPad. They were in Brittany's office going over the final notes for the festival.

"I was saying that the fire department will be sending a couple of guys to man a booth *and* they're even bringing one of the fire trucks for the children to tour."

"They're gonna love that," Misty murmured, while wondering if Leon would be in attendance.

"I heard that Leon is going to be there," Brittany stated as if she'd read her mind.

"Misty, how are you doing with everything?"

"I'm fine," she responded. "John not being here still doesn't seem quite real. Even though we were divorced, he was still the father of my child and it hurts me when I see her sad. She misses him a lot."

Brittany nodded in understanding.

"Leon has been great by stepping up as her godfather. I reconnected with my grandmother, so now Talei has her Nana, aunts and a host of cousins. But the reality is that none of them can replace her father."

"She's adjusting well. At least from what I

can tell," Brittany said. "She's a very happy and secure little girl."

Misty smiled. "Thank you for saying that."

Brittany's phone rang.

"Girl, I'm sorry. I need to take this."

When she finished her call, she stated, "Now back to business. This year's festival is going to be huge. We are expecting twice the attendance of last year."

Misty broke into a grin. "That's great news. I've really enjoyed working on this event."

"I'm glad because I'd really like for you to stay on the board." Brittany broke into a grin. "And not just for the tasty snacks you always bring."

"Miss Eleanor told me that you're the reason the Polk Island Children's Festival exists in the first place," Misty said. "You never told me."

"I worked the one they have in Charleston and thought it would be nice to have an annual one here on the island. Now we're in our second year." Brittany took a sip of her smoothie. "I hope I'm not being too nosy, but I just have to ask. Are you interested in Leon?"

"Why would you ask me that?"

"Because you get this certain look in your eyes whenever his name is mentioned."

"I like him," she confessed. "I feel like we're building a friendship." Misty was fine with this as she had to fight her own battle of personal restraint. She was unable to give herself completely to any man at this time, so friendship was good. She was pretty sure Leon felt the same way.

Changing the subject, she asked, "Did you ever hear back from Robert with the petting zoo?"

"Yeah, I did," Brittany answered. "We're good on that. He will be bringing his animals."

"Talei is going to be thrilled. She loves animals."

"Petting zoos seem to be a popular attraction for children."

An hour later, Misty and Brittany ended their meeting.

Brittany slipped her purse over her left shoulder. "We'll have one final meeting the day before the festival with the rest of the staff."

"Great," Misty murmured. "I'll finalize the list of vendors and send that to you later this evening."

"Your mom is one, right?"

"Yes. She's going to sell some of the fringe dresses and ribbon skirts she's made. They will be in both children and adult sizes. She may have some blankets, as well."

"I'm so excited."

Misty smiled. "Me, too."

She walked out of Brittany's office. "I'll talk to you later."

The July weather was nice and sunny, which had prompted Misty to walk from the café to her friend's place of business.

She strolled along the sidewalk on Main Street, enjoying the feel of the sun on her face and arms. As much as she wanted to stop and peruse some of the boutiques along the way, Misty needed to get back to the shop. Some of the men were coming to work on the repairs.

She heard the blaring sound of a siren blasting. It was coming from the fire station located a couple of streets over. Her immediate thought was of Leon, and she hoped he would be safe.

One of their customers came in not long after Misty got back to the café. "There's a fire over on Oak Street. The fire department got there just in time."

"Was it a big one?" Misty inquired.

"No, I think it was pretty much contained to one room, but the owner of that house is in her nineties. She was able to get out with the help of her neighbor."

"That's great," she said.

"First the bakery and now poor Mrs. Warren's house. Hopefully, this doesn't become a trend. I hate fires."

Misty walked outside in time to see the fire

truck on its way back to the station. Leon stuck his head out of the window on the passenger side and waved.

Smiling, Misty waved back.

CHAPTER FIFTEEN

TRUE TO HER WORD, Eleanor had given Rusty's proposal a lot of thought. She'd called him earlier, inviting him to dinner.

Eleanor eyed her reflection in the full-length mirror. The emerald-green color complemented her complexion. She ran her fingers through her short salt-and-pepper curls.

The answer to his proposal had come easily. She and Rusty had been friends most of their life. Eleanor had always felt an eager affection coming from him. The night he took her to their junior prom, she assumed he would declare his feelings for her, but Rusty said nothing, leading Eleanor to believe that she had been wrong.

In recent years, every time Rusty's gaze met hers, Eleanor's heart turned over in response. Whenever she thought of him, she felt a tingling in the pit of her stomach, although she tried to dismiss it as something else.

"I'm thrilled you could join me for dinner, Rusty," Eleanor said when he arrived thirty minutes later. Her heart jolted and her pulse pounded.

"I was glad to receive your invite." Rusty's stare was bold as he assessed her. "Ladybug, you look beautiful."

His words sent her spirit soaring. "You look pretty sharp yourself," Eleanor responded. "Why don't we sit down in the family room and talk while we wait for dinner to be ready. It shouldn't be much longer."

Rusty sniffed the air. "You made my favorite meal," he said with a grin. "I love your home-made chicken potpie."

Eleanor smiled. "I had to look up the recipe. I couldn't remember all the ingredients. It's so frustrating at times."

Rusty took her hand in his. "I know but we're going to find out what's going on and then we can put together a plan of action."

"I'm really grateful to you for going to see the neurologist last week. I'm tired of all these tests but I know they're necessary. I just need answers."

"We will get them," Rusty assured her.

Eleanor rose to her feet. "It's time for the food to come out of the oven."

"Let me help you," Rusty said, following her into the kitchen.

They took their plates to the dining room table and kept the conversation light while they ate.

"I made enough for you to take the leftovers home," Eleanor said.

"Thanks, Ladybug."

After dinner and dessert, they settled down into the family room to talk.

"I've done a lot of thinking about your proposal. Rusty, do you really want to be tied down to a woman who may have Alzheimer's or dementia?"

"I want you to be my wife for better or worse. In sickness and in health, but even if you refuse to marry me, I intend on being by your side no matter what." Rusty kissed her. "The real question is do you think you can wake up to my ugly mug every day?"

"You're nowhere near ugly," she murmured. "You were handsome all those years ago and, in my opinion, you've improved with age. I don't have a problem waking up next to you for the next fifty or sixty years. I plan on living a very long time. You know Polk lived to be over a hundred years old and Hoss was almost ninety-six when he died."

Rusty looked hopeful. "Does this mean…"

Eleanor nodded. "I want to marry you, Rusty. I don't want to face whatever this is alone, and I don't want to be a burden to Leon. But let me be clear. It's not the only reason I want to be married to you. You're my best friend and I care deeply for you."

He couldn't stop grinning. "You have no idea how happy you've made me."

Her eyes clung to his, analyzing his reaction. "I'm very happy about this, too."

"How do you think Leon and Trey are going to take the news of our getting married?"

"Trust me, they will be surprised for sure, but no doubt pleased. They think the world of you, Rusty."

Rusty's large hand took Eleanor's face and held it gently. "I can't wait for you to be my wife." He kissed her slowly and thoughtfully.

The kiss sent the pit of her stomach into a wild swirl. Eleanor hadn't felt this way since she was in high school. It was a feeling she never thought she'd experience a second time.

ELEANOR AND RUSTY invited Leon and Misty to join them for dinner the next day.

When they arrived, she stated, "Rusty and I have some news we'd like to share." Eleanor could barely contain her excitement over her engagement. She didn't want to hold off telling the people she cared most about.

Leon looked from one person to the other. "What's going on?"

"We're getting married."

Misty gasped in surprise while Leon's mouth dropped open in his shock.

When he found his voice, he asked, "When did this happen? Don't get me wrong—I'm happy about it. I just didn't think you wanted to remarry, Auntie."

"I'd been thinking about it for a while," Eleanor responded. "I just didn't know if I'd meet someone special enough, but Rusty has been here all along. He finally spoke up."

Leon laughed. "Took you long enough."

Seated side by side, Eleanor said, "We're thinking of something small and intimate at the church and a dinner at the café. Rusty called Pastor Nelson and we can get married August 8."

"That's the Saturday after the children's festival," Misty stated.

"Wow," Leon uttered. "You're not wasting any time."

"We've already done a lot of that," Rusty said as he took Eleanor's hand in his.

She agreed.

"This is wonderful news," Misty said. "I'm thrilled for you both."

Leon got up and walked over to his aunt. "Congratulations. You know I want you to be happy."

Shaking Rusty's hand, he said, "I'm happy for you both. Man, it's about time…"

They laughed.

THE NEXT DAY, Eleanor and Rusty announced their engagement at the shop to the staff. She wanted to tell them before the rest of the locals found out. Her employees were her extended family. Leon stopped in that morning for the announcement.

Misty walked him out to his truck afterward. "I had no idea your aunt was dating Rusty," she said. "Did you know?" They didn't have much time to talk after the dinner because she had to leave to pick up Talei.

"No clue. I'm thinking they've known each other forever that they're just heading straight to matrimony with no stops along the way," Leon responded. "He's her best friend and I know he's been in love with her for years. I suspected Aunt Eleanor had feelings for him as well, but she kept denying it."

"Well, I'm really excited for them both."

"So am I."

"It was sweet of Miss Eleanor to ask me to design the wedding cake."

"I'm not surprised. You know that she's your biggest fan."

"I feel the same way about her," Misty said.

"I need to call Trey. Hopefully, he'll be able to come home for the ceremony," Eleanor interjected when she walked out of the shop to join them. She gave a short chuckle, then said, "Lawd my sister is going to faint when I tell her Rusty and I are getting married. I'll call her and Estelle after I talk to Trey."

"Don't forget Howard," Leon said.

"I won't," she responded. "It's going to be nice having the family together. So much to do in a short amount of time."

Misty gave her a reassuring hug. "I'm here to help in any way I can, Miss Eleanor. Your wedding is going to be the talk of the island."

Leon turned the ignition in his truck. "Ladies, I need to get out of here. Love you Auntie. Misty, I'll call you later."

They watched him drive down Main.

"Before too long, I suspect there's going to be another wedding we'll be planning." Eleanor met Misty's gaze. "Mark my words."

CHAPTER SIXTEEN

"LEON AND I are working the first shift at the Fire and Safety Booth," Charles announced after they finished their meal. "Al and Rob have the second shift…"

"If anyone wants to take my place, they can," Leon said. He wasn't comfortable with the idea of having to interact with a lot of children. Until he met Talei, he didn't think he could ever spend more than a minute around a child, especially one close to the age that his own daughter would've been.

"Kids love you," one of his coworkers commented. "You're a natural."

Leaning over, Leon whispered, "Charles, I'm not sure I'm really ready for this."

"You are," his friend reassured him. "Look how you are with Misty's little girl. Besides, the kids will be more interested in the truck than two boring firemen."

Leon chuckled. "You're probably right."

He strode into the kitchen, preparing to clean up. He tackled the dishes first, then the pots and pans. Suds and soapy water up to his elbows, Leon found his thoughts turning to Misty and his growing affection for her.

Everyone seemed to think he and Misty were a perfect match, and he liked her a lot. In truth, he was developing strong feelings for her. But Leon felt they were building a great friendship, and no way would he risk ruining that.

As soon as his shift ended, Leon left the station and went home to take care of some tasks around the house. He wanted to get them out of the way before going to his aunt's shop. He hoped to be able to start painting the kitchen today. The new appliances were scheduled to be delivered at the end of the week.

Rusty was inside sweeping up debris when he arrived shortly after two o'clock. "The construction crew just left not too long ago."

Leon surveyed the area. "It looks good in here."

"Your aunt keeps wanting to come see the place," Rusty said. "I don't know how long I can keep her away. I told her to focus on the wedding planning and let me take care of the shop."

Leon sighed. "I keep telling her that we want to surprise her. Don't worry—I'll talk to Aunt Eleanor."

Rusty pointed to the two paint cans in the corner. "They're ready for you."

"I brought a jumpsuit to change into," Leon said. "The last time I messed up a good pair of jeans."

"If you want, I can stay a while longer to help."

"Rusty if you don't mind putting down some tape on that side—that'll help me a lot."

"I got you."

An hour later, Leon was ready to paint. He was glad that Rusty had been able to match the original color, which was what his aunt wanted. She wanted the appliances updated but the style to reflect the way the kitchen looked before the fire.

Sweat poured off him as he worked to finish the painting in a few hours. Leon glanced at the clock. It was close to four o'clock.

He slid the roller upward, then down, leaving a trail of dove-gray paint on the wall.

Leon heard the front door open and close.

"Hey, you," Misty greeted as she walked cautiously around a ladder. "Wow… The kitchen is really coming together."

"We've been working hard at it."

She discreetly admired his physique as he pulled off the jumpsuit to reveal his T-shirt and jeans. "I'm sure your aunt truly appreciates all you've done. I know that I'm looking forward to getting back to work."

Misty walked out of the kitchen and sat down in one of the booths.

Leon washed his hands before joining her. "How is Talei?"

"She's doing great. Every now and then she mentions John, but she's adjusted well."

"That's good to hear," he responded.

"I don't think I've asked, but how are you dealing with John's death?"

"I miss my friend," he admitted.

"Despite everything John and I went through, I miss him, too."

Leon studied Misty. He could see the truth of her words in her eyes. "Hopefully, he's at peace now."

"I certainly hope so," she said. "That's all I ever wanted for both of us. Just not together."

"Do you have any plans for tomorrow evening?" Leon asked. "There's a new Disney movie playing. I thought we could take Talei."

Misty broke into a smile. "She would love that."

"So, what do you say?"

"I say let's do it," she responded. "It's a date."

LEON PICKED UP Misty and Talei a few minutes before 6:00 p.m. the next day. They had pizza for dinner, then walked across the street to the theater.

He carried a sleeping Talei to the car when they emerged two hours later. "She'd held on as long as she could."

Misty chuckled. "My baby put up a good fight. She stayed awake for most of the movie, though."

Leon was able to put Talei in her car seat without disturbing her sleep. "She's such a beautiful little girl. She's funny, too."

"She's learning the art of manipulation," Misty said.

He laughed as he opened the door to the passenger side for her. "I'm sure. I think that's one of the first lessons all children learn. How to manipulate their parents."

"You're probably right. I'm going to have to ask my mom if I did that. I know I tried in my teens."

On the drive to her place, Misty said, "We had a wonderful time, Leon."

He glanced at her. "So did I."

"You did a great job painting. You think I can convince you to paint my bathroom?"

"When would you like me to start?"

Misty gave him a sidelong glance. "Are you being serious right now?"

"Yeah. I enjoy painting. I'd do it for you."

Leon parked in front of her building. "Do you want me to carry her inside for you?"

"If you don't mind," Misty responded. "Thank you."

He carried Talei into the condo and laid her on the sofa. "We'll have to do this again sometime."

Smiling, Misty said, "I'd like that."

At home, Leon showered and prepared for bed. He was scheduled to work the next morning.

Although he'd enjoyed seeing the movie with Misty and Talei, he was left feeling conflicted. His emotions were all over the place where she was concerned. Leon didn't want to tamper with their friendship—it meant too much to him. But he was extremely attracted to Misty; he couldn't deny it.

Just let go and enjoy the journey.

Leon had heard this on more than one occasion. Time for him to really act on it. He was tired of living with loneliness. If he wanted to have a fragment of happiness back in his life, then he had to reclaim it.

CHAPTER SEVENTEEN

WHAT IF A relationship with Misty doesn't work out? How will this affect Talei?

It was a question that haunted Leon. The little girl lost her father—he didn't want her to lose someone else in her life. It was the main reason why he was constantly debating whether to pursue a relationship with Misty. His feelings for her were growing, but deep down he feared becoming too attached to Talei. Leon also didn't want to cost Misty or her daughter any heartache; he also wanted to spare himself more pain and loss.

He left the firehouse, grateful that he was off work for the next two days. Instead of going home, he drove to the cemetery.

Leon stopped by his parents' graves and then headed over to Vera's. Before taking a seat on the bench, he placed the dozen roses he'd bought at Vera's headstone.

"Hey, Vee. You know I had to come out here to wish you a happy birthday in heaven. I brought you your favorite roses—the pink ones.

I can't tell you how much I miss you. Vee, you deserve to be here, enjoying life and raising our daughter… I will never understand why you had to leave me," Leon said. "I know you don't want me mourning you forever. I'm doing my best to move on. I even met someone. The thing is that she was married to John. Her name is Misty. You'd like her, Vee."

Leon pulled a weed from the grass and tossed it. "John's gone now, too. I can't remember if I told you when I was here the last time. I've lost too many people and I'm tired of it." He shook his head. "I know all about the circle of life and that this is a journey that we all have to take, but Vee… Dying's not the hard part. It's surviving the death of the people you love—it's not easy.

"Spending time with Misty and her daughter has helped me through some pretty tough days. I've developed feelings for Misty and I'm crazy about her daughter. But I do worry what might happen if it doesn't work out. I know what you'd say. You'd tell me to just take it one day at a time."

His eyes traveled to the flowers. "Here I am talking about my issues when it's your special day. I came here to tell you that I'm so happy to have been your husband, even for the short time we were married. There's not a day that I don't think about you, Vee. You were the love of my life."

Leon rose to his full height. "That will never change."

He could see himself spending the rest of his life with Misty. While Vera was his first love, he now realized that there was room in his heart to love another. He just had to have the courage to walk the journey.

THE FIRST SATURDAY in August brought with it lots of sunny weather for the second annual children's festival. Misty and Brittany did one final walk through the area secured for the event.

"All the vendors are set up and ready. The authors are in the VIP area near the stage," Misty said as she went through her checklist.

"This is gonna be huge," Brittany said. "People are already lining up to get into the festival."

"Talei was very excited this morning. She wants to see the pink dinosaur from that TV show and the petting zoo. My mother is bringing her. They should be here shortly."

"Look who's here all nice and early," Brittany said, gesturing toward the fire truck.

"Leon Rothchild."

"He told me that he'd be working the festival today, but only until noon."

"I'm really glad we were able to get the fire department to come out here today."

Misty eyed Leon as he arranged stuffed Dalmatians and teddy bears on a table behind the booth. She had known there was something special about him from the very beginning. Quickly, she banished the thought. They were friends. Nothing more.

"There's that look again," Brittany said. "You like him more than you'd care to admit."

"Can we talk about something else?" Misty asked.

Her friend chuckled. "Sure. Why don't we go check out the petting zoo?"

Misty held up the map of the festival. "Sounds good to me."

She glanced over her shoulder. Leon was so preoccupied with his tasks that he hadn't even seen her. Misty wasn't concerned because she'd stop by the booth at some point during the festival to say hello.

"Looks like everything is in order," Brittany said. "We're ready to get this event started."

LEON ARRIVED AN hour early to set up the booth for the children's festival. They hadn't allowed anyone entry yet, so the area was quiet, yet very colorful. There were balloons and cartoon characters everywhere.

He poured a large bag of assorted candies in a bowl, an easy way to summon the children.

Leon looked around at the different vendors. He caught a glimpse of Misty with Brittany, but they looked deep in conversation. He'd heard that they were part of the committee who coordinated the event.

Charles arrived. "Everything looks great. The truck is on its way."

"They're starting to let people in," Leon observed aloud. A wave of apprehension flowed through him at the sight of two small children running toward their booth.

"Can I have a fire hat?" the little boy asked.

Wearing a smile, Leon responded, "You sure can. Do you want to be a fireman when you grow up?"

"Yeah."

"What would you like, young lady?" Charles inquired.

In a sudden bout of shyness, the little girl covered her face with her hands.

A woman walked up, gently scolding them. "I told you two not to run off."

Charles held up a stuffed Dalmatian. "Would you like one of these?"

She nodded.

"Here you go…"

The fire engine arrived and parked beside the booth.

Within thirty minutes, there was a host of children lined up to tour the truck. Leon liked that they were busy. It helped to pass the time.

If Vera and his daughter had lived, the three of them would have attended this festival as a family. Every time Leon saw a father with his wife and daughter, he felt a stabbing pain in his chest. He would never understand why his parents died when he was only ten or why he had to lose his uncle five years after that, but he'd refused to lose hope. Leon always believed his life would get better. For the most past, it did, especially when he met Vera.

His life with her was perfect.

When Vera told him that she was pregnant, Leon doubted life could get any better, but then tragedy struck, and his life came to a crashing halt. Where hope once resided, there was none.

It was hard to picture life without his beloved Vera. During that first year, there were days when Leon felt each crushing breath would be his last. Somehow, he managed to make it to the second anniversary of her death. He'd spent most of it angry and bitter. It wasn't until the third year that Leon found acceptance.

CHAPTER EIGHTEEN

LEON ROTHCHILD.

Courageous, handsome and of high moral character. Misty watched him navigate coolly through the growing sea of children wanting a tour of the fire truck to the booth. When his dazzling gaze latched onto hers, the bustle and noise of the kids running ahead of their parents all faded into the background.

"How's it going?" Misty inquired as she glanced around the booth. "Looks like it's been busy over here."

"It's the fire engine," Leon said. "They love getting inside and climbing to the top. We practically have to beg them to take one of the stuffed dogs. We're already out of the toy engines and fire hats."

Misty chuckled.

"You've been one busy lady," Leon said. "Every time I looked up; I saw you running from one place to another. You did a nice job with this festival."

"This is my first year on the board. I've really enjoyed working on this event."

"We've got a great turnout. Congrats to you and the staff."

Misty was touched by the compliment. "Brittany would love to hear that."

"I'll make sure to tell her," he responded.

"Did you go by the bakery booth?" Misty asked. "Your aunt is there with an assortment of cupcakes and slices of cake. She has that lemon one you love so much."

"I'd better run over there right now," Leon responded. "I'm done here for the day."

"I'm actually on my way there. Want to join me?"

He smiled. "Sure."

Leon and Misty made their way through the crowd to get to the food area.

"Her booth is over there."

His eyes scanned the table. "Aunt Eleanor, I came to get some lemon cake, but looks like it's all gone."

She smiled. "Now, you know I saved you a couple of slices."

"Thanks, Auntie."

A volunteer walked over to Eleanor saying, *"De chillun full' up wid baa'becue."*

Misty glanced up at Leon, who said, "You'll

hear the Gullah language spoken from time to time from some of the older people."

"Sounds like she was saying that the children were full of barbecue."

"Close enough," Leon replied. "She said the children filled their stomachs with barbecue."

"You speak the language?"

He gave a slight nod. "Some."

"I don't know much about it," Misty said. "Just that Gullah refers to the people and culture along the coastal landscape of South Carolina, Georgia and the Sea Islands."

"Only a handful of old-timers still speak Gullah. They spoke it really heavy when my parents were growing up," Leon said. "Now, it's fading. We attended school on the mainland and the teachers would make us speak proper English."

"I find that fascinating. My mom has always wanted me to learn the Tsalagi language. She had the same experience when she was in school. That's why she believes it's important to keep our Cherokee language and traditions alive."

"I agree," Leon said. "The love for our history is something we have in common."

"It's important that we know where we come from," Misty responded. "That's the one regret I have about my father. I don't really know his side of my family."

"You can always change that."

"You're right."

"Where's Talei?" Leon inquired. "I saw her for a few minutes when she came to see the engine."

"I'm pretty sure we'll find her and my mother at the petting zoo," Misty said. "We weren't sure we'd be able to get the animals this year, but we were lucky. They had a cancellation."

Just as Misty said, Talei and Oma were at the petting zoo, which included twenty rare and exotic animals from around the world.

Talei pointed at the potbellied pig named Jake. "Mommy, look…pig."

"Yes, I see him."

"Eon, I like pig," she said happily.

He grinned. "He's as big as you are, little one."

"I like him."

"His name is Jake," Misty said.

"Jay…" Talei repeated as she waved. "Hey, Jay."

The pig was ushered over so that she could pet him. Talei touched him, then burst into giggles.

After she spent some time with Jake, Oma convinced her to visit with Rascal, the fox in the next stall.

"She seems to love animals," Leon said.

"She does," Misty responded. "Especially rabbits."

Misty watched Talei reach tiny fingers in to touch the baby rabbits. For the moment, the little girl was laughing and happy.

"You're doing so well with that rabbit."

"Her so cute," Talei said.

Smiling, Oma patted her back. "Be careful with her."

They went to the stall where the camels were kept.

"Mommy, I wanna ride horse."

"That's a camel, baby girl. That's Bubba. He's not a horse."

"I wanna ride cammer," Talei stated. "Eon, I wanna ride."

Leon read the sign. "It says here that Bubba drinks Diet Coke."

"Really?"

He nodded.

Misty chuckled. "Okay, then. I have to say that's new to me. A camel drinking Diet Coke."

They stood in the line for rides, and when it was Talei's turn, Leon helped lift her onto the back of the camel.

Misty and her mother both took pictures of the little girl riding with Leon and the owner on either side of her.

Oma took Talei home around four o'clock,

leaving Misty to finish her day working the festival.

"I'm here if you need any help with the cleanup," Leon said.

"That's really sweet of you, but I wouldn't ask this of you."

"You didn't ask," Leon responded. "I offered."

"Then you'll have to let me buy you dinner."

He smiled. "That's an offer I can't pass up."

Two hours later, they sat in a seafood restaurant enjoying their meal.

"You're very good with children," Misty said.

"It's hard sometimes being around them," he confessed. "It's a reminder of what I'm missing. I've always wanted my own family."

"I'm sorry."

Leon shrugged, then finished off a glass of ice water. "Life goes on. At least that's what I've been told."

"It does," Misty said. "You just have to take it one day at a time."

Leon gazed at her. "That's exactly what Vera would've said."

Misty wiped her mouth on the edge of her napkin. "They say great minds think alike."

Leon ordered dessert. "I hope you're going to help me with this walnut blondie brownie."

"You really have a sweet tooth." Misty took a sip of her tea. "I called to check on John's parents the other day. Clara's still a bit emotional and Elroy was just rude as always."

"It's kind of you to even call them after everything that's happened."

Misty shrugged. "Clara's always been pretty decent to me. It's her husband who has always been the issue. I've done everything I could to be nice to him, so I just gave up. As long as he's good to my daughter, I'm good."

"I have to say that I admire you, Misty. You've been a pillar of strength through everything. I find strength in a woman a very attractive quality."

The waiter arrived with the dessert and two spoons.

"Did you know that John made me a beneficiary of an insurance policy?" Misty inquired. "I didn't expect that at all."

"All he ever told me was that he intended to make sure you and Talei were taken care of if anything happened to him."

"Do you think he's at peace now?"

He nodded. "I choose to think so—otherwise his death wouldn't make sense to me."

They finished off the brownie and ice cream.

Oma was in the kitchen when Misty arrived home an hour later.

"Hey, Mama. Where's Talei?"

"She's in her room watching a movie. I just came down to make her some warm milk."

Oma retrieved a carton from the refrigerator. "How was your dinner with Leon?"

"Nice," Misty murmured. "It was great being able to have a meal and conversation with a man with no expectations. Leon doesn't drink. That was kind of nice, too. For the first time, I was able to see what it feels like to have a normal relationship with a man. Leon's still grieving some, but he has such a kind heart."

"Don't judge him for what others have done to you in the past."

"I'm not, Mama," Misty said. "I'm not rushing into anything with Leon. We're just building a friendship. If it goes further than that, then it does. I'm focusing on the present."

She went to check on Talei.

"Mama, why didn't you ever remarry?" Misty asked when she walked into the dining room.

"My focus was making sure you were going to be okay. I didn't have time to meet men and determine if they were worthy of being in our life."

"What about now?"

"I'm happy with my life the way it is, Misty. Your father was a good man, but then the alcohol changed him. It became his god. He chose it over his family. Then he started running around with other women. When I got the phone call from that woman bragging how she was pregnant with his child. I was done for good."

"All I remember of my dad is that he was mean-spirited. I remember the way he used to treat you."

"You have to forgive him, Misty."

"I'm trying, Mama. I'm really trying to forgive him and John."

When she was upstairs in her room, her cell phone rang.

Misty grinned when she saw the ID of the caller.

Picking up, she said, "Leon, hello."

"Thanks again for having dinner with me."

"I enjoyed myself," Misty responded.

"Look, I'm not really good at this—more like out of practice—but I'd like to get to know you better," Leon said. "I'm really not good at this at all."

She smiled. "You're doing fine. I want to get to know you better, as well."

He released an audible sigh. "Now that we got that out of the way, I can relax some."

Misty chuckled. "I know the feeling. It's not like it's been all that long, but it feels like it's been a while since I've been on a date."

"Maybe it's because we're both anxious about what could come of our dating."

"I'm hoping for something good," she confessed.

"I don't intend to do anything to hurt you or Talei," Leon stated. "I want a relationship of substance—something real."

"We're definitely on the same page, then."

They talked for the next hour, discussing books, the island history and the things they had in common.

Misty fell asleep with thoughts of Leon dancing through her mind.

MONDAY AFTERNOON, MISTY met Brittany at a shop downtown for some retail therapy.

"Let me just get this out of the way by telling you that Leon and I have a date tomorrow," she announced. "We're leaving early and spending the day in Savannah. He's going to be busy the rest of the week with Miss Eleanor and Rusty."

"That's right. The wedding is Saturday," Brittany exclaimed as they wandered around the clothing boutique. "I'm not surprised that you're going on a date with Leon. Girl, I knew you had a thing for him."

"Okay you're right. I really, *really* like him but I'm so nervous," Misty confessed. "It's actually been a while since I've been on a date. I know this is last minute, but do you mind watching Talei?"

"I don't mind at all. That's my little princess."

"What should I wear?" Misty picked up a red sundress. "You like this one?"

"I like this better." Brittany help up a strapless dress in yellow.

"It's nice, but not appropriate for a day trip to Savannah."

"Make sure you wear comfortable walking shoes with something cute. Those cobblestone streets are agony on your feet."

"I remember. That's why I need to find something to go with my walking shoes. I'm looking for something in red or navy." Misty walked over to the next clothing rack. "Congratulations again on making partner. It's well deserved."

Brittany held up a shirt against her body and eyed her reflection in the full-length mirror. "Girl, thank you. I'm excited about it. We're actually planning to expand our office to Charleston."

"Oh, wow. That's wonderful."

"Mary's boyfriend lives there, and he's asked her to marry him."

"So, she plans on running that office while you manage the one on the island?"

Brittany nodded. "Exactly."

"Thank you for babysitting Talei. You know how much I appreciate you."

"Talei and I are gonna have a good time.

Enjoy your day with Leon. Don't worry about rushing back. She can just stay the night and I'll drop her off at school. She and I will be fine. Talei loves her auntie Britt."

Misty smiled. "Yes, she does. That's because you spoil her."

They left the store and walked across the street.

"Let's try this place here," Misty said. "I need to find something in the next ten minutes. I have to get back to work."

Later that evening, Misty tried on the two different outfits she'd purchased earlier. She was having a difficult time trying to find the perfect one for her date with Leon.

It was past eleven o'clock by the time she chose the sundress in a hot pink color with white sneakers. Misty also retrieved a light white cardigan to take with her.

She climbed into bed and exhaled a long sigh of contentment. Misty propped herself up against her pillows and relaxed for a few minutes, then she slid out of bed.

Misty went downstairs to the kitchen. She'd made a decision to bake lemon cupcakes for Leon.

Misty wanted to do something special for him.

ELEANOR HANDED HER nephew a cup of coffee to go with his dessert. "So, you're going out with Misty."

"We've been spending time together," Leon told his aunt. "We took Talei to see a movie, and we were together at the children's festival… I'd like to get to know her better."

"I had a feeling you two would be getting together," Eleanor said.

Holding up his hand, Leon uttered, "Whoa, Auntie… We're just learning more about each other. We're not a couple or anything like that."

"I have an instinct about stuff like this. You two gwine be a couple before long. Mark my words."

Leon chuckled. "Do me a favor and don't tell Misty any of this—I don't want you to scare her off."

"It's good to see you going out. It's about time."

"Aunt Eleanor, I'm not going to rush into anything with Misty. I'm not even sure if I'm really ready for this, but I'm going to give it a shot. I can't get her out of my head. I think about her all the time."

"Vera never wanted you to become a hermit. You're not the type of man meant to be single. You're a family man, Leon."

"I know, but Vee was the love of my life. Maybe that's all we get—that one great love."

"Sometimes that's all we get," Eleanor said.

"But there are times when life surprises you with a new love…a new beginning."

"I miss Uncle Walter."

"I do, too," Eleanor said with a soft sigh. "We used to close the shop, turn on our favorite songs and we'd just dance… Those were some good times."

Leon chuckled. "I remember this one time when Trey and I were in the office—we heard y'all talking and laughing. We crept out and saw Uncle chasing you around the room. He caught you, then you two started kissing. Back then, Trey and I thought it was gross, but now I realize it was a really romantic moment between the two of you."

"Your uncle was a very romantic man," Eleanor murmured as she sat down at the table facing Leon. "I'm very lucky to have another good man to spend my life with. All those happy memories I have with Walter—they're in my heart."

"I know what you mean, Auntie. I keep all the memories I have of Vee close to mine."

Eleanor reached over and took Leon's hand. "She was a wonderful person."

"Yes, she was," he agreed. "We had so many plans for our life and our family. I never once thought Vee wouldn't be here."

"So, what do you really think of Misty?"

"I think she's a nice person," Leon said. "She's attractive and appears to be a wonderful mother. I just want to get to know her better. I have no other expectations."

"But are you open to the possibility?"

"Aunt Eleanor, I have to admit that I'm dealing with some guilt about seeing Misty. I feel like I'm cheating on Vera."

"You loved being married, son. I don't think I'd ever seen you so happy. You were meant to share your life with someone special."

"I don't know if I ever want to love that much again," Leon confessed. "Losing Vera and Selena... My heart is still in pieces."

"I have a feeling Misty may be the one to help put those pieces back together, sugar."

"You are forever the matchmaker, Auntie."

Eleanor broke into a grin. "It's a gift. I have a real instinct about two people who belong together."

He didn't look convinced.

"Leon, just give yourself a chance to find love again. Be open to it."

"I'll try, Auntie."

Eleanor pushed away from the breakfast table and rose to her feet, then frowned. "I was just about to do something but for the life of me, I can't remember what it was. Rosemary told me

I need to take fish oil, I think. She said it would help keep your memory sharp."

"You should try it, Auntie," Leon said. "But I don't think you have anything to worry about. There's nothing wrong with you."

CHAPTER NINETEEN

MISTY CURLED HER hair with a curling wand and applied her makeup with a light hand. She looked forward to spending this day with Leon. Misty decided not to look too much into the swirling emotions she felt—she had to take things slow. She couldn't afford to make another relationship mistake.

Leon picked her up at 8:00 a.m. for the drive to Savannah.

They began their day in Forsythe Park.

Misty ran over to the nineteenth-century cast-iron fountain that was designed to resemble the grand fountain in Paris. She found it breathtaking. Camera in hand, she snapped several photographs.

They were surrounded by other couples lounging on colorful blankets beneath green shade trees.

"So, you're a photographer, as well?" Leon asked.

"I guess an amateur one. I enjoy taking pictures," Misty said. "I took a course online and watched YouTube. I mostly take pictures of nature—mostly flowers. I still have a lot to learn."

"I'm sure you do a much better job than I can," Leon said. "You're the official picture taker on this trip."

Misty chuckled. "Okay."

When they sat down at a picnic table to have lunch, Leon said, "I noticed the white box you brought to the car."

"I made lemon cupcakes for dessert."

Leon smiled. "I could kiss you right now."

"What's stopping you?"

His kiss was sweet, surprisingly gentle and a delicious sensation.

After lunch, they strolled along the tree-lined pathways of Chippewa Square. Did you know that the north side was one of the locations in the film *Forrest Gump*?"

"I have a confession to make," Misty said. "I have never seen that movie."

Leon looked completely shocked. "We have to remedy that. You *have* to see *Forrest Gump*."

"Why?" Misty inquired. "What makes this particular film so special?"

"*Forrest Gump* is one of those inspirational movies that show us how to turn our greatest weaknesses into our greatest strength. Forrest accomplished a great many things while facing adversities."

"I'm willing to give it a shot, Leon. We'll have a movie night one-night next week when you're off."

"Make sure you have a box of tissues on hand. You're gonna need them."

At dusk, they took a private carriage ride along the cobblestone streets to view some of the historic mansions.

"I have to say that you did a great job planning out this day," Misty said. "I've really enjoyed myself."

"I'm glad," Leon responded. "This city is one of my favorite places to visit."

"You showed me a side of Savannah I hadn't really noticed before."

"We're going to have dinner at Elizabeth on 37th," he announced. "It's off the beaten path, but I'm sure you'll appreciate the atmosphere and the cuisine."

The moment they arrived; Misty instantly fell in love with the twentieth-century mansion that housed the restaurant.

Leon ordered the half-moon river clams with roasted Vidalia onions, country ham and truffle oil for the appetizer.

For her entrée, Misty ordered the spicy Savannah red rice with shrimp while Leon chose the roasted chicken with wild mushrooms.

When their appetizers arrived, Leon offered a quick prayer of thanksgiving.

"This is sooo delicious," Misty said.

Leon nodded his agreement.

The entrées looked equally wonderful. Leon sampled the braised collards and corn bread dressing before cutting into the chicken breast. He glanced at her. "How is your food?"

Smiling, Misty responded, "I can't complain about a thing."

MISTY HAD A wonderful sense of humor. Leon couldn't remember the last time he'd laughed so much. He was truly enjoying himself.

"I'm stuffed," she murmured.

"You only ate half of your food."

"I eat until I feel full. Don't worry, it's not going to waste. I'm eating the rest of it tomorrow for lunch."

Misty's smile warmed him. Leon had no idea why she affected him the way she did, but instead of dwelling on the thought, he pushed it to the back of his mind and focused on enjoying the rest of his evening with her.

Misty fell asleep in the car during the drive back to Polk Island.

She woke up just as they were about to turn on her street. "Oh, Leon… I'm sorry for falling asleep on you like that."

"You're fine. It's been a long day."

"Thank you for making today so special and memorable."

Leon got out and walked around his car to open the door for Misty. "Don't forget about planning movie night for next week."

"Oh, I won't," she promised. "I'm actually looking forward to seeing *Forrest Gump*." She kissed his cheek, then gave his hand a little squeeze. His flesh prickled at her touch, and his heart hammered in his chest at a steadfast rate.

Focus.

It's what Leon kept telling himself, but it wasn't that simple. Misty made him feel things he'd never experienced before. Or maybe it was because he was so out of touch with these particular emotions.

RUSTY HOSTED A family dinner the night before the wedding at his home. Maggie, Eleanor's sister and her cousin Estelle arrived earlier in the day. Rusty also had a couple of relatives coming to the island from out of town. Many of his family members were local residents.

Leon received a text stating that his second cousin Howard had gotten in late the night before and was staying at the hotel on Main. He texted that he'd come to Eleanor's house after his son and daughter's flight landed. Trey's flight was scheduled to land a couple of hours after the dinner.

He stopped by the church because he knew that Eleanor would be there with the florist going over the decorations.

Leon was surprised to see Misty with Eleanor, but it really wasn't that surprising. She was always willing to help his aunt. She had such a warm, loving spirit and was always smiling. He loved her sometimes-quirky sense of humor, and the sense of freedom she seemed to have in her life. Not only was Misty beautiful, but she was intelligent and caring, as well. The more Leon got to know her, the more he wanted to know about her.

I have real feelings for this woman.

The silent declaration shocked him, but Leon didn't bother to deny the truth.

He'd come to offer his assistance, but it looked like the women had everything under control. Leon decided to check on Rusty before meeting Howard at the hotel. He would see Misty tonight at the dinner. The next day, they were planning to help with last-minute wedding arrangements, which included moving Eleanor's things into Rusty's house. She'd decided to close up her house for now. They would decide later what to do with it.

CHAPTER TWENTY

ELEANOR WOKE UP feeling what she could describe only as a bit fuzzy in the brain. She stared at the simple lavender-and-silver dress hanging on the door of her closet.

It was her wedding day.

She sat up with a start at the sound of the knock on her bedroom door.

Leon stuck his head inside the room. "You up, Auntie?"

"C'mon in, sugar." Eleanor glanced at the clock on her nightstand. "How long have you been here?"

"Long enough to make you some breakfast," he announced, entering with a tray.

"Thank you, son."

"How did you sleep?"

"I think I was out almost immediately. I slept pretty good considering I was up well past midnight talking with Maggie and Estelle."

"I'm still surprised that Aunt Maggie drove all the way from Raleigh," Leon said.

"Although cousin Estelle said she slept the whole way down."

Leon positioned the tray on the bed so she could eat comfortably.

Eleanor chuckled. "Must've been some good sleep 'cause she tried to keep us up all night. I kept trying to tell them I don't need any more luggage under these eyes."

Trey knocked before walking inside the bedroom. "Good morning, beautiful." He planted a kiss on her cheek. "I need to know something before Leon and I walk you down the aisle."

She picked up her fork. "What is it you want to know?"

"Do you love Rusty?"

"I do," Eleanor responded. She met his gaze straight on. "Trey, I've always loved him. Not in the same way that I loved your uncle, but I have deep feelings for him. I'm always telling Leon that he should move on. Well, I realized that I needed to do the same."

"I'm glad to see you're taking your own advice."

Eleanor swatted at Leon. "Alright, smarty-pants." She smiled at her nephews.

"I want y'all to know this day couldn't be more perfect. I have my two boys here to share in this special moment of my life."

Trey kissed her cheek. "I have to fly out tomorrow morning, but there was no way I was going to miss your wedding, Auntie. I'm glad you've found a good man to share your life with. I've always liked Rusty except when he was my football coach in middle school."

Eleanor laughed. "I'm so happy you're here."

"Me, too," Trey stated. "Especially since I'm going to deploy to Afghanistan in a couple of weeks."

Eleanor gasped and her eyes filled with tears.

He sat down on the edge of her bed. "Auntie, don't cry. Everything's gonna be fine. I wouldn't have told you if I'd known it would upset you."

"I'm just gwine miss you so much. I know that's your job, but I hate you have to go over there."

"I'm gonna be careful and I know you'll keep me covered with your prayers. Today is your wedding day. Let's focus on all of us being here together—family."

"Finish your breakfast," Leon said. "We leave for the church in less than two hours. Aunt Maggie needs to hem Trey's pants. They're too long."

Trey stood up. "That's right. I need to see if she can get started on that right after breakfast." He walked briskly out of the room.

"Auntie, Trey is gonna be fine. Don't get yourself worked up over his deployment. Not today."

Eleanor smiled. "I won't. I just won't think about it today."

Leon made his way to the door. "Good."

He went downstairs.

Eleanor finished off her food, then climbed out of bed.

After a quick shower, she slipped on a flowy caftan and went downstairs. Leon jumped up from his seat to take the tray from her.

She sat down beside her sister, who asked, "Did you get any sleep?"

"Some. I wouldn't have gotten any if I'd left it up to you and Estelle."

ELEANOR AND RUSTY had both decided to keep their wedding a simple affair. However, the sophistication of the event would be carried throughout the ceremony and old-fashioned champagne and cake reception. Eleanor felt the intimate setting would emphasize what was important to her and Rusty as a mature couple versus the frills that most young couples often preferred.

She and Rusty both owned homes so they politely asked invited guests to opt out of bringing gifts. While planning the wedding, Eleanor chose not to have any bridesmaids.

She decided on a lavender-colored gown because it was the same color of the dress she wore to her junior prom with Rusty—the one and only time they ever went out.

It was time to leave for the church.

Eleanor headed to the dressing room with Leon in tow, carrying her gown and tote packed with other essentials.

Ten minutes later, Misty arrived to help with hair and makeup.

"If I'd had a wedding party, Talei would've been a gorgeous little flower girl."

"She's at home with my mama. They're going to Charleston to buy fabric and some other materials. By the way, I ran into Rusty when I stopped by the café. He looks so handsome in his charcoal-gray suit. His shirt is the exact shade of your dress. Great job on the coordination."

"We didn't coordinate what we were wearing—he has no idea the color of my gown."

Misty's eyebrow rose in surprise. "Really?"

Eleanor broke into a smile. "These are the colors we wore to our junior prom."

"This is so incredibly romantic, Miss Eleanor. It's a sign that you two are meant to be together."

She laughed. "It means we're two old sentimental fools."

Misty shook her head in denial. "This shows

that you both put a lot of thought into the start of a new life together. *I love it.*"

Eleanor wanted her hair pulled back into a bun. Misty stuck pearl-tipped hairpins around it to match her earrings and necklace.

Surveying Eleanor's face, Misty said, "You don't need much more than a little powder, some mascara and lipstick."

She handed Eleanor a mirror. "What do you think?"

"I love it. Thank you, sugar."

Misty glanced around the room. "Where's your bouquet?"

"I'm not carrying one," Eleanor responded. "I don't need all that." She had also decided against walking down the aisle. As soon as she was dressed and ready, Eleanor left the dressing area with the photographer to take a few pictures outside the church.

"You look so beautiful and happy," her friend Rose said. "You certainly made poor Rusty wait long enough. That man has loved you forever."

"Everybody seems to have been aware of his feelings but me."

"Well, you know he's always been shy and then when you met Walter, Rusty didn't stand a chance."

"I think this is the perfect time for us to start our lives together," Eleanor said. "I'm not sure

I would've really appreciated him or been able to give him what he needed before."

Rose smiled. "Better late than live a life alone with nothing but memories."

Leon joined them, saying, "Pastor Nelson just arrived. Rusty's on his way inside. The photographer took some photos of him outside the church."

MISTY SPIED TREY standing near the door with an arrangement of orchids and lilies. She walked up to him, saying, "Your aunt just told me that she wasn't carrying a bouquet."

The florist made this for her."

Smiling, Misty said, "I'm glad. Make sure Miss Eleanor carries it."

"Have you met my aunt?" Trey asked with a chuckle.

"All you have to do is give her one of your winning smiles."

"Okay, I see how you wrapped my brother around your little finger. You bat those long lashes of yours and stroke his ego…"

"Trey, I have no idea what you're talking about." Amused, Misty walked away in search of Leon.

She found him standing outside while Eleanor was being photographed in her gown.

He glanced over his shoulder at her, smiling.

"She looks beautiful," Misty said.

Leon nodded in agreement. "She sure does."

"The florist sent over a bouquet for her to carry. Trey has it—I told him to make sure she carries it down the aisle."

Leon gave her a sidelong glance. "You've worked with my aunt long enough to know she's gonna do what she wants."

"I'm telling you the same thing I told your brother—flash one of those charming smiles of yours."

Leon pulled her into his embrace.

She settled there, loving the feel of his arms—she felt safe and secure. In this moment there was no other place she wanted to be.

CHAPTER TWENTY-ONE

Rusty's nephew played several selections on the violin while guests took their seats to wait for the ceremony to begin. A Rothchild cousin to Leon and Trey would perform a sax solo near the end of the service.

It was time for the ceremony to begin, Eleanor realized.

When the music started, Leon and Trey stood on either side of her.

"My brother and I are going to walk you down this aisle," Leon stated. "We insist on it."

"And the florist made you this bouquet, Auntie," Trey said. "I really think you should carry it."

Eleanor looked at the flowers. "It *is* pretty."

"It looks really nice with your dress," Leon contributed.

"Since she went through all this trouble, I'll carry it."

The doors to the sanctuary opened.

Escorted by her nephews, Eleanor teared up

when she glimpsed Rusty up front with the minister.

Misty was right. He looked handsome in the dark gray suit. His silver cuff links complemented the silver studs on her gown.

He met her as she neared the altar. Taking her hand, Rusty said, "I've always loved that color on you."

"Same here," Eleanor murmured.

They had both agreed to forgo writing their own vows, sticking to tradition.

Eleanor blinked back tears of joy as she and Rusty repeated their vows. She forced away all thoughts of her medical condition and what it meant for her future. She just wanted to revel in this shared moment of pure happiness. The love she saw reflected in Rusty's eyes was burned into her memory. It was a look she never wanted to forget.

After the ceremony, Eleanor and Rusty took more photographs before heading to the café for the reception.

"Mrs. Joshua Henry Sanford… Since everybody calls you Rusty… maybe I should just introduce myself as Mrs. Rusty Sanford."

"I love them both," he said, beaming with pride.

Placing a hand to his cheek, Eleanor said, "I

adore everything about you—especially that sandy-red hair and your freckles."

He kissed her. "You've made me the happiest man alive."

"I pray we have a long life together."

"We will, Ladybug. I believe this with my whole soul." Taking her arm, he said, "It's time for us to head to the shop for the reception."

They walked over to the waiting car. Trey sat behind the wheel grinning. "Alright, you two lovebirds. Time to party."

There was no evidence of the fire that had ravaged the kitchen a few weeks ago. Shiny new appliances, new cookware, plates and silverware…all purchased by Leon and Trey. She'd tried to talk them out of spending so much money, but her boys wouldn't take no for an answer. Rusty had been generous with his donation of the supplies necessary to repair the shop. A group of men from the community volunteered long hours during the week to make sure the repairs were completed in time for the wedding.

I'm so blessed to be surrounded by loving family, friends and a caring community.

When they arrived at the café, Eleanor smiled and murmured, "All of you did a beautiful job in here."

"We left the decorating up to Misty," Rusty said with a chuckle.

In the center of the room, round tables were covered in white tablecloths with gardenia and orchid centerpieces. Place settings included dessert plates and champagne glasses. The tables in booths had been covered as well with elaborate candle displays in the center. Balloons and streamers hung from the ceiling. Soft music flowed throughout, a combination of jazz and R&B that could be enjoyed by guests of all ages.

Rusty and Eleanor navigated around the room, greeting and thanking their guests for coming. They made their way over to the booth where Leon sat with Misty.

"You did a fabulous job with the decorations." Eleanor gestured toward the small table in the center holding the wedding cake. "It's beautiful. I appreciate everything you've done."

Rusty agreed. "Thank you for everything, Misty."

"I didn't do it by myself. Leon and Brittany helped."

Eleanor smiled. "I love y'all so much."

Rusty took her hand. "We need to speak with the pastor before he leaves, Ladybug." He pulled an envelope from a pocket inside his jacket.

"This is one of the happiest days of my life," she whispered.

Rusty kissed her cheek. "I feel the same way. I've waited most of my life for this day. I love you, Ladybug."

"Never let me forget it."

"THE CEREMONY WAS so sweet and romantic," Misty said. She reached up and grabbed the string of a floating balloon.

Leon took a sip of punch. "Aunt Eleanor looks very happy. So does Rusty for that matter. I've always believed that those two belonged together." He hadn't realized how much he'd wanted to see his aunt sharing her life with someone who truly adored her.

"Look."

He followed Misty's gaze. Rusty and Eleanor were in the middle of the room dancing. As he watched them, Leon felt a bottomless sense of peace.

"I've enjoyed meeting other members of your family," Misty said. "They really know how to have a good time."

"It's great seeing Aunt Maggie and everyone. We've always been a close family." Leon stepped over a pair of shoes on the floor where someone had kicked them off. "I used to wish that they'd all move back to the island when I was younger, but now I realize we all have to walk our own paths even if they take us away from Polk Island."

"I can tell family's very important to you."

He nodded. "You feel the same way."

"I do," Misty said. "I don't know my relatives on my father's side very well. They live in and around Atlanta. I've spent most of my time with my mother's family. Most of my summers were spent in North Carolina with my grandparents."

"Do you miss your dad?" Leon inquired.

"Not really. I've been so angry with him for so many years for the way he mistreated my mom. I used to adore him when I was younger, but my feelings changed when I was able to understand what was happening."

"Understandable."

After a slice of wedding cake and the champagne toast, Leon asked, "Would you like to dance?"

"Sure." Misty slipped off her shoes.

He got up and led her to the dance floor. They danced until she needed to get some air.

They walked outside and sat down on a bench near the shop.

Fanning herself, Misty said, "Whew... I needed this little break. My feet were begging for it. I can't hang like I used to—I could stay on the dance floor for a couple of hours straight."

"I know what you mean," Leon said. "I'm starting to feel old."

She laughed. "Well, I'm not claiming that. You're by yourself with that."

"I love hearing you laugh. It's like you're free and just at peace."

"I haven't felt like this in such a long time," Misty said. "This is what life should feel like, Leon. It's liberating."

"I used to feel like that, but then tragedy struck, and things changed for me. Since I've met you, my life has gotten better. You're a great example of moving past adversity. You inspire me."

Misty was touched by his words. "That's really sweet of you to say that."

Rusty and Eleanor left the shop an hour later.

Leon hung behind to help with the cleanup, which thrilled Misty. She wasn't ready to part company with him just yet.

"I'm meeting Howard, Junior and Renee for breakfast tomorrow morning. If you're free, I'd like you to join us," Leon said when they walked out of the shop.

"I'd love to join you," Misty said. "And the timing is perfect. I don't have to work until noon."

"Who watches Talei for you when you work late?" Leon inquired.

"My friend Brittany."

"She used to date my brother, you know."

"She told me."

Once the café was restored back to its normal look, Misty had no reason to keep Leon with her. She consoled herself with the fact that she'd see him in the morning. "I'd better get home. My mom has been dealing with Talei all day. I'm sure she's ready for a break."

Leon kissed her on the lips. "I'll see you tomorrow for breakfast."

THE NEXT MORNING, Leon and Misty met Howard and his children at the hotel for breakfast. They were seated in a booth near the window.

"Trey had an early flight, so he wanted me to pass on his farewells."

"It's wonderful being back on the island," Howard said. "I hadn't realized how much I missed being here."

"Maybe you'll consider moving back," Leon suggested.

Howard laid down his menu. "To be honest, I've been thinking about it."

"I've been thinking about it, too," Renee interjected. "I'd like to open a clothing boutique on the island—it would be my designs, though."

"My daughter is a fashion designer," Howard said. "You should see some of her work."

"I'd love to see them," Misty responded.

"I have some on my phone." Renee passed her cell to Leon, who gave it to Misty.

She scanned through the photographs. "Oh, wow, these are all beautiful. I think you'd do well on the island."

Leon agreed. "We could use a high-end boutique around here. All the locals end up going to Charleston or Savannah to shop. It would be good to keep that revenue on the island."

"The space next to the bakery is available," Misty said.

Renee's eyes widened in surprise. "Really?"

Misty took a sip of her juice. "If you have time, I can take you to check it out."

"I'd love that. My flight isn't until noon. I can just take an Uber later to the mainland."

"I can drop you off," Leon offered. "I'll take you to the airport."

CHAPTER TWENTY-TWO

"So, how long have you and Leon been seeing each other?" Renee inquired. "I couldn't help but notice how close you two seem to be at the wedding."

"For a few weeks," Misty responded.

"It's really nice seeing him happy again."

She smiled. "Leon definitely makes me happy."

Misty parked curbside. "Are you seriously considering moving to the island?"

"I am," Renee said. "I want to start over some place fresh. Polk Island is my home—it's the best place for a new beginning."

"I called the owner and had him unlock the door for us."

Once they were inside, Renee's gaze bounced around the empty space. "This is perfect for what I envisioned."

Misty hung back, allowing her to wander about the shop. A boutique next door to the bakery and café would bring in more business for them both. It would also make Leon happy. She was a witness to the joy being around family brought him.

"I really like this spot."

"Do you want the owner's information?" Misty asked.

"Yes."

They walked out of the vacant space and headed back to the car. "I'd like to show you one other place that might fit your needs. I don't think we'll be able to get in with this being Sunday, but I can try to see it tomorrow and get some photos for you."

Renee smiled. "Great. I'm getting excited. You have no idea how bad I want to move back here."

AFTER SEVERAL DIAGNOSTIC tests and multiple visits to her doctor, and a neurologist, Eleanor and Rusty were back at the doctor's office for the results. They had just returned from a week in Hawaii for their honeymoon.

"No matter what, we're gonna be just fine," Rusty assured his wife.

She nodded in agreement, but deep down she was scared.

Her doctor entered the room and didn't waste any time with the diagnosis. "What we suspected has been confirmed…"

"I have early onset Alzheimer's," Eleanor stated as calmly as she could manage.

"Yes," her doctor said. He then lapsed into the treatment plan.

Eleanor sat there listening and numb.

Holding her hand in his, Rusty did the talking. He asked questions; lots of them.

She sat there thinking about all the plans she had for her golden years; plans for the shop. Her condition was going to change everything. She now had to attend to practical matters such as putting a plan in place to protect her financial assets.

When they were back at the house, Eleanor said, "I want to keep this just between us for now. Trey is deploying soon and Leon—with the jobs they have, they have to stay focused."

"Ladybug, you know your nephews are gonna want to know what's going on with you. They're gonna be mighty upset when they find out. This is not something we can keep to ourselves for too long. Besides, friends and family are some of the best medicine that any of us will have, in a journey such as this one."

"I hear what you're saying, Rusty, but I stand by what I said. It's not the right time." She paused a moment. "I'm going to turn my house over to Trey. He can decide if he wants to keep it or sell it. As for the shop, I'm thinking of talking to Misty about buying it. She told me when she began working for me that she wanted to own her own bakery one day. She has a great head for business and Lawd knows, the girl has a gift when it comes to baking. She's a good cook period."

"Are you sure you want to sell your shop? It's been in your family for years."

"Nobody in my family is interested in running it. Maybe if my brother had lived… Maggie loves her life in Raleigh." Eleanor took Rusty's hand in her own. "I know Misty will take care of the shop. I can see that she loves it as much as I do. Besides, she and Leon seem to be getting close. Perhaps it will stay in the family after all."

She suddenly grew quiet. Eleanor put her hands to her face and groaned.

Rusty was instantly concerned. "What's wrong, Ladybug?"

Placing her hands on her lap, she said, "I was about to do something, but I can't remember what it was."

"Close your eyes and quiet your mind. Think of someplace peaceful," he suggested.

Eleanor did as he said. She thought about their time in Hawaii. It was like they were in their own little paradise. She and Rusty enjoyed the different fruit stands and boutiques.

A smile tugged at her lips as she thought about the tiny roadside shack on the side of one of the roads that sold the best banana bread—it even rivaled Misty's delicious banana bread.

"I bet you're thinking about Hawaii."

Eleanor opened her eyes. "How did you know?"

"Because you had the same expression on your face just now that you had the whole time we were there."

Smiling, she said, "Maybe we should go back."

"We will," Rusty said. "But right now, why don't you lie down for a bit while I go pick up your medicine."

"I think I will. I was going to check in on the shop, but it's probably best if I don't. I don't quite feel like myself."

While Rusty was gone, Eleanor sat in bed contemplating her situation. Although she hadn't wanted to admit it before, she had begun to recognize changes in her own behavior, like her ability to manage multiple projects. There were a couple of instances when she found herself veering off course when she was supposed to be headed to a specific location.

Early onset Alzheimer's.

Eleanor wondered how long it would take before the reality of her fate really sunk in. She had zero control and this feeling of helplessness scared her. Her doctor mentioned an Alzheimer's Association chapter in Charleston. At this point, Eleanor wasn't sure she'd reach out—the thought was overwhelming.

There is no known cure, so I might as well accept what I can't change. I just worry about my family, especially Leon and Trey. Rusty... dear sweet Rusty. He was her rock. He had always been a man of strong faith, but she was afraid that this test would prove to be too much for even him.

Her eyes filled with tears. *Maybe I shouldn't have married him. It isn't fair for Rusty to have to witness my decline. I know he loves me, but he deserves a wife who is healthy.*

Eleanor knew what Rusty would say if he could hear her thoughts. They'd talked about this at length before the wedding. He assured her that he wanted to spend the rest of his life with her. She believed him—it was just a lot to ask of anybody. Yet, if it was the other way around, she would never abandon Rusty.

She heard him enter the house and make his way up the stairs. A smile tugged at her lips.

Rusty made her feel safe and she was glad he was home.

"I thought you'd be sleeping."

"I couldn't," Eleanor said. "I had a lot on my

mind. This is just so much to take in and I have a lot to do before my condition gets worse."

"Do you have plans for this weekend?" Leon inquired. His gaze traveled over her face and searched her eyes. They had just gotten back to her place after seeing a movie.

"I'm going to a powwow in Charleston. Talei and I are competing."

"Really?"

Misty nodded. "Yeah, it's something I've done since I was five years old."

"I've never been to one, but they seem to be pretty popular. Tell me… What exactly is a powwow?"

"It's a traditional gathering. A time for nations to come together to share songs and dances," Misty explained. "It's fun, it's sacred and it's social. If you're not busy, Talei and I would love to have you there."

"I'll be there."

"Since this is your first time, there are some things you should know. If you're asked to dance by an elder, do so. It's considered rude and disrespectful if you don't."

"I'm sure I don't know how to do any of the dances."

Misty met his gaze. "How can you learn if you turn the elders down? Our dances are more of a ceremony and a prayer… Some dances are old, and some are brand-new."

Leon grinned. "I guess you have a point."

"When the master of ceremonies calls an intertribal dance, it's expected that all visitors get out on the dance ring. The reason for this is that it's not considered polite to just watch as others perform. It's about honoring the circle." She smiled. "You still interested in coming?"

"Yeah, I'm actually intrigued. I know John loved to dance," Leon said. "I'm surprised he didn't try to steal the show."

"He never wanted to come," Misty said. "Talei and I always went with my mother."

"Oh."

"He was never into learning anything about this part of my culture, but it was more because he knew Elroy would've pitched a fit. His dad was always quick to remind me that my father is Black. I guess he thought that outweighed my Native heritage."

Leon frowned. "I don't understand that."

"I didn't either."

"We've been told that Polk's grandmother was Seminole, but there's nothing to back up the claim. Aunt Eleanor said Polk and Hoss wanted to make sure they documented our history going forward, so that we would at least know as much of it as possible. We can go all the way back to 1830."

"That's huge," Misty said. "Some people can't get past the 1900s."

"Aunt Eleanor has some quilts with pictures showing the history of Polk Island. She keeps them under lock and key. The director of the cultural center here has asked to display them, but she refuses."

"I'm sure she worries that they might end up damaged or, worse, stolen."

"Probably. I've been thinking of turning the church into some type of museum—one run by the Rothchild family."

"Leon, I think that's a fabulous idea. You should do it."

"I'll have to talk to the rest of the family first. I think we need to be all in if we want this to work."

Leon settled back against the couch cushions. "So, do you want to give me a preview of what I'm going to see at the powwow?"

"I think it's best to just let you experience it firsthand. No preview."

"Chicken," Leon said with a chuckle.

Misty's mouth dropped open in shock. "I can't believe you just said that. No more lemon cupcakes for you. When you attend the powwow, you'll understand why I'm not performing it for you right now."

"Since I can't get you to dance for me, can we just sit here and cuddle?"

She grinned. "Yes, yes and *yes*."

CHAPTER TWENTY-THREE

Misty and Oma picked herbs from her mother's indoor aero garden. She sniffed the basil. "I might have to try my hand at this, but I can't deal with bugs."

"You're bigger than the bugs."

"Doesn't matter, Mama. They gross me out."

"You've passed your fear on to your daughter," Oma said. "The last time she was here, that poor child worked herself into a frenzy over a fly."

Misty burst into laughter.

She carried the bowl of herbs to the sink to rinse them off. "Leon's coming to Charleston for the powwow tomorrow."

"Eon…" Talei said with a smile as she played with her two favorite bears.

Scanning her face, Oma asked, "I know you've been seeing quite a bit of Leon. Is this getting serious?"

Misty shrugged. "I don't know. Both of us have been through a lot, so we're just taking things slow. I want to really take time to get to know him. I've always rushed into my past relationships."

"Are you interested in something more with him?"

"I enjoy his company, Mama. I'm good with the way things are between us. I don't want any drama—I just want to have a good time."

"I can tell you like him, though."

Misty chuckled. "It's true. I like Leon a lot."

"One thing you have to learn to do is trust your heart and your gut instincts. There were red flags with the other guys you dated, but you ignored them."

"You're right," Misty mumbled. "I wanted to believe in the good I saw in them, but I found out that it was mostly an act. Thankfully, there haven't been any red flags with Leon. He seems pretty normal and well-adjusted. It's such a relief, Mama."

"Enjoy the journey."

"But I have to remember that he's not perfect. Leon has to have flaws. We all have them."

"True. Just make sure you're not waiting for something bad to happen. That's no way to enjoy a relationship."

"I'm very optimistic about dating Leon, Mama. But I'm also being realistic."

Misty helped Oma prepare a light meal for

the three of them, ate and then settled in her mother's sewing room.

She watched her mother sew ribbons on the bottom of a blue skirt and said, "It's beautiful."

Misty fingered one of the ribbons that represented prayers. "Are you wearing that tomorrow?"

"Yes," Oma responded. "Prayer is needed more than ever in this world."

"Are you going to have some for sale?"

Her mother pointed to a stack of clothing on a nearby chair. "I'm also selling the other ones I made along with some of the fringe dresses."

"Do you have any more of the quilts you made? I'd like to buy one for Miss Eleanor. She gave me one of hers—it's so pretty. I'll have to send you a picture of it."

"Take the one with the indigo blue flowers. I think she'll like that one."

Misty opened her purse, but Oma stopped her by saying, "It's a gift for your employer."

She gave her mother a hug. "*Wado*, Mama."

DRESSED IN NATIVE regalia in vibrant rich colors, Misty and Talei met Leon at the entrance of the grounds where the powwow took place. Talei's hair was in two braids with ribbons entwined while Misty's hair was pulled back into a bun with an eagle feather sticking up.

Leon picked up Talei. "Hello, pretty girl."

"*Oseeyo*, Eon." She pointed down to her moccasins. "Cute."

"Yes, they are. I see they match your mom's. You think they have some to fit my feet?"

"Yes." Talei pointed toward the area where the vendors were set up.

Leon met Misty's gaze and laughed. "She should get commission. You look beautiful, by the way."

She smiled. "Thank you. My mother wore this dress when she used to perform the healing dance."

"That sounds spiritual. Is that why you wouldn't dance for me the other night?"

"Yeah," she responded. "It's a sacred dance."

Leon glanced around the grounds. "This is amazing. I'm looking forward to this event. I especially can't wait to see this little one out there dancing."

Talei giggled.

"C'mon. I want to take you to see Mama. She wants to say hello."

Oma was with a customer when they walked up.

While they waited for her to complete the sale, Leon and Misty strolled around the tent, looking at the clothing, blankets and quilts.

"These are beautiful," he told Oma when she joined them.

"Mama, this is Leon Rothchild."

"It's nice to finally meet you," Oma stated.

He smiled. "Same here."

The powwow began with a grand entry. Leon watched as all the dancers entered the circle led by the veterans and head dancers. He stood up along with everyone in attendance when the opening prayer was said.

When it was time for the intertribal dance, Oma took Leon by the hand and led him into the arena. Talei joined him and Oma as the music began.

"I have no clue what I'm doing," he said in a low voice.

"Just walk with the beat," Oma advised.

He studied the man in front of him and mimicked what he did. Out of the corner of his eye, he saw Oma give a slight nod of approval.

When they left the arena, Leon said, "I probably looked crazy out there."

"You did great," Oma said. "I have to go back to my tent, but I'll be back when Talei dances."

He never knew that powwows were so sacred and spiritual. He'd just assumed they were nothing more than entertainment.

Leon felt a surge of fatherly pride as he watched Talei in the arena with the other children doing the candy dance. She looked like she was having a wonderful time. He had been so intent on watching her that he didn't notice Oma sitting beside him.

"Talei did a fantastic job," he said. "How long has she been dancing?"

"This is her second year competing, but she's been dancing since she was big enough to walk. She would watch Misty and try to imitate her."

Leon watched Talei line up a second time with the other children. She was the smallest, so she was right behind the head dancer holding eagle fans.

"This is called the Eagle Dance," Oma responded.

Leon grinned, watching Talei mimic the leader's movements, extending her arms to soar and spiral, before bringing them closer to her body and crouching on the ground. The line of children winded their way around the circle, surrounding the head dancer when he kneeled.

Talei waited until she exited the arena before running over to Oma and Leon. Misty was on the other side of the arena with a group of female dancers.

Oma planted a kiss on Talei's forehead, then returned to her tent.

Talei sat in the chair beside Leon. "Mommy dance."

"I can't wait to see that." He turned to face the little girl. "You did a great job out there. I'm so proud of you."

She grinned. "I not scared."

"I could tell," he said. "You're such a brave little girl, Talei."

"Hot dawg and fench fries, pleeze."

Leon burst into laughter. "C'mon, little one."

They returned to their seats in time to watch Misty perform the Dance of Life.

He was mesmerized by her graceful movements.

When she joined him and Talei after the dance, Leon said, "Wow… You were amazing."

"Amazing," her daughter repeated.

"I'm glad I came out here today. I've learned a lot."

"This is a huge part of who I am—I wanted you to experience it with me," Misty stated.

Talei got up and crawled onto Leon's lap so her mother could sit down.

The male dancers in fancy regalia entered the arena to perform.

Misty pointed to the dancer closest to where they were sitting. "My mom made his clothing."

"She's very talented."

By the end of the event, Leon found all of the dancers awe-inspiring. "When is the next pow-wow?" he asked.

"There's going to be one in Savannah next month," Misty said. "Interested in joining us?"

"I'm there," he responded with a grin.

TODAY THE STATION house was a busy one.

Leon and his coworkers started off washing engines one and two, then inspected their personal protective equipment. They had to be ready for any calls for assistance.

"Don't forget we have training in thirty minutes," Lizzie reminded him as she poured out the pail of dirty water. "Today is on special operations."

"Yeah," Leon uttered. They trained three days a week at the station. "I hope I can stay awake."

"Late night?" she asked as they strolled into the dorm.

Leon sat down on his bunk. "I went to a powwow in Charleston. I was there all day long."

"I haven't been to one of those in a long time."

"It was my first. I really enjoyed it. Misty and Talei performed."

Lizzie smiled. "I bet Talei was adorable."

Leon swept the kitchen area before heading to the training room.

When the session ended, he and the other firemen returned to dusting, sweeping and mopping the station. Charles did the laundry before leaving to talk to students at a community center about fire prevention and how to use a fire extinguisher as part of the station's public outreach program.

Leon spent the next hour working out with Lizzie and another member of the unit. They were required to exercise for one hour each shift.

"So, have you said those three little words to Misty?" Lizzie inquired.

He pretended not to know what she was talking about. "Huh?"

She laughed.

"I don't know what you're waiting for. We can see how much you care about Misty."

"Lizzie, have you told Rob how you feel?" Leon countered.

She stepped off the treadmill and wiped her face with a towel. "It's not the same."

He reached for his water bottle and took a long drink before putting it back down. "When the time is right, I'll tell Misty how I feel about her," Leon stated. He picked up a couple of hand weights. "Things are great between us, but we've only been together a short while. Neither one of us wants to rush the relationship."

CHAPTER TWENTY-FOUR

"MISTY, WHEN YOU get a minute, I'd like to talk to you."

"I have some time now, Miss Eleanor."

"Great, let's talk in my office."

Eleanor closed the door behind them, then sat down at her desk.

"Is everything okay?"

"Now that Rusty and I are married, I've been thinking about the future. One thing I want to do is to spend more time with him."

Misty smiled. "Ah…the honeymoon phase."

"It's more than that, sugar," Eleanor said. "There are some things that have come up in my life and it's changed my focus. I'm actually thinking of selling the shop to you…that is if you're interested."

A soft gasp escaped Misty. "You're not serious. This place has been in your family for years."

"I know that you will take care of it."

"Miss Eleanor, what's really going on?"

Misty inquired. "I know how much this place means to you."

"I'm gwine retire and spend time enjoying life with Rusty."

Misty shook her head in denial. "I'm not really buying that story. There's something more going on. I'm not trying to get in your business, Miss Eleanor, but I know you wouldn't just up and sell the shop like this. Don't get me wrong. I would love to buy this place from you. John left me and Talei well taken care of, so the money isn't an issue."

"Misty, I owe you the truth. What I'm about to tell you, I need you to keep to yourself. Rusty and I are the only ones who know this information."

"I won't say a word," Misty said.

"This means you're going to have to keep a secret from Leon," Eleanor clarified.

"He would want to know what's going on with you. You know that he adores you."

"I know but he can't know about this just yet. I have early onset Alzheimer's," Eleanor announced. "We just found out a couple of days ago and I need some time to process the news myself before I start telling everybody."

Misty's body stiffened in shock. "Miss Eleanor… I don't know what to say…"

Eleanor gave a slight shrug. "It's fine, sugar.

But I hope you can understand why I want to sell. There's no way I can keep up with the demands of the shop. I would take great comfort in knowing that I've left it in good hands with you, Misty. I know you want your own business. What do you think?"

"I never expected this," she responded. "Are you sure you want to do this, Miss Eleanor?"

She nodded. "Rusty and I discussed it at length. You have a brilliant mind for business and you also have a passion for what you do."

"But what about your other family members?"

"None of them are interested in this shop. I couldn't get not a one of them to work when I needed extra help."

"Not even Leon?"

"He has enough on his plate, Misty. So does Trey. He's committed to the marines and looking to make a career of the military."

"Please give this some serious thought and let me know, Misty. I don't want to sell to strangers."

"I don't have to think about it," she said. "I'll take over the shop, Miss Eleanor. I love it here."

MISTY LOOKED DOWN at the baggy sweatpants and T-shirt she was wearing. Leon was due to arrive at any moment. They were staying in tonight and she wanted to be comfortable.

Maybe I should change clothes.

She dismissed the thought as quickly as it had come. *Why am I worried about what he's going to think?* This was part of her normal routine. "Might as well let him see the real me," she whispered.

The doorbell sounded.

Misty opened the door and threw herself into his arms. Leon gave the best hugs.

Once they were seated in the living room, Misty stated, "I was thinking we could make homemade pizza."

"Works for me."

Talei walked into the room. "Mommy... Eon..." She climbed into his lap with her stuffed bears. "I playing with Pooh Bear and Eon," she said, pointing to the bear in the fire department T-shirt.

"You named him after me?" Leon asked.

"Yes," Talei responded.

"I'm honored."

Talei grinned, then laid her head on his chest.

Misty's heart warmed as she watched her daughter with Leon. The two had really bonded over the past few months.

"Who's ready to make pizza?" she asked.

"Me," Leon and Talei responded in unison.

Laughing, they made their way to the kitchen.

Leon set Talei on a stool while Misty gathered the ingredients.

"Pepperooni."

"You want pepperoni pizza, Talei?"

"Yes. Mommy like pepperooni, too." Talei picked up the packet from the counter and tried to open it.

"Let me help you," Leon said.

She gave him the bag of pepperoni slices. Pointing to a blue container, Talei inquired, "What that?"

"Mushrooms," he responded. "I like them on my pizza."

She made a face, prompting laughter from Leon. "Do you like olives, little one?"

Frowning, Talei shook her head no.

"She's a plain pepperoni-and-cheese kind of girl," Misty said.

When it was time to put the toppings on her pizza, Talei placed one mushroom and one olive on hers.

"Look at my brave girl," Misty said. "I'm so proud of you for trying new things."

"When Daddy come home from heaven?" Talei blurted when they gathered at the dining room table. "Daddy got hurt in car."

Misty glanced over at Leon, then said, "Sweetie, your dad isn't here."

"Your daddy's in heaven watching over you," Leon stated.

After they finished eating, Misty turned on a Disney movie for Talei to watch.

Keeping her voice low, she said, "I think I made a mistake."

"What do you mean?" Leon asked.

"I told Talei that John went to heaven. She thinks he's coming back."

"If you'd like, we can try to explain it to her together."

"Come here, honey," Misty said. "We want to talk to you about Daddy."

"Okay." Talei climbed down from the sofa. She skipped back to the table where they were sitting.

"You remember the car accident?"

Talei nodded. "Daddy got hurt. Eon help Daddy."

"That's right. He was taken to the hospital. The doctors tried to make Daddy better, but they couldn't. He was too hurt." Misty paused a moment, then said, "Daddy *died*. He didn't want to die, but he was too hurt."

"Your mom's right," Leon said. "Your daddy never wanted to leave you. I know that he misses you very much because he can't see you or your mom again."

Talei's eyes filled with tears. "He not coming back."

"When you die, you can't come back. You go to live in heaven. It's okay for you to miss him."

"Your dad's up there watching over you," Leon said. "He will always live in your heart, little one. His love for you will never stop."

"We still have pictures and memories of Daddy," Misty stated. "You will always remember how much he loved you."

"I want Daddy." Talei began to cry.

Leon embraced her. "He loved you so much. Your daddy was crazy about you. He made me promise to look after you when he was gone. I'm going to keep my word to your daddy. I will always be here for you." He wiped away her tears. "It may not seem like it now, but it's going to be okay, little one."

Talei eased out of his lap and ran off to her room.

Misty shook her head. "This is so hard."

After a while, Talei returned with her bears Pooh and Eon. Without a word, she climbed into Misty's lap. "I wanna watch Minty Mouse."

"Me, too," Leon said with a grin.

Misty planted a kiss on Talei's cheek.

"Do I get one of those?" he asked.

She kissed his cheek in response. "Thank you."

Misty felt guilty about the secret she was keeping from Leon. He deserved to know about his aunt's condition, but Eleanor wasn't ready to tell him. Misty had no choice but to respect her decision.

Inside, she felt terrible about it.

Misty also worried that she could lose Leon once he knew the truth about the shop and Eleanor's condition. She prayed he would understand that she was only honoring his aunt's wishes.

"What's on your mind?" Leon asked, cutting into her thoughts.

"It's nothing," she replied with a smile.

He scanned her face. "You sure you're okay? You look a little troubled.

"I am. Everything is fine. I'm just tired."

"I've been meaning to ask how my aunt's been doing at the shop. I know she's been a bit forgetful."

Misty chewed on her bottom lip and pretended to be interested in watching television. "I've been forgetting stuff myself. That's why I have to write everything down."

"I know she runs herself ragged at times."

"I've been trying to get Miss Eleanor to slow down. Now that she's married, I think she will."

"I hope so," Leon said. "I offered to help out on days when I don't have to work."

"You're such a sweetheart."

"Aunt Eleanor took care of me and Trey when we lost our parents. When Vee and my daughter died, my aunt wouldn't let me quit on life." Leon eyed her. "Misty, I was in so much pain." His voice broke.

Misty hugged him. "I'm so sorry for all you've been through."

"Aunt Eleanor moved in with me because she was so worried about me. My coworkers checked on me to the point they were getting on my nerves. I owe them so much."

"I understand what you mean," Misty said. "The good thing is that you had so many people rallying around you."

"I had a lot of people. The whole community was here for me."

"Hearing this lets me know that I chose the perfect place to raise my daughter. This is the way it should be."

LEON COULDN'T ESCAPE the feeling that Misty was hiding something from him. He didn't know if it had to do with her feelings or something else. She seemed troubled or uneasy, but he couldn't get her to open up to him.

He decided to give it one more shot. "Misty, how are you feeling about us?"

She looked perplexed by his question for a brief moment, then responded, "I love the way things are between us. We have a great time together. We have a lot in common and there's no drama." Misty scanned his face. "Why do you ask?"

"I just wanted to make sure we're on the same page," Leon said. "I really like you and I need to know that you're as invested in this relationship as I am."

Smiling, Misty said, "You don't have anything to worry about. I'm very invested."

Leon believed her, but still couldn't shake the feeling that there was something more going on. He intended to find out what Misty was hiding. He didn't like secrets.

"So, WHAT ARE you gonna do about the shop?" Brittany asked. "It would be a great investment for you."

"I don't know," Misty said with a shrug. "I want to buy it, but I just feel that Miss Eleanor's going through a lot right now. I'm not sure she's thinking clearly about everything. This is not a decision to make while emotions are high."

"I hope it's nothing serious."

"She's starting a new life with Rusty. Miss Eleanor deserves to spend every moment making new memories, but the shop has been in her family a few generations."

"Apparently, she's fine with selling it, Misty.

I just wonder how Leon's gonna feel about all this. He's big on family. So is Trey for that matter."

Misty shrugged. "Miss Eleanor made it clear that it's *her* decision."

"Okay, then. There you have it."

After she left her best friend, Misty decided to pay Leon a visit.

She found him working in the yard. "Hey, you."

"Hello," he responded.

"Want some help?"

"Sure."

She started weeding across the garden from him.

He hunched over, his hands resting on his thighs. "You're not working today?"

"No. I'm taking Talei to the doctor later this afternoon and I ran some errands this morning." She couldn't tell him that she spent her morning working out the financing for the shop.

"When you're done, you wanna come do mine?"

The voice, from a passerby, prompted Leon to look up and see who was talking to him. "Hey, Pete."

Leon pushed to his feet and walked down the driveway, leaving Misty to continue her task. She didn't pay much attention to them.

"How could you take advantage of my aunt like that?" Leon demanded when he returned. He glared at Misty with burning, reproachful eyes.

She shielded her eyes from the sun as she looked up at him. "What are you talking about?"

"My great-great-grandparents opened that shop. Aunt Eleanor loves that place. She wouldn't sell it to *anyone* unless she was manipulated." A sudden thin chill hung on the edge of his words.

Misty seethed with disappointment and anger. She stood up to him. "Do you really think that I'm the type of person who would do something like that?"

"All I know is that she would want the shop to stay in the family."

"It's clearly time for me to leave," Misty said. She wasn't about to stand there and argue with him. "For the record I didn't steal your aunt's business." She felt weak and vulnerable in the face of Leon's anger. "You will have to ask her about why she wants to sell."

"I never said you were stealing anything."

"You're an idiot," Misty uttered. "You don't have to worry, Leon. I don't need to buy it—I can open my own somewhere else."

"Aunt Eleanor loves that place. It doesn't make sense that she would want to sell it. That's all I know."

"Miss Eleanor knows that she's not able to keep running it, Leon."

"Why not?" he asked.

Misty hadn't meant to say that much. "You'll have to ask your aunt."

"I'm asking *you*. Why would my aunt suddenly decide to up and sell her business? I know that there's something you're not telling me."

"Miss Eleanor came to me, Leon. If you want to know more, ask her." Misty wiped her hands with a nearby towel. "Goodbye… Oh and lose my number."

CHAPTER TWENTY-FIVE

Upset, Misty left Leon's house and drove to see Eleanor. The last thing she wanted was to cause friction in their family. It was better to take herself out of the equation.

Eleanor opened the door and stepped back to let Misty enter the foyer. "What a pleasant surprise. C'mon in, sugar."

They sat down in the living room. "Miss Eleanor, I thought about it and I don't think it's a good idea for me to buy the shop."

Eleanor looked disappointed and near tears. "Why not? You seemed pretty excited about it when we had our discussion."

"I was… I am… The truth is that Leon's not really happy about the idea. In fact, he accused me of manipulating you to get you to sell to me."

"*What?* How in the world did he find out?"

"One of his neighbors mentioned it. I think his name is Pete."

"He works at the law firm. My lawyer must have mentioned it to him, but you don't have to worry about my nephew. I'll set him straight."

"Leon's right about how much you love the shop, Miss Eleanor. Maybe there's another way…"

"Misty, the only person I'd trust with the shop is you. I know that you love it as much as I do."

"I do love this place, but I don't want to cause friction between you and Leon. In fact, I'm thinking about moving back to Charleston."

"Misty, I hope it doesn't come to that."

"Miss Eleanor, you didn't see the way Leon reacted. He really hurt my feelings."

"Don't make any decisions just yet. I'll straighten everything out, Misty. The bakery and café are mine to do what I will with it. I don't need my nephew's permission to sell."

"Regardless, the damage is already done. Leon and I won't be seeing each other anymore."

"I know that you care for Leon. Don't give up on him."

"I can't make any promises, Miss Eleanor. I refuse to date a man who thinks so little of me. I don't know what John told him about me, but apparently he believes it."

"I'm so sorry, sugar."

"Miss Eleanor, it's not your fault. I'm actually glad it happened. I needed to know who I was dealing with."

Eleanor took Misty's hand in her own. "I

want to sell my shop to *you*. I will only have peace if I know it's in your hands."

"I'll think about it and give you a call tomorrow."

"Even if you decide not to buy the shop, I know you love this island. Don't let what happened run you off."

"Miss Eleanor, I can't imagine living so close to Leon and not being with him. It would hurt too much to see him around town... My feelings for him are strong." She paused a moment, then said, "I'm in love with him."

"I can see that clear as day."

"That's why his actions today hurt so much." Misty stood up. "I need to get home, but I'll give you a call tomorrow to let you know what I decide."

LEON WAS IN search of answers.

"Rusty, do you know anything about my aunt selling the shop?" Leon asked. "Pete told me that she met with her lawyer about it."

"Have you spoken to Eleanor?"

"Not yet," Leon responded. "Is this because the two of you got married?"

"Eleanor will be home soon," Rusty said. "You should talk to *her*."

"What's with all the secrecy?" Shaking his

head in frustration, Leon stated, "I just hope this wasn't Misty's plan all along."

"You don't really believe that, do you?"

Leon shrugged. "I don't know what to believe. John used to tell me that she used manipulation to get whatever she wanted from him."

"John also took his own daughter without Misty's permission," Rusty said. "I would say his credibility was questionable at best. He was your friend, but clearly there was a side to him that you didn't know about."

"All the more reason to wonder if there's a side to Misty that I have no knowledge of—don't you think?"

"Has she ever lied to you?"

"I don't think so," Leon responded. "Rusty, I know where you're going with this. Believe me, I want to give Misty the benefit of the doubt."

"Join us for dinner tonight," Rusty suggested. "You can talk to your aunt and get all of your questions answered."

Leon nodded. "I'll definitely be back."

None of this made sense to him. He would never believe that his aunt would just up and sell a business that had been in his family for generations. She wouldn't do something like that unless she was somehow forced into it.

He would find out the truth in a few hours.

WHEN LEON ARRIVED, Eleanor had the food prepared and was ready to serve. He washed his hands, then joined them at the dining room table.

Rusty said the blessing.

Leon sampled his food. "Auntie, everything is delicious."

He tried to keep the discussion light while they ate, but questions hammered at him.

Halfway through the meal, Eleanor glanced over at Rusty, then said, "I hear Pete opened his big mouth before I had a chance to talk to you. There's something you should know."

Leon wiped his mouth with his napkin. "Is this about the shop?"

"Yes," she responded. "First off… You were wrong for blaming Misty for anything. It was my idea to sell the shop to her. She's the perfect person to take ownership because I know she'll take care of it. Rusty and I talked about this at length. It's what I want to do, and you have no say-so in the matter."

"But why do you suddenly want to sell the shop?" Leon inquired. "This didn't come up after the fire. I don't understand."

"There's something I need to tell you, son."

The expression on her face made him ask, "What's going on, Auntie?"

"I have early onset Alzheimer's," Eleanor announced. "I thought I was just getting forgetful…that it was because of my age… I never considered that it would be something more. I wake up in the morning sometimes and I don't feel rested. But mostly, I don't know what day of the week it is…the date or even the month. There are times when I don't remember what I planned for the day."

"Sometimes I have days like that, Auntie. I think everyone goes through times like this."

"I didn't realize until today that I get up and wear one of three outfits all the time, Leon. I have a closet full of clothes. This morning at the café, I couldn't remember where the coffee was, and I couldn't remember where I keep the flour. I found myself reading the same article over and over again this afternoon."

"I'm so sorry, Auntie."

"I'm sure you've noticed I ask you the same questions over and over again. This is my life."

"Why didn't you tell me you were going through this?" He gazed at Rusty. "Did you know?"

"Yes," Rusty answered.

"Leon, I didn't want to worry you, son," Eleanor stated. "I didn't want you worrying about me. And don't be upset with my husband—he wanted to tell you but respected my decision to tell you when I was ready."

"That's not your call, Auntie. I love you so I'm always gonna worry about you."

"Now I need you to not say anything to Trey. I want to tell him in my own time, Leon. He's over in Afghanistan. I need your brother to keep his head straight so he can be safe."

"I won't say anything," Leon provided. "I was just thinking how I made a fool of myself with Misty. I owe her a huge apology."

"Well, you better do it soon. Misty's thinking about leaving the island," Eleanor announced.

Leon's eyebrows shot up in surprise. "What are you talking about?"

"She told me that she might be moving back to Charleston. I don't know what happened between you two, but she was really hurt by it."

Leon laid down his fork. "I never meant to hurt Misty. I accused her of manipulating you into selling the shop."

"Boy, you done lost your mind. Yeah, you need to make it right or you stand to lose her forever. *Mark my word.*"

"I will," he said. "I'll go by her place when I leave here."

Leon's heart was in a panic at the thought of losing Misty. He had to talk to her—to make things right.

CHAPTER TWENTY-SIX

LEON SAT OUTSIDE her condo for ten minutes, trying to figure out the best approach. He had been a complete jerk to her. He prayed he could repair the damage done.

"I apologize for just showing up, but I really wanted to talk to you," Leon said when Misty opened the front door. "May I come in?"

"I'm not sure we have anything to discuss."

She was still clearly upset with him. "I want to apologize for the things I said earlier."

They settled in the living room.

"I just left my aunt's house," Leon began. "She told me everything. Misty, I'm very sorry for the way I treated you."

"You should've known better," she said. "The fact that you think I'd do something like that—it really bothers me."

"Misty, I honestly don't know why I said that to you—it just didn't make sense that my aunt would even think of selling her shop. I'm so sorry."

After a moment, she said, "I accept your apology."

"I assume my aunt told you why she wants to sell you the shop."

Misty nodded. "I know she has Alzheimer's. For the record, she wanted me to keep her secret until she was ready to tell you. She didn't want you to worry about her."

"She told me the same thing, but it doesn't matter. She's my aunt and I care what happens to her."

"Miss Eleanor knows that," Misty said. "I have to be honest, Leon. You really hurt my feelings. I have always wanted my own business, but there's no way I'd swindle Miss Eleanor out of her shop. Or anyone else for that matter. I'm not that type of person."

"I know that," he responded. "For the record, I never thought you cheated her."

"Maybe not, but you did accuse me of manipulating your aunt. That sounds just as bad, Leon. Just so you know, I backed out of buying the shop."

"Aunt Eleanor made it clear that she wanted you to take over the bakery. Now that I know everything, I agree with her. You should buy it."

"I don't know."

"Misty, can we get past this?"

She met Leon's gaze. "What happened has made me realize that you don't really know me."

"I want to get to know you more. I admit that I messed up, but I'm hoping you'll give me another chance. I should say give *us* another chance."

"I need some time to think about it, Leon."

He gave a slight nod. "I understand. I'll give you some space."

Leon rose to his feet.

"Don't leave," Misty said when he reached for the doorknob. "I don't want you to go."

He came and sat back down beside her.

"If we're going to see each other, I need you to trust me unless I prove to be untrustworthy. I don't know what John told you about me, but whatever he said must have colored your opinion of me."

"I agree," Leon said. "You deserve that and more. As for John—he had nothing to do with what happened. I jumped to conclusions without all the information. I won't make that mistake again. I give you my word."

"Thank you for coming here to make things right. I appreciate that."

"Were you seriously thinking about moving back to Charleston?" Leon asked.

"I was," she responded.

"And now?"

"I thought about moving, but the truth is that Talei and I love it here. I'm not leaving. Polk Island has become our home."

"I'm happy to hear you say this," Leon said. "I don't want to lose you or Talei. You've both come to mean a lot to me."

"I need to know something. If I buy the bakery and café, how will you feel about it? I want you to be honest."

"I'll be okay. I know you'll be great."

"You really mean that?" Misty asked.

"I do."

Misty picked up the television remote. "I was just about to watch a movie. Would you like to stay?"

"Sure. I can't think of a better way to spend the evening."

They watched in companionable silence until a commercial break.

"How was your day?" Leon asked.

"It was great," Misty responded. "The shop was busy nonstop. I picked Talei up from day care, we got ice cream, then walked the beach."

She turned down the volume to the TV while they talked.

"Leon, how are you feeling about your aunt's diagnosis?"

"I need to learn more about the disease," he responded. "I'm worried for her. I know Rusty's there for her, but I can't abandon her either. I just don't know what I can do to help my aunt."

Misty took his hand in her own. "I read somewhere that they are making great strides in slowing down the progression of Alzheimer's. You can't lose hope."

"One thing I've noticed is that whenever we watch the news, I can tell my aunt gets bothered—she doesn't like hearing about all the bad things happening in the world. Minutes later, Aunt Eleanor didn't even remember what it was that bothered her. She asks the same question over and over again. She can remember things she did as a child…"

"Her short-term memory is affected by the disease," Misty said. "What can I do to help?"

"I don't know," Leon responded. "I'm glad she has Rusty because I'm not sure how much longer she could've lived alone." He released a long sigh. "I wish I knew what to do to help her. She's always been there for me."

"You have to allow her to live as normal a life as possible, Leon. My grandmother had dementia and my mother was her caregiver. As her disease progressed, there were days she didn't recognize her own daughter. It was hard on my mom because of Granny's inability to communicate her thoughts or remember faces and names." Misty pasted on a smile. "Your aunt is one strong-willed lady. She is going to fight back with her entire being."

"She's tough," Leon agreed.

"Make sure she takes her medicine. My granny hated taking hers. There were times when she'd get violent with my mom." Misty took Leon's hand in her own. "I'm here to help in any way I can. I know Rusty has to run his business and you're working at the station."

"You're going to be running the shop and you have Talei. I can't intrude in your life any more than that."

"You're not," Misty responded. "I'm offering."

"I guess we'll both just have to wait and see how this disease progresses. Aunt Eleanor was herself when I went to see her earlier. She made dinner and it was delicious. She looked good. Misty, she looked really happy."

"That's good to hear, but you may notice her asking you the same questions repeatedly or she may be confused or forgetful—those are the things you have to be on the watch for with Miss Eleanor."

"I'm scared of losing her, Misty."

"Don't think that way. Just take it one day at a time. Learn about the disease. You might want to join a support group if that will help."

"I'm glad that I have you, Misty."

"I'll always be here for you, Leon. Don't ever forget that."

He pulled her into his embrace, holding her close. No words were necessary.

RUSTY COULDN'T LEAVE work so Leon picked up Eleanor for her doctor appointment. During the fifteen-minute drive, she asked the same question four times. "Where are we going?"

"To see your doctor, Auntie."

"Is it time for my physical?" She frowned. "Seems like I already did that. I saw Dr. Allen last month."

"We're going to see Dr. Grady," Leon announced.

"Ooh…" she responded. "I like Dr. Grady. I need to talk to her about getting my license back."

"Auntie, you don't need to worry about driving. I'll take you anywhere you need to go."

"Sugar, you have to work. I don't need you running me around. I can drive myself."

Her determination filled Leon with angst. He didn't want to upset her, but there was no way he'd let her get behind the wheel of a car in her condition. However, he couldn't tell her—she would be angry and devastated.

After the appointment, Eleanor asked, "Where are we going?"

"Home. We just left your doctor's appointment," he responded patiently.

"We did?" Eleanor appeared confused.

"Yes, ma'am."

"I just saw Dr. Allen. I think it was last month."

"We saw Dr. Grady, Aunt Eleanor."

"What did she say? Did she give me my license back? I don't know why she took it in the first place."

Rusty had prepared him that his aunt would have moments like this. Still, Leon found it heartbreaking to see her going through this.

"How about I make you some lunch?" Leon suggested when they arrived back at the house.

"Sure," Eleanor responded.

He found some chili in the refrigerator and heated it up.

She ate only half of what was in the bowl.

"You're not hungry?"

"It didn't have a lot of flavor," Eleanor responded.

"I've never been the cook that you are." Leon didn't have the heart to tell her that she'd made it. She was right, of course. It wasn't the same recipe she often used in the past—it was missing something.

"Sugar, I'm sorry. I wasn't trying to hurt your feelings."

"You didn't, Auntie."

"Where's Rusty? I thought he'd be home by now."

"He should be here soon," Leon said. "I'm gonna hang around until he gets here to keep you company."

"Great," Eleanor murmured. "Sometimes I don't like being here alone."

She finished off her water, then asked, "How are things going with Misty?"

"Fine," Leon responded. "We're in a good place."

"You two make such a lovely couple. It's good to see you smile again. Misty is perfect for you, but then you know this already. She's been through so much in her lifetime. She's a survivor…that one."

THE NEXT DAY after Rusty left for work, Eleanor began to have dark, negative thoughts. She had no idea why. She checked the locks on the doors and the windows. She was safe.

Her emotions ranged from feeling depressed, angry, even crying. Oftentimes music lifted her spirits. Eleanor didn't venture to the café as much now because she wasn't able to drive, and she didn't want to burden anyone with chauffeuring her around.

She spent the rest of her afternoon figuring out word games in a puzzle magazine Leon purchased for her. When she grew bored with that, she attempted to read a book but lost the narrative after a few pages.

Eleanor picked up her phone and tapped on a number.

"Ladybug, I was just about to call you. I was going to pick up lunch from the café. You know how much I love Josh's brisket sandwich."

"That's fine," she responded. "Just get me whatever you're having."

"Did you need something?"

"No, I was just checking to see when you'd be home. I miss you."

"I'll be there shortly."

"Tell Josh to make sure he checks behind Silas. I don't want any of my customers ever complaining about dirty silverware."

"I'll let him know."

"Ladybug, you sold the shop to Misty, remember?"

"Oh, yeah. That's right."

When she hung up, Eleanor burst into tears.

CHAPTER TWENTY-SEVEN

OMA WAS VISITING for the weekend.

"I'm so glad you're here, Mama."

"Misty, how are you doing really? I know how much you internalize things."

"I'm fine," she responded. "Moving here was a good choice for me. This is probably the first time in a long while that I've felt safe and at peace."

"How do you feel about John's death now?"

"I hate that he's not here, Mama. This isn't the way I wanted Talei to grow up, without her father. I just hoped he'd get it together." She paused a moment, then said, "There's something I've been wanting to ask you."

"Go ahead. You know you can ask me anything."

"Mama, did daddy ever hit you during your marriage?"

"No. Your father always had a temper and sometimes he was verbally abusive, but he never laid a hand on me."

"I promised myself that I would never marry

someone like him. I was so sure I knew the man I'd fallen in love with. John was such a sweetheart when we dated. Like Daddy, he had a bit of a temper, but he seemed to manage it well until we got married." Misty shook her head. "I was such a fool."

"John's father was a trigger for him. Y'all were fine until that man started interfering in your marriage."

"He never thought I was good enough for his son."

"He was wrong," Oma uttered. "You were too good for John Hayes."

"I dread the thought of having to deal with his parents, although his mother has been pretty nice since John's death."

"She doesn't want you to keep her grandchild away. You see John's sister doesn't have anything to do with them."

"Sherry didn't come to the funeral, but she did call me. She refuses to have her children anywhere near her father."

"He's nothing but a bully."

"I don't mind Talei spending time with her grandmother, but Elroy... I'm not so comfortable with him."

Later when Misty climbed into bed, she retrieved her journal from the nightstand and began to write.

Everybody keeps asking me how I'm dealing with John's death. I tell them I'm fine, but is that really the truth?

I haven't told anyone, but I feel like John's death is on me. It's my fault that he felt desperate enough to kidnap Talei. If I hadn't pushed for supervised visitation, he would probably still be alive.

When Talei asks about her daddy, there are days it's hard for me to look her in the face.

She misses him so much. How can I ever make this up to her?

How can I ever forgive myself for John's death?

I can't talk about this to anyone because they just won't understand. I didn't want anything bad to happen to John. I didn't want to fight with him over custody. I wanted our marriage to work, but I couldn't live with the man he had become. All I wanted was for John to get the help he needed so he could be a good father to Talei.

Elroy blames me for John's death. I refuse to give him the satisfaction of knowing that I blame myself, as well. I will never get the chance to tell you this, so I'll write it here:

John, I'm so sorry. I didn't want to hurt you, but I couldn't live with you hurting me. I feared that you would one day hurt our daughter. If

*you hadn't threatened to take Talei from me...
if you hadn't threatened my life... We wouldn't
have been in this space. You made me afraid
of you. I'm tired of being afraid. I don't want
to be a victim anymore. I want to live in peace
and without drama.*

*I hope that you have finally found the peace
that escaped you in life, John. I'm so sorry for
everything. I promise Talei will never forget
you. Leon has stepped up to be her godfather.
I can clearly see why you chose him. He's good
to us.*

THE NEXT MORNING, Eleanor woke up early. It
took a minute or so to recognize her surroundings. She eased out of bed and went to the bathroom. She heard the lawn mower and stole a
peek outside.

She watched Rusty as he mowed the grass, a
smile on her lips.

Fifteen minutes later, she strolled into the
kitchen to prepare breakfast. She hit a wrinkle
in her preparations because Eleanor was unsure of whether she'd already put in the right
amount of baking soda. She was making Belgian waffles for Rusty with fresh berries and a
homemade strawberry glaze.

"Why can't I remember something so simple?" Eleanor whispered. The feeling of frustration left a lingering effect.

"Good morning, Ladybug."

She pasted on a smile. "Rusty... What time did you wake up?"

"I got up around five thirty. I wanted to get that grass cut before it got real hot out there."

"For all your hard work, I was going to make you some Belgian waffles, but I'm having trouble remembering all the ingredients." Tears filled her eyes. "Rusty, I hate being this way."

He embraced her. "Honey, it's gonna be okay. The meds they're giving you will help slow down the progression. As for breakfast, I can help you with that."

"But you shouldn't have to, Rusty. I'm your wife. I'm not helpless," Eleanor stated. "I've made Belgian waffles for as long as I can remember."

"The truth is that I've always wanted to learn how to make them." Rusty placed his arms around her, whispering, "You know I love *cooking* with you."

"I don't know if I put in all the right ingredients," Eleanor said.

"It's fine. We can start over," Rusty responded. He pulled out his phone. "I'll find a recipe that's close to yours and we'll use that one. If it's not right, you can change it." He kissed her cheek. "Now stop crying, Ladybug. *We got this.*"

"I'm very lucky to have you in my life. I've always known that. I want to go to the café today," Eleanor announced. "I feel like I need to stay busy today."

"If you're sure you're up to it," Rusty responded. "Don't forget to take your medicine."

"I better get it now." She rose to her feet and left the dining room.

Eleanor returned a few minutes later with medication in hand. "If I don't take it now, I'll forget." She paused to look at him. "Rusty, I'm scared."

"I know, Ladybug. Just remember that you're not alone. You have me."

LEON WATCHED MISTY as she held the ball straight, her arms fully extended. Her right hand supported the ball underneath. She looked as if she knew what she was doing. He, on the other hand, hadn't played in a while but used to be on the bowling team with some of his co-workers.

Aware that his gaze had traveled from the back of her head downward to the curve of her hips, Leon forced his attention back to the game.

Misty released the ball, rolling a perfect strike. "Yes. Let's see if you can match that."

It was his turn.

His ball left three pins standing. "I guess not."

"It's okay, Leon," Misty murmured. "You can knock them down."

"I appreciate the encouragement."

She kissed him on the cheek. "I heard you were on a bowling team."

"Aunt Eleanor talks too much."

Misty chuckled.

Leon placed the bowling ball on the rack before drawing Misty into an embrace. He pressed his lips against hers, and then gently covered her mouth. Leon kissed the top of her nose, then her eyes, and finally, he returned his attention to her lips.

After they left the bowling alley, they went to Misty's condo.

She quickly prepared a simple fare of shrimp alfredo over pasta, a garden salad and garlic bread.

Misty watched him as he took a bite. "How is it?"

"Delicious," Leon responded.

She felt a warm glow go through her, prompting her to take several sips of her iced tea. Misty couldn't keep from peering at him throughout dinner. She'd never felt this way about any other man.

Swallowing hard, she forced those thoughts out of her mind.

Misty breathed a sigh of relief when Brittany brought Talei home.

CHAPTER TWENTY-EIGHT

ELEANOR WALKED OVER to the French doors leading to the patio and stared out. Rusty was at the grill making burgers and chicken. "Leon just arrived with Misty and Talei."

She was looking forward to spending the day with family and friends. It was something Eleanor hadn't done in a while. Before her symptoms appeared, she would often have gatherings on Sunday afternoons.

She gave the patio one last glance, then joined Leon in the kitchen. He was putting a bowl of potato salad in the refrigerator.

"Don't worry, Misty made it."

Eleanor chuckled. "Thank the Lawd…"

"Is there anything I can do to help?" Misty inquired.

"Rusty will probably need more burgers."

"I'll make them," Misty said. She quickly washed her hands, then reached into the bowl containing ground beef. She and Leon made small talk while forming the meat into patties.

"Thanks for having us over, Auntie."

"I'm so glad y'all could come," Eleanor said.

Talei skipped into the kitchen. "I want juice."

Misty smiled at her daughter. "Is that how you're supposed to ask?"

"May I have juice?"

"That's better."

Eleanor picked up a paper cup. "I have some apple juice, Talei."

"*Wado*, Miss Ellie."

Rusty's nephew and his family were the next to arrive.

Eleanor felt blissfully happy in this moment. She felt like herself before the memory loss. Before the diagnosis.

Rusty entered through the patio doors. He gave her a huge smile. "You look like you're having a good time."

"I am," she responded. "There's no confusion. I feel fine, Rusty. Maybe the medication is working." Eleanor gloried in this shared moment. "This is a perfect day."

LEON HADN'T HAD this much fun in a long time.

He played a couple of rounds of basketball with the guys while Misty and the other women sat around the pool chatting.

Eleanor strolled outside carrying a plate stacked with corn on the cob. She handed it to her husband.

Leon glanced around the yard, looking for Talei. He found her with the other kids kicking around a ball.

His heart sang with delight at the sound of her laughter.

Thirty minutes later, the game ended and the men, with T-shirts drenched in perspiration, dispersed.

"I'm going to take a quick shower," Leon told Misty. "I'll be back in a few."

When he returned, he found her and Talei seated at one of the picnic tables eating.

"We couldn't wait for you," Misty said. "Sorry."

"That's fine."

Leon fixed a plate, then walked over to join Misty and Talei. "I think my basketball days are over. My body feels like it's on fire."

"Did you stretch beforehand?"

"I did," Leon said. "I don't think it helped."

"I want chicken, Eon." She pointed to the drumstick on his plate.

He stuck his fork into the meat and put it on hers.

"Wado."

"This is such a beautiful day," Misty said. "We'd better enjoy it while we can before the weather starts to change."

Leon took a sip of his iced tea. "The fall weather is usually pretty mild."

He embraced her. "I don't care where we are as long as we're together."

Rusty found two decks of cards, prompting a discussion of who was good when it came to playing spades.

"You don't want none of this over here," Leon said with a grin. "Misty and I play well together. We don't lose."

"That's because you haven't played me and Sarah," Luke countered.

Rusty laughed. "Nephew, I don't know. When was the last time you played?"

"It doesn't matter," Misty said. "We got this."

Leon's features became more animated. "Yeah, I'm definitely the right man for this woman."

THE FOLLOWING WEEKEND, they decided to dine at a local Italian restaurant. Afterward, they were going to the park for the last outdoor concert of the year.

"I really like this side of you," Misty commented as she scanned her menu. She took a sip of her iced water.

He laughed. "I take it that you thought I was pretty boring."

"Not really," she replied. "No, I didn't think that. I felt like you were still grieving."

"Do you still feel that way?"

She met his gaze. "I feel like you're at the stage where you've accepted your wife's and child's deaths."

"I have," Leon confirmed. "They're gone, but it isn't the end of the world. When they died, it sure felt like it. I'm at the point where I know it's okay to move on with my life."

He picked up his menu and looked it over. "I think I'm having the chicken Marsala," he said. "Do you know what you want?"

"I'm in the mood for the shrimp scampi."

They gave the waiter their orders when he returned to the table.

"Misty, you don't have to worry about me. I did right by Vera and our child. I feel good about moving on with you."

"That's very sweet of you to say," Misty stated with a tender smile. "I was a little afraid of getting involved with someone else. I was concerned how Talei would be affected if things didn't work out for us."

"I will always be her godfather, Misty. However, I intend to make sure on my end that we work."

The waiter returned with their food on a tray. Leon blessed the food.

Misty sampled her food. "This is delicious. I love it when I can taste the garlic and other spices in the scampi sauce."

"Mine is really good," he responded. "I love chicken Marsala."

She smiled. "Is that a hint?"

"Yes, it is," Leon answered. "This is like my favorite meal of all time."

Misty looked around the dining area. "It feels good being out on such a beautiful night. I'm excited about the concert. I can't wait to see Kem perform. I love all his music."

After signaling for the check a short time later, Leon inquired, "Are you ready to party?"

She awarded him a smile. "Definitely."

They left the restaurant and drove down the street to the park. There were cars everywhere, but Leon found an empty space a block away from the location.

He held Misty's hand as they walked.

"You were lucky to find that parking space. I thought we'd end up having to walk at least three or four blocks."

"I'm glad we left the restaurant when we did," Leon said. "Great timing."

At the park, Leon set up their chairs.

Misty settled in her seat. She closed her eyes, savoring the feel of the night air on her face while enjoying the music on the deejay's playlist. The concert wasn't due to start for another forty minutes.

Leon brought her hand up to his lips and placed a gentle kiss on it. "I can't believe that I found someone as wonderful as you."

She felt a warmth wash over her like waves.

Turning her to face him, Leon leaned over and kissed her softly on the lips. "I have been wanting to do this from the moment I arrived at your place to pick you up."

In response, Misty pulled his head down to hers. Their lips met and she felt buffeted by the winds of a gentle harmony.

Breaking their kiss, Leon said, "I love you."

His words caught Misty by surprise. Tears glittered in her eyes as she responded, "I love you, too."

CHAPTER TWENTY-NINE

MISTY FELT LIKE she was floating on a cloud. Her evening with Leon couldn't have been more perfect. Sharing delicious food and great music with the man she loved equaled the making of wonderful memories.

She checked on Talei when she got home, then had a glass of wine with Brittany.

"Thank you so much for watching her."

"We had a good time. She was showing me how to do the candy dance. At least I think that's what it was called."

Misty laughed. "She performs it at the pow-wows."

"We also did some shark dance, too." Brittany sat her glass down on the counter. "Girl, I'm tired."

They broke into laughter.

After Brittany left, Misty went upstairs to her room and showered.

She came out of the bathroom ten minutes later and checked her phone. Misty smiled when she read the sweet good-night text from Leon.

Tonight was perfect!

LEON WENT TO the cemetery to clean up around the graves of his parents and Vera. He also wanted to put out some fresh flowers. After pulling all the weeds and tossing them in a garbage bag, he took a seat on the cement bench at the foot of his wife's grave.

"I can't put into words how much I miss you, Vee. Not a day goes by that I don't think of you and our daughter. I wanted to let you know that I finally have the strength to move on. I told you about Misty… Well, we've been seeing each other, and things are good between us. I love her, Vee, and I'm happy."

He sat there, taking in the warmth of the sunlight. "I feel like you're looking down on me and smiling. Probably giving me your *I told you so* look."

"I had a feeling I'd find you here."

Leon glanced over his shoulder. "Auntie, you had a mind to come to visit the family, too?"

"I did," she responded. "The weather's nice today. I figured I'd come put some fresh flowers on Walter's and my parents' graves, then I saw you sitting over here."

Eleanor sat down beside him. "It gets a little easier with each passing day."

"Yes, it does," Leon said. "Spending time with Misty has helped. I still grieve, but it's not as intense as it was before."

"Do you still feel like you're cheating on Vee?"

He nodded. "A little. I know she's gone and it's okay for me to date in my heart—I just need my mind to fully catch up."

"Why don't we get out of this cemetery," she suggested. "Let's go grab some lunch."

Leon stood up, then assisted Eleanor to her feet. "I think we should hire a groundskeeper. I'd like to have flowers on all the graves. Maybe we can plant a garden over there near Polk's grave."

"I agree," Eleanor said. "That's a good idea."

"Where would you like to eat?" Leon asked.

"I'm in the mood for seafood."

He chuckled. "You always want seafood. That's not surprising."

The only vehicle parked on the street was Leon's truck. "You walked here?"

"Yeah," Eleanor answered. "It's so nice out."

He unlocked his truck and opened the passenger side door.

Eleanor climbed inside.

They drove to an oceanfront restaurant.

"Thank you, son" she murmured, taking a seat in the chair Leon pulled out for her.

He walked around the table with the vibrant red tablecloth and eased into a chair facing her. Leon picked up his menu. "I always have a hard time deciding what I want to eat whenever I come here. Everything is delicious."

"I can tell you and Misty are becoming close," Eleanor said. "You're falling in love with her."

He gave a slight nod. "Not falling, Auntie. I'm in love with her."

"I'm relieved to hear this. I had hoped this was the case and not because you want to take care of her and Talei out of loyalty to John."

"I think it may have started that way," Leon confessed. "I really have strong feelings for Misty. It's crazy, but whenever I'm with her, the world feels different. I'm sure that makes no sense at all."

Eleanor smiled. "Actually, it makes a lot of sense. That's what happens when you fall in love."

Leon laid down his menu. "Misty told me that she loves me, too."

"You seem surprised."

"I guess I shouldn't be," he said. "I know she cared something for me, but I wasn't a hundred percent sure that it was love."

MISTY SHOWED BRITTANY the cake she'd designed for the historical society gala taking place tomorrow night. "What do you think?"

"It's beautiful. Meredith is gonna love it."

She closed the box back up. "Thanks for the

referral. Miss Eleanor said this is the first year that we were asked to do the cake."

Lowering her voice, Brittany said, "Meredith broke up with the guy who provided the cakes in previous years."

"Oh, wow."

They sat down at an empty table in the bakery area.

Brittany chuckled. "I take it that things are still good between you and Leon?"

"They are," Misty stated. "Our relationship has hit another level."

"Another level…meaning?"

"We love each other."

"So, you've said the actual words?"

She nodded. "Yes."

"Leon is one of the good ones."

"That's the biggest relief," Misty said. "After all the bad choices I've made in my past relationships… It's great to have someone so nice in my life."

"He's got you glowing, that's for sure."

"I feel really good about us. Life is so drama-free and I love it."

"Well, all the bad stuff is over now," Brittany said. "Enjoy."

Misty smiled. "I intend to do so. Now we're supposed to be talking about your wedding cake. Do you know what you want?"

"Nothing too fancy," Brittany said. "Rick and I both want carrot cake—it's our favorite. I was thinking that we could have cupcakes for the guests that may want something different."

"I like that," Misty said. "Do you want the frosting to match your wedding cake?"

"Yes. And can we have flowers instead of the bride-and-groom topper?"

"Sure. You can have whatever you choose. I can create them, or you can have your florist create a topper with the wedding flowers. I'll need it the day before the ceremony." Misty quickly typed in notes on her iPad.

"I'll see her when I leave here, so I'll get back to you on that," Brittany responded. "You know I want you to be in the wedding. I'd like you to be a bridesmaid. My sister is my maid of honor."

Misty was genuinely touched by her offer. "I'd be honored to be a part of your wedding. Thank you."

"Girl, thank *you*. We're not having a big wedding. I want to keep it small and intimate with three in my wedding party only because Rick has three brothers. Some of my friends are seriously tripping and arguing about who should be in *my* wedding. I told them to be happy that they're getting an invite." Brittany shook her head sadly. "Unnecessary drama."

Misty chuckled. "Wow."

"Oh, and I want Talei to be my flower girl."

"Oh, my goodness! She is gonna love that, Britt. We won't be able to convince her that she's not a princess."

"March can't come quick enough for me. I'm so ready to become a wife."

Smiling, Misty nodded in understanding. "I loved being married—it just wasn't to the right man. I haven't given up on love everlasting though. Even if it turns out that Leon and I aren't meant to be, he's given me a peek into what it looks like. I'll always be grateful to him because of that."

CHAPTER THIRTY

WHEN LEON AND MISTY entered the ballroom, they were immediately enveloped in a warm haze of music and happy voices. A harpist played something slow and lovely in the background beneath a strong undercurrent of conversation that rose and fell like waves crashing against the shore.

There was a sea of people dressed in tuxes and bright, colorful dresses roaming around talking and taking photographs. Leon saw it all, yet the woman on his arm kept his full attention. Misty stood out. Each time he looked at her, he felt a strange mixture of calm and excitement churning through his bloodstream.

Misty, dressed in a deep purple gown, did one final check on the cake. She wanted it to be perfect for the gala. Her hair was a tumble of soft curly tendrils that called out to him to run his fingers through their silkiness. Leon inhaled the light floral perfume Misty wore, flavoring his very breath with her scent.

Fresh flowers in vases and small plants graced every tabletop, and the soft lighting reflecting off the mauve wallpaper created a magical glow.

"You need to relax," Leon said. "The cake is beautiful, and it looks delicious. Half the people in here have tasted your baked goods. You have nothing to worry about."

"Thank you for saying that," Misty responded. "I'm just nervous because this is the first time they commissioned us to do the cake." Her gaze traveled from his head to his shoes. "Oh, my… You look so handsome."

"And you're stunning in that dress." In truth, Misty was electrifying.

Smiling, she lifted her chin, tossed her hair away from her face and placed her hand in his. "We should find our table."

Leon looked down into Misty's sparkling brown eyes.

He was in deep trouble. His feelings for her were intensifying so much that the very air around him seemed electrified.

She picked up her wineglass and took a sip. "You do realize that you're staring at me."

"I'm sorry," Leon responded. "I don't mean to stare but I can't help it. You're a beautiful woman." Everything took on a clean brightness when she was with him. Each time Misty smiled at him, the pull was stronger.

They made small talk with the other guests at the table while dining on filet mignon, baby asparagus and large, fluffy baked potatoes.

"Now you're the one staring," he said, feeling the heat of her gaze on him.

"Guilty," Misty murmured.

"Would you like to dance?" Leon asked when the deejay put on a popular R&B song.

"I'd love to," she responded as she rose to her feet.

Swaying to the music, Misty took his hand and led him to the dance floor. "I love dancing."

Leon smiled. "I know."

They danced through two songs, then returned to their table.

All around them, people were enjoying themselves, leaning toward each other, smiling, laughing, talking. The clink of glassware and the waves of conversation became a white noise pulsating in the background, but Leon had eyes and ears only for Misty.

He stared into her eyes and resisted the urge to reach out and touch her face. There was so much Leon wanted to say to Misty, but it would have to wait until later when they were alone.

The music called out to them once more, prompting their return to the dance floor.

AT THE END of the night, Leon parked at the curb outside her condo.

Even in the moonlight, he could see the colorful flower beds nestled around the grounds.

Leon's gaze stayed on Misty as they made their way to her home and she unlocked the door.

He walked in behind her, taking in the eclectic decor and artistic pieces of Native American art displayed around the living room.

When Misty hit a switch, pools of golden light fell across the hardwood floors.

Leon removed his tuxedo jacket and draped it across one of the dining room chairs before joining her on the dark green leather couch.

"You really mean the world to me, Misty," he murmured without thought. "I wasn't expecting this. I never thought I'd feel this way again. I didn't think it was possible."

Leon pulled her in close and kissed her, then said, "You and Talei are an important part of my life. Misty, I'm not looking for something recreational. I loved being a husband and I wanted to be a father. I want all that again." Leon paused a moment. "I hope I'm not scaring you. I'm not real good at this, but I want to make sure we're on the same page."

Misty smiled. "We're definitely on the same page, Leon. I'd never really given much thought to the idea of getting married again...until I met you." She leaned into his embrace, enjoying the feel of his arms around her.

"Do you have any plans for tomorrow?" Misty inquired.

"Nothing concrete. What's up?"

"Clara called me earlier and asked if I'd bring Talei for a visit tomorrow. I told her I'd come, but I would like you to join us."

"What time do you want to leave?" Leon asked.

"I was thinking around nine in the morning."

"I'll be here."

She smiled. "*Wado*, my sweet Leon."

"*Hawa.*"

LEON GLANCED OVER at Misty and asked, "Ready?"

"I'm as ready as I'll ever be," she responded. Biting her lip, Misty looked away. She wasn't worried about Clara, but Elroy... Misty would've preferred to have avoided him at all costs.

"I ready," Talei interjected from her seat.

"Let's hit the road, then."

They weren't down the road a good thirty minutes before Talei was sleeping.

Amused, Leon glanced up at the rearview mirror. "That didn't take long."

"Thank you for coming with me," Misty said. "I didn't want to deal with Elroy alone."

"I understand," Leon said. "When I first met Elroy, I felt like he couldn't stand me. It took a minute, but he eventually warmed up."

"Well, he hates me," Misty stated. "From the moment John introduced me to his family, that man never had a kind word to say about me. I'm to the point that I don't care how he feels about me personally—this is about my daughter."

He wasn't going to let Elroy attack Misty any longer. Leon fully intended to speak up on her behalf. He hoped it wouldn't come to that, but he was prepared if it did.

They talked, sang along with the radio, then talked some more, but the closer they got to Orangeburg, the quieter Misty became.

"You okay?" Leon inquired.

"I'm just bracing myself mentally for whatever Elroy has to say. I haven't spoken to him since that day at the funeral home. Clara and I communicate regarding Talei. But since I'm going to be at his house, I'm sure Elroy won't hold his tongue."

Leon parked in front of the Hayes' ranch-style house.

Misty got out of the vehicle, saying, "Here goes…"

She gently woke Talei. "Hey, sweetie. We're at Paw Paw's house. You ready to see Grandma and Paw Paw?"

Talei nodded, then stretched and yawned.

Clara opened the front door. "Leon, hello. We didn't expect to see you."

She stepped aside to let them enter.

"I asked him to come with me," Misty interjected. "I hope that's okay."

"Of course," she responded. "C'mon in. He is always welcome here."

Clara led them to the den. "Make yourselves at home."

"Looks like you two have gotten mighty close," Elroy stated when he walked into the room.

Misty stirred uneasily in the chair. Before she could respond, Leon said, "We're dating."

Talei ran over to him. "Paw Paw."

"Hey there, baby girl. I've missed you something fierce."

"Would y'all like something to drink?" Clara inquired, breaking the tense silence that enveloped the room.

"I'm fine," Misty and Leon said in unison.

"I just want to make sure I understand what's going on. Are you two involved?"

"Why is that important, Clara?" Misty asked. She and Leon weren't doing anything wrong and she refused to allow her ex-in-laws to make her feel otherwise.

"I'm sorry if I'm being intrusive."

"Don't you apologize," Elroy uttered. "It's our right to know who's hanging around our grandchild."

Leon opened his mouth to speak, but Misty gave a quick shake of her head. It wasn't worth the drama. "Clara, the answer is yes as Leon already told you. The two of us are dating."

Elroy muttered something under his breath, then abruptly left the room.

Misty sighed, clasped her hands together, and stared at Clara.

"He's not been feeling well lately," Clara offered as an excuse. "That's why I asked you to bring Talei for a visit. I thought seeing her would cheer him up."

Elroy returned, cold fury in his eyes. "How can you do this to John? He was your friend."

"Do what?" Leon asked, keeping his voice low.

"Is that why you moved to that island? Elroy accused Misty. "To be with *him*? I told my son you were no good."

Clara pulled Talei close to her. "Don't do this in front of this child."

"She's right," Leon stated, rising to his full height. "You and I can have this conversation outside." He'd had enough of Elroy's rudeness.

"Leon, it's okay," Misty said. Her anxiety level increased with each passing moment.

"Sweetheart, it's not okay and it stops today."

CHAPTER THIRTY-ONE

WHEN THEY WERE OUTSIDE, Leon said, "Tell me something. Elroy, how can you treat the mother of your grandchild like that? What did she do to you?"

He looked indignant. "You may have been John's friend, but you have no right to talk to me like this."

"I'm making it my right. Look around you. Look at what your anger has cost you. Your daughter left and never looked back. She won't even bring her family around you. John wanted to leave but he didn't want to break your heart."

Elroy frowned. "What are you talking about?"

"John never wanted to leave school, but he felt like you'd given him no choice—you threatened to cut him off financially." Leon paused a moment before saying, "You know he hated being a truck driver."

"He was weak."

"John was loyal to you," Leon countered. "But you never appreciated him. All he ever wanted was your approval."

"If that's true, then he should've listened to me when I told him to stay away from that girl. Because of Misty, my son is dead."

"What is your problem with her?"

"She just wasn't right for John. Now she's running after you. I guess you turned out to be the *best man* after all."

Leon clenched his lips together and struggled to maintain his calm.

"You know I always thought you were smart—"

"I'm not going to let you finish that thought," Leon interjected. "One thing you need to remember right now—I'm not John. What I do is my business and you have nothing to say about it. Elroy, I've done my best to remain neutral in this situation and I've tried to see both sides... You're blowing your chance to have a relationship with your granddaughter. Instead of bashing her mother to me, you should be inside that house enjoying time with Talei."

After a moment, Elroy said, "I'm not going to be disrespected on my property."

"And I'm not going to stay here and allow you to disrespect Misty. We're leaving." Leon headed back inside the house.

He entered and looked at Clara. "I'm afraid we need to head back to the island."

Tears sprang into Clara's eyes. "Noo... Please don't leave."

"Let 'em go," Elroy yelled from the outside.

"I'm sorry, Clara. This is for the best." Misty sighed, picked up Talei and followed Leon to the front door.

Leon wrapped an arm around her.

Standing a few feet away, Elroy suddenly collapsed to the ground.

Leon sprang into action. "Call the paramedics." He glanced over his shoulder at Misty, who was buckling Talei in her seat.

Clara came running out of the house. "What's wrong with him?"

Elroy looked as if he wanted to say something, but he couldn't get the words out.

Leon glanced over at Clara. "I think he's had a stroke. The paramedics are on the way."

Elroy was transported to the hospital with Clara by his side.

"He may have had a stroke," Leon said, following behind the ambulance.

When Misty didn't respond, he glanced over at her. "Did you hear me?"

"Yeah, I heard you. I'm just trying to remove the image of Elroy on the ground like that. I had to shield Talei from seeing him."

"He was getting so worked up over nothing."

"It was a mistake coming here," Misty said. "I should've known better."

"This isn't your fault. You know that, right?"

Misty didn't respond.

"Where Paw Paw?" Talei asked when they arrived at the hospital.

"He's with the doctor," Clara said.

"He sick?"

"He's just getting a checkup, sweetie," Misty interjected. "Your Paw Paw is fine."

"Why would you tell her that?" Clara asked in a loud whisper. "We have no idea what's wrong and if he'll come out of it okay."

"I don't want to traumatize my daughter. The last time she was in a hospital, John died."

Clara walked over to a nearby window and stared out.

Leon took Talei and sat down in the waiting area.

Misty stood beside Clara. "I'm sorry about all this. I don't think it was a good idea for us to come."

"I invited *you*. I thought seeing Talei would make Elroy feel better. Since John's death, the business has suffered. We keep losing drivers and contracts… He's been under a tremendous amount of stress," Clara wiped away a tear. "I tried to get him to let me help. I grew up around trucks. I did all my daddy's paperwork for him until I married Elroy." She glanced over her shoulder at Leon, then said, "I don't think he should've come with you. This was the last thing my husband needed."

"Leon and I have nothing to hide, Clara."

After a moment, she responded, "You're right. Of course, Misty. Leon is a good man and after what my son put you through… Well, you deserve to be happy. It's just that Leon was John's friend."

"You're entitled to feel how you feel, but it has nothing to do with me," Misty stated.

Clara glared at her. "John always said you were selfish. He said that you only think of yourself and what *you* want. I've tried to give you the benefit of the doubt, but I'm beginning to see just how right he was about you."

Misty wasn't about to make a scene, so she walked away with uttering a response.

"Leon, I think we should just head home."

He stood up. "Is everything okay between you two?"

"I just need to get out of here."

Misty was quiet most of the ride back to Polk Island.

"Are you okay?" Leon asked.

"I'm… I've just been thinking."

"About?" he prompted.

"I can't do this—any of it," Misty said. "All I want is to live a peaceful life, Leon. *That's it.* I'm not going to have it as long as I have to deal with Elroy and Clara. As long as we're together, they are not going to let me live in peace. I need to be completely free of my past and the hell that came with it. Unfortunately, this means that you and I can't see each other either."

"Because of my relationship with your ex-husband, we can't be together—that's what you're saying. Right?"

Misty ached with an inner pain. "I think it's b-best." Her voice broke miserably. Clara's words had wounded her deeply. Maybe she was being selfish. She hadn't contemplated how being with Leon would disturb them. Misty hadn't considered how taking Talei and moving away would affect John.

She wiped away her tears. "I'm sorry but I just can't do this, Leon."

"I'm at a loss here."

"I have to get Talei in the house," Misty said. "I'm sorry."

MISTY PUT TALEI to bed.

Inside her room, she removed her clothes and padded barefoot into the bathroom to take a shower.

Warm tears streamed down her face, merging with the water from the showerhead.

Run?
Panic?

Escape?

Why was that always her first instinct?

Misty shook off the questions. *I did the right thing. I can't live with that type of turmoil in my life. Clara was right about my being selfish. I have to consider everyone in this situation. As much as I care for Leon, he's an innocent partner in my turbulent relationship with the Hayeses. I just hope one day we can get past this—maybe even be friends.*

One thing was abundantly clear. Shadows still clung to her heart. The ones Misty thought she'd banished with counseling, determination and the new life she'd built.

She picked up her phone and saw that she had a text from Clara informing her that Leon was right. Elroy had a stroke but fortunately it left little effect to his body.

Misty sent a response saying she was relieved to hear that he would recover. She couldn't think of anything else to say so she left it at that.

Sleep did not come easy for her. Every time she closed her eyes, she saw the hurt and disappointment registered on Leon's face. The last thing she ever wanted was to break his heart. Her selfishness taunted her.

"THANK YOU FOR letting me know, Clara." Leon's throat ached with defeat.

Leon laid his phone on the wireless charger, then got up to remove his clothes.

He had chosen to love again. To hope again.

Then the waves of heartbreak came crashing all around him. He'd allowed Misty into his life and now she was gone.

Frustrated, Leon tossed a pillow across the room.

He had no idea what Clara had said to Misty at the house, but it clearly upset her, and he couldn't get her to tell him anything. Before today, they could talk about any and everything. This time she just shut down completely.

Her rejection hurt, wounding him to the core of his soul. Misty wanted out of their relationship and there was nothing he could do about it.

He told himself that it was best that it happened now rather than later.

Leon's heart ached as it yearned for the woman he thought he'd one day marry. He'd allowed himself to believe that he could have a second chance at love.

He thought about Talei and felt another throbbing ache. Leon wasn't going to abandon his goddaughter—he just had to find a way to erect a wall around his heart where Misty was concerned.

He vowed to never give her a chance to hurt him again.

MISTY HIRED TWO part-time employees to help out in the shop. She had three weddings on the schedule, an anniversary celebration and several other events requiring cakes and other baked goods. She planned to expand their catering menu to include sandwiches and other specialties.

At two o'clock, Misty left the shop to pick up Talei. They were going to visit with Eleanor. Although she was the new owner of the Polk Island Bakery & Café, Misty continued to seek guidance from her.

Eleanor embraced Talei, then Misty. "I'm so glad to see y'all. I made some lunch for us."

Lunch turned out to be parmesan chicken, wild rice and mixed greens. She'd even made a cheesecake for dessert.

Misty said, "You didn't have to go through all this trouble but thank you."

"It wasn't no trouble. I try to keep busy, but I can't stand being in this house all day long."

They sat down at the table to eat.

"Miss Eleanor, you're supposed to be a lady of leisure."

She chuckled. "That just sounds boring to me." Eleanor paused a moment, then asked, "Have you seen Rusty? I thought he was in the yard working. I want him to eat while the food's hot."

"I think he's at work, Miss Eleanor. I saw his car there when we were driving here."

"Oh, that's right. I can be so forgetful at times."

Misty smiled. "I have days like that, too."

"Rusty has me working on puzzles. He says it helps improve your memory."

"I'm going to have to give it a try."

"How's the shop?"

"It's going well," Misty said. "I just hired two part-time employees, but to be honest, we all miss you not being there."

"Maybe I could come in a couple days a week to help out. Just to get me out of the house. I hate being here alone all the time."

Misty smiled. "That would be great."

The doorbell sounded.

"Would you like me to get it?" Misty asked.

Eleanor nodded. "I'm not expecting anyone."

Misty opened the front door to find Leon standing there.

He seemed just as surprised to see her.

"Hello, Leon."

When he looked at her, she could see the pain reflected in his gaze. "I didn't expect to see you. I came to see my aunt."

"Talei and I stopped by for a visit." Misty stepped back so he could enter.

"I'll just come back later." He spoke calmly, with no light in his eyes, no smile of tenderness.

"Leon, you don't have to leave. It doesn't have to be this distance between us. We're still friends, I hope."

"I can't have this conversation right now."

"Can we talk later?"

Leon eyed her. "You made a decision about us without talking it through with me, Misty. This was *your* decision. We both have to live with it." He glanced down at his watch. "Tell my aunt I'll be back in an hour."

Her throat closed as she watched him walk away, shoulders squared, back straight—a picture of strength.

Added to her disappointment was a feeling of guilt.

When Misty returned to the table, Eleanor said, "I take it things are a little bumpy between you two."

"It's worse than that," she said. "We're not seeing each other anymore. I ended it because I thought it was the best thing to do."

Eleanor eyed her. "You're not looking like you really believe that. You love him, and I know he loves you, Misty. Don't make the same mistake I did for years. Work it out."

Her eyes filled with tears. "It's too late for that."

Smiling, Eleanor said, "It's never too late for love."

CHAPTER THIRTY-TWO

"A FEW OF us are going out tonight," Charles announced when their shift ended. "Care to join us?"

"Not tonight," Leon responded. "Next time, though. Right now, I'm not in the mood to be around people." All pleasure left him the night Misty ended their relationship. He needed more time for his raw emotions to heal from the shock.

"Trouble in paradise?"

"I don't know what to call it, truthfully." He shrugged. "But it is what it is…" His attempts to figure out how he and Misty had come to be in this space left his thoughts painful and jagged.

"Leon, I don't know what happened between you and Misty, but don't give up on the relationship. You two are good for each other. And that little girl… She adores you."

"That's the hard part," Leon confessed. "I miss Talei."

"What about her mom?" Charles asked. "Do you miss her, too?"

"I miss them both."

"Maybe Misty got scared."

"She wanted out and it was after she had a conversation with John's mother."

"I'm sure they're not happy about her moving on with their son's best friend," Charles stated.

"You're right about that, but I can't understand why Misty would suddenly start caring about what they think."

"Leon, I have a feeling she's going to have a change of heart once she has a chance to think things through."

His life was once again a bitter battle and his sense of loss went beyond the hurt he felt. "I opened myself up once to her, Charles. I'm not going to make that mistake a second time."

"Are you really going to give up so easily on her?"

"Look how easy it was for her to give up on me," Leon replied in sinking tones.

THE NEXT DAY, Eleanor spent most of the morning observing Misty. She'd never seen her look so sad.

She called Leon and invited him to have lunch with her. "I'm at the shop."

"What are you doing there?"

"I'm not one for being home all the time," Eleanor said. "I come here three days a week just to get out of the house."

"I'll be there at noon."

"See you then, son."

When Leon arrived, Eleanor gestured for him to join her in a booth near the huge window in the front of the shop. "I know I have trouble with my memory, but one thing I'm pretty clear on right now is that something's going on between you and Misty. You want to tell me what happened?"

"I wish I could, Auntie. I don't fully understand it myself."

"Is it fixable?"

"Both people in a relationship have to want it to work."

"You love her?"

"I do," Leon said. "I never thought I'd ever feel this way again. To be honest, I wasn't sure I wanted to love another woman like this. I took the leap and now it's bitten me in the behind."

"Son, I can't believe you're giving up so easily. Misty loves you, too. Y'all have something worth fighting for. You're letting your fears get in the way."

Eleanor rose to her feet. "I almost forgot. I need to make another lemon pound cake. We sold the last one earlier."

"Auntie, you don't have to worry about that,"

Leon said gently. "You sold the shop to Misty, remember?"

She wore a confused look on her face. "I did?"

"Yes, ma'am. You wanted to spend more time with Rusty. I hear you're going to Hawaii in a couple of weeks. Let's order some lunch. They have some new items on the menu."

"That's right," she murmured. "We're going on a cruise to Hawaii."

"Have you started packing yet?"

Eleanor chuckled. "No. I have to make a list of everything we're gonna need. It's been a while since I was on a cruise ship."

"If you'd like, we can get started on that list right now," Leon suggested. "I can tell you right now that you need to make sure you pack your medications."

"You sound like Rusty." Eleanor pulled out a small notebook and a pen.

MISTY TOOK TALEI to Atlanta for the Labor Day weekend to see her grandmother. She needed some time away from the island.

"Honey, there's something I need to tell you," Waverly said when they arrived.

Concerned, Misty asked, "What is it? Are you okay?"

"My mother's fine," a voice said from behind her.

Shocked, she turned around to face her father. "Hello, Misty."

Waverly took Talei by the hand and led her into the house, saying, "Nana's got some lunch for you."

"You gonna say something to your daddy?"

"No, I'm not. I don't have anything to say to you." The disdain in her voice was ill-concealed.

She heard his quick intake of breath before he said, "You owe me a measure of respect."

Misty burst into a short laugh. "*Respect?* Mike, I don't *owe* you anything. I lived in fear because of you. You talked to my mother like she was nothing and you disrespected her with other women until she finally had the good sense to leave you. You were nothing more than an alcoholic and cheater. What is there to respect?"

He flinched at her words but recovered quickly. "I'm not that person anymore."

"You kept your family away from me," Misty uttered, her breath burning in her throat. "You cut me out of your life."

"No, your mother did that," Mike stated. "She didn't want any part of us."

Misty eyed him. "That's not true and you know it. What we're not going to do is lie about what happened. If you have truly changed, tell the truth."

He looked taken aback by her response.

"You wanted to hurt my mom—that's why you shut us out." Shrugging, Misty said, "It doesn't matter anymore because we survived, Mike. We made it in spite of *you*."

"Why are you coming around now?" he asked. "What do you want from my mother?"

"I don't want anything other than a relationship with my grandmother."

"Misty, I admit I had some problems in the past, but I'm not that man anymore."

"I'm sure your family's very happy about that," she countered icily.

"I came here to make amends. I've missed you, Misty."

She waved off his declaration. "I don't believe that."

"Please hear me out."

"Mike, what else is there really to say? I'm a grown woman with a child of my own. I don't need a daddy now."

"Let me start with the admission that I was a terrible husband and father. I drank too much. I hurt your mom—"

Misty interrupted him by interjecting, "You humiliated my mother."

"Yes, I was wrong. I need you to understand

that I've changed. I've been sober for over twenty years."

"Congratulations," she said tersely.

"I'm sorry for what I did to you and your mom. It is my hope that one day you'll find it in your heart to forgive me."

Misty didn't respond.

"My family is here with me. I want you to meet Jennifer and your siblings. Maybe talking to them will convince you that I'm no longer the monster you believe I am."

Arms folded across her chest, Misty responded, "I can't make any promises, Mike." She wasn't going to allow him to manipulate her into just believing his words. It was about action—she'd learned that from her marriage to John.

"Fair enough."

"I know it's hard to believe, but your daddy is telling the truth," Waverly said in a low whisper. "He is a changed man."

Misty glanced over her shoulder to find Waverly standing in the doorway.

"Grandmother, it remains to be seen. I don't just want to hear about it."

"I can't prove it to you if you won't give me a chance," Mike stated.

A girl who appeared to be in her late teens walked out of the house.

"Misty, I'm Sierra...your sister. I've been wanting to meet you for a while."

Mike and his mother left them alone on the porch to talk.

They sat down on the swing. "He told you about me?"

"Yeah, he did, but last night was the first time he told us about all the horrible things he did to you and your mother."

"I have to be honest with you, Sierra. I don't trust Mike and I'm not sure I ever will."

"I can understand why. It may take some time."

Misty eyed her sibling. "How was he as a father?"

"He's good to me and Michael. For me, it's really hard to reconcile the father I have to the man he used to be."

"As you know it's the reverse for me. I will just have to see what happens from this point forward."

"I'm hoping you and I will be able to have a relationship regardless. I've always wanted a sister."

"Of course. I want to get to know you better, Sierra."

"Talei is adorable," she said. "I can't believe I have a little niece."

"How old are you?" Misty inquired.

"I'm twenty," she responded. "Michael is eighteen."

"Are you in college?"

Sierra nodded. "I'm in school at UNC Greensboro."

"What are you studying?"

"Psychology. I want to be a psychiatrist."

Misty chuckled. "Sign me up for the friends and family rate."

Sierra laughed. "From the way you handled our dad, you're good."

Mike returned with a woman and a teenage boy.

"This is my mom, Jennifer," Sierra said, making the introduction. "And our brother, Michael."

Smiling, Misty responded, "It's nice to meet you both."

Michael gave her a hug. "*Osiyo*. I read that was the way to say hello in Cherokee. Did I pronounce it correctly?"

"It was perfect," she murmured.

"It's such a pleasure to finally meet you, as well," Jennifer said. "You're very beautiful, Misty. I saw pictures of you when you were little. You were a beauty even then."

"How long have you known about me?"

"About a year after I met your father."

"So, you were okay with the way he just disappeared from my life?"

"Misty…" Mike began.

"No," Jennifer interjected. "It's a fair question. Misty, I've been on Mike for years to reconnect with you. It was the one thing we've always disagreed on."

"I was afraid you'd reject me," Mike confessed. "I was ashamed to face you, Misty. That's the truth."

In that instance, she believed him. His eyes were glittering ovals of shame and regret.

"I'd like to speak to my dad in private, please."

When they were alone, she said, "Mike, you have a beautiful family."

"They're your family, too."

"True and because of you, I've missed out on so much with them. However, I'm really grateful to finally have the chance to get to know all of them. Thank you for coming here today."

"I hope you mean that, Misty. I can't change the past, but I really would like a second chance with you. I'd like to be a part of my granddaughter's life. She's so beautiful."

"Talei lost her father a few months ago."

"My mom told me. I'm so sorry."

"I want to have a life of peace," Misty stated. "I'll give you that second chance, but I'm telling

you now—any sign of the old you… I'm gone.
I'm not that little scared girl anymore."

"I know it doesn't matter but I'm very proud
of the woman that you've become."

Talei ran out of the house. "Mommy…"

"Hey, sweetie, I'm right here." Misty picked
her up. "I want you to meet my daddy. This
is…"

"Grandpa if that's alright with you."

"This is Grandpa."

"Gandpaw," she repeated.

"So, what do you say to him?" Misty asked.

Grinning, Talei said, "*Oseeyo*, Gandpaw."

He smiled. "*Osiyo*, my beautiful granddaughter." A lone tear slid down his face. "I am truly
sorry for everything I've done, Misty."

"We're not going to live in the past. We have
this chance to start over and I'd like to do that.
But I have to be honest. I'm gonna have to work
hard on forgiving you. I'm just not there yet."

"I understand completely." He kissed Talei
on the cheek. "I'm warning you now. I'm gonna
spoil this little girl."

She gave a short laugh. "She's already spoiled."

CHAPTER THIRTY-THREE

"I SAW MY DAD, Miss Eleanor," Misty announced when she returned to work on Tuesday. "We spent the weekend getting to know one another."

"I guess it was bound to happen with that being his mama's house and all. How do you feel about him now?"

"He's not the same man I grew up fearing," Misty said. "He seemed truly repentant. I told him I'd give him a second chance."

"Good for you," Eleanor responded. "It was the right thing to do."

"I'm cautiously optimistic."

"I would be too, sugar. We have to forgive, but we don't have to be blind to reality."

"I also met my siblings," Misty announced. "I have a brother and a sister."

Eleanor grinned. "You seem happy about it."

"I am. I never wanted to be an only child. And I'm glad Talei has an aunt and uncle on my side of the family. John's sister has nothing to do with his family."

"I'm glad to see things working out for you, Misty."

"Everything is great except with Leon. Miss Eleanor, I messed up big-time with him and I don't know if I can fix it. I thought we could at least try to be friends."

"Give him some space, sugar. Leon will come around."

"I hope so," Misty responded. "I really miss him."

Eleanor slipped out of the booth. "Time sure flies. It's almost time for the lunch crowd to come rushing in."

"Everything's ready, Miss Eleanor. Just sit and relax."

"The shop won't run itself."

"Miss Eleanor… Remember you sold the shop to me," Misty said. "You don't have to worry about anything. The staff here is great."

Eleanor looked confused. "What are you talking about? I sold my shop?"

"Yes, ma'am."

Rusty walked in, humming softly.

Misty gestured for him to join them.

He greeted his wife with a kiss. "Hey, Ladybug."

"Rusty, did I sell the shop?"

He sat down at the table. "Yes, you did. With

your health, you thought it best to turn it over to Misty. She's done a great job, too."

Eleanor smiled. "I remember now... I'm sorry, Misty."

"No need to apologize."

"You're really doing a fine job. I was right to sell this place to you."

When Rusty excused himself to go to the restroom, Eleanor said, "I'm scared this disease is progressing."

"Why do you say that?"

"I've been having some difficulty writing a simple check. I have to have Rusty review it to make sure it's the right amount and date. Some days I can't even plan a meal. I didn't even remember that it was Labor Day weekend, Misty."

"Have you shared any of this with Rusty?"

Eleanor nodded. "He's such a sweet and patient man. He makes time to go grocery shopping with me or he'll do it alone. He always offers to help with the cooking. It just makes me sad that I'm not the wife I want to be for him. I feel so useless." Her eyes teared up.

Misty reached over and took her hand. "Miss Eleanor, you're anything but useless. You're still that amazing woman I met when I came here looking to relocate and find a job. You're not going to let this disease take over your life—fight back."

"What if I get to the point where I can't fight anymore?"

"Then we will all fight for you."

"Thanks for coming to my birthday celebration," Lizzie said. "My family enjoyed meeting you. I talk about you all the time—they were beginning to think I'd made you up."

"I appreciate you inviting me," Leon said. "Otherwise, I would've spent the day on my couch binge-watching Netflix."

"I heard that you and Misty broke up. I don't get it. You're a good man. Any woman would be lucky to have you."

Leon smiled through his confusion. He and Lizzie had worked together for two years and he considered her a friend, but from the way she was looking at him right now, he wondered if she was interested in something more.

"I've always liked you, Leon. I never said anything because I didn't think you were ready to start dating…"

"Lizzie, you're my friend and we work together."

"You don't date your coworkers."

"I don't," Leon confirmed. "Besides, I still have feelings for Misty."

Smiling, Lizzie responded, "I hope things won't be weird between us now."

"They won't. I take it as a compliment."

"If Misty is as smart as I think she is, she'll be back, Leon."

MISTY DROVE TO Charleston to see her mother the following weekend.

They sat down on the patio. "You were right, Mama. You said Mike was going to show up one day. He was in Georgia last weekend."

"What did he say?" Oma asked.

"First he tried to put the blame on you, but I nixed that immediately," Misty said. "Then he admitted fault, apologized and asked for forgiveness."

"Really?"

She nodded. "I couldn't believe it myself, and I thought it was all a lie, but now I really think he was telling the truth."

Oma looked skeptical.

"Mama, you didn't see his face. I talked to his wife and his children—Mike's been a great husband and father to them. They adore him. Oh, he's been sober for twenty years."

"That's good to hear."

"I'm tired of holding on to all the anger, the fear and the hurt," Misty said. "If I really want to move on with my life, I have to find a way to forgive Mike."

"You're right," Oma responded. "I forgave

him a long time ago, but I know it's been hard for you."

"I'm not going to let my past interfere with my future anymore. Leon was wonderful to me and Talei. Breaking up with him was the biggest mistake I've ever made, Mama. I love him. I can't see my life without him in it."

"So, what are you going to do about it?" Oma asked.

"I've got to find a way to fix this."

"Just tell him what you've just told me."

"First I have to find a way to get him to talk to me," Misty responded. "The last time I saw Leon, he made it clear he wanted nothing to do with me."

"I'm sure he's hurt and confused by the abrupt way you ended things with him."

What in the world was I thinking? Things were perfect between us and I ruined it.

"At the time I thought it was best. I was wrong."

MISTY STRODE INTO the kitchen dressed in a pair of jeans and carrying a bag of groceries. Josh greeted her before turning his attention back to stacking plates on the counter. "We needed more tomatoes, onions and mushrooms," she said. "I also bought some other stuff that was on sale."

"We have a delivery scheduled on Wednesday," Josh stated.

"I know, but it's not like we can't use this stuff. We've had a really busy past few days."

The to-go order sitting on the counter caught her attention. "Who is this for?"

Josh responded, "It's for Leon. He should be here any minute."

Misty yearned to see him. She missed the sound of his voice, his laughter and the feel of his arms around her.

She pasted on a smile when he burst through the door of the shop a few minutes later. "Hey."

"I came to pick up an order," Leon said.

"It's ready," Misty said.

Josh strolled out of the kitchen. "Here you go, Leon."

Misty stepped out of the way so that one of the servers could ring up his ticket.

She moved from behind the counter to try to talk to Leon, but he brushed past her. Misty wasn't about to let him walk away a second time.

Warm air fanned over her as she followed him outside the restaurant. "Leon, I know things are tense between us right now, and that's on me, but I'd like the chance to explain myself."

"You made yourself pretty clear, Misty."

"Please hear me out."

A look of tired sadness passed over Leon's features as he unlocked his truck. "You want to do this now?"

She shook her head no. "Not here. Can you come by my place tonight?"

After a moment of tense silence, he asked, "What time?"

"Six thirtyish."

"I'll see you then."

Misty released a short sigh of relief. At least Leon had agreed to meet with her. Now all she had to do was convince him to give her another chance.

CHAPTER THIRTY-FOUR

MISTY SPENT THE late afternoon planning the menu for dinner. She flicked through several cookbooks, trying to work out what she could pull together given the limited supplies in her refrigerator. Talei wanted to go to the pool when they got home, so Misty didn't have time to go grocery shopping. She settled for a pasta dish—tortellini with salami, goat cheese and Kalamata olives, and fresh bread.

She began prepping for dinner at five o'clock so she could take her time and enjoy the process. Misty was both excited and nervous about seeing Leon tonight. She forced herself to remain hopeful that they could work things out and start over.

Misty had everything ready by six o'clock, the table set by a quarter past.

In her bedroom, she decided to slip on a flowy sundress that was comfortable and made her feel elegant. She paired it with a pair of sandals.

Misty ran nervous fingers through her hair as she eyed her reflection in the full-length mirror.

Leon arrived promptly at six thirty.

Misty stepped aside to allow him to enter her condo. "Thank you for coming."

They sat down in the living room.

"I made dinner. I figured we could eat first, then talk after."

"Where's Talei?" Leon asked as he rose to his feet.

"She's having dinner with Rusty and Eleanor." Misty smiled. "She has quite the social life."

Leon pulled out a chair for Misty at the dining room table, then sat down across from her.

They made small talk while eating.

"I made a key lime pie for dessert," she announced.

"Maybe later," Leon said.

He helped her clear the table.

"I'll put everything in the dishwasher later," Misty said. "We can sit in the living room to talk."

When they settled on the sofa, she was the first to speak. "Leon, I first want apologize to you for the way I handled this situation. You deserved better and I'm so sorry."

"I understand that John and his father put you through a lot—I get it. What I don't get is how I was thrown in with them. I've never done anything to intentionally hurt you."

"I was overwhelmed by all the drama in that moment. Leon, I grew up with an alcoholic and verbally abusive father. After that, it was a string of toxic relationships—the very thing I wanted to avoid. I started to feel like a magnet for the worst choices of men." Tears filled her eyes. "I was relieved when she finally chose to leave him, but deep down I wanted him to change and come after us. I wanted him to love us enough to become a better man. Leon, I wasn't going to allow Talei to grow up in that type of environment."

"My aunt mentioned in passing that you'd been through a lot."

"I had no real idea of how toxic his relationship with his father was until a few months before our wedding. I wanted to call off the engagement. John promised me that we'd be okay, but things only got worse. He started drinking and that's when the abusive behavior began."

"John loved you and when you divorced him, he felt betrayed."

"He said I was selfish. Clara said the same thing at the hospital, and it made me question all of the decisions I'd made, including wanting to be with you," Misty said. "It was not my intention to keep my daughter away from her father. I wanted to push John to get some help.

"Leon, I spent two years in therapy, learning to move past all this stuff. I saw my father a week ago for the first time in twenty years. We talked and I'm finally able to work toward forgiving him. All I ever wanted was a better life for me and Talei. I wanted to feel a sense of normalcy." Misty met his gaze. "I wasn't being selfish. I was trying to survive."

"Misty, we can't help who we fall in love with—I never thought I'd feel this way about anybody after Vera. I never want to bring chaos into your life."

"You haven't," she said. "Things just got out of control when we went to see Elroy and Clara. I was overwhelmed, confused and I panicked. But I want you to know that I'm clear on what I want regardless of what they think."

"What are you telling me?"

She hesitated a moment, measuring Leon for a moment. "I love you. Being apart from you showed me a few things. I always felt so safe with you and peaceful—everything I've always wanted in a relationship. I regret not realizing it sooner."

He didn't respond.

Misty chewed on her lip and stole a look at him.

"It was a lot for me to open my heart to loving someone again." Leon's voice was carefully colored in neutral shades.

"I know," she murmured. "I'm hoping you will trust me with your heart again. I'm asking for a second chance."

He was staring as if assessing her.

"Please say something, Leon." Misty tried to sheath her inner feelings.

He reached over and took her hand in his own. "When you broke up with me—I told myself that was it. I was done."

Her eyes filled with tears.

"But the more I tried to forget about you, the more I realized that what we have between us is worth fighting for," Leon said. "I'm not ready to give up on love."

Tears streaming down her face, she said, "I love you so much and I want to be with you."

"I need you to be sure of what you want, Misty. No more flip-flopping."

She wiped away her tears with the back of her hands. "I am very clear on this. I want you and me. *I want us.*"

Leon leaned over and planted a kiss on her lips. "You take my breath away every time I see you."

"I missed you so much," she whispered against his mouth.

"I really missed you, too."

He captured her mouth with his own a second time.

When they parted, he said, "I love you, Misty, and it's very real."

She placed a hand to his cheek. "I know. I feel it even when we're not together."

During dessert, Misty said, "Your aunt's birthday is coming up at the end of October. Rusty came to see me earlier. He wants to surprise Miss Eleanor with a party at the shop. She's been so good to me—I told him I'd be happy to plan it. What do you think?"

"I think it's a good idea."

"Great," she said. "Once I have a solid plan, I'll go over everything with Rusty."

"I've been trying to figure out what to get her for her birthday."

"You have all those family pictures and Miss Eleanor has a bunch. What about putting together a memory book for her?" Misty suggested. "We can have the photos scanned. We can organize them online and put names, dates—anything you want."

"Will they put it in book form?" Leon asked.

"Yeah. They can do it anyway you want."

"I'd love to do that for Aunt Eleanor. Maybe it'll help if she starts to lose some of those memories."

"WHERE ARE YOU off to in such a hurry?" Charles inquired, blocking Leon's path. "You're running outta here like you have a hot date or something."

Leon broke into a grin. "I have to be somewhere. I'm actually on my way to the jewelry store."

"Really?"

"Yeah. I love Misty and I want to spend the rest of my life with her and Talei."

"My man…"

"I'm going to propose after my aunt's surprise party."

"Congratulations, Leon. I'm happy for you."

"I hope she's ready for this next step."

"Misty loves you. She's gonna say yes. I'm sure of it. I bet Vera's smiling down from heaven seeing you happy. She would've wanted you to keep living. For a while there, you had me worried."

"I couldn't imagine loving anyone other than Vee," Leon responded. "We'd made so many plans for the future—it was supposed to be the two of us against the world." He chuckled. "That sounded so cliché."

"Yeah, but it's true. It's the same with me and Betty. I never thought I'd come home one day to her wanting a divorce."

"I see she's been coming around a lot," Leon said. "Are you two getting back together?"

"We've been going to counseling," Charles

said. "I want my marriage. Betty says she does, too. I guess we'll see."

"I hope it works out for you both."

Leon left the station and headed to the mainland. He was going to see the jeweler who'd designed Eleanor's wedding ring in Savannah.

He hadn't been this happy in a long time. Leon was actually looking forward to the future now that he'd found the person who gave his life new meaning. He even toyed with the idea that it was fate that had kept him from meeting Misty while she was married to John. Otherwise, they would be in a different space.

Leon didn't question whether John would approve of their relationship—he knew that John would understand. That was all that mattered.

"Josh, do we have everything we need for the party tomorrow?" Misty asked, checking her watch. "I'm meeting Leon at noon for lunch. I can pick up the stuff we need after that."

"As far as I can tell, we're good," he responded. "I'll text you if we're missing anything."

She removed her apron, then went to the bathroom to take off her plastic cap and fluff her hair.

Misty walked out saying, "I have to get out of here."

She walked the two blocks to the restaurant. Leon was already seated when she arrived.

"How long have you been here?" Misty asked.

"Just a couple of minutes," Leon said. "I actually just got off the phone with Clara."

"How is Elroy?" Misty asked.

"He's coming along. Clara is running the business and even Elroy had to admit she's doing a great job. She's hired more staff and they are busier than ever. I had no idea that she used to drive for her father's trucking company whenever he needed an extra driver."

Misty's eyes widened in surprise. "Really? I had no idea that she drove a truck or that she worked for her father. I know she's always wanted to help with the business."

"Elroy apologized and he wants to talk to you. He asked me to bring you and Talei for a visit. He realizes now that he'd allowed his frustrations to take over his life. He says the stroke humbled him. He wants to make amends if possible. He understands that it may take some time for you to feel comfortable around him."

"If he's willing to make peace, then I'm all for it. He is Talei's grandfather and I want them to have a relationship."

A server came over with glasses of water. While she was there, they gave her their order.

"Is everything ready for the party?" Leon asked when the server left the table.

Misty nodded. "Yes. I've already prepared the trays of lasagna. They're in the freezer. I'll have the cake ready by tomorrow morning."

"When will your mother arrive?"

"She got here this morning," Misty responded. "She and Talei were putting together a puzzle when I checked on them a few minutes ago."

"Are you sure you want to cook dinner tonight? I don't mind picking up something for us."

"Mama actually made dinner for us," she said. "Wait until you taste her brisket and garlic mashed potatoes… I'm telling you, Oma Brightwater is a fantastic cook."

"Apparently you inherited her skills."

"Thank you." Misty looked at the clock on the wall. "I have to go back to work, but I'm looking forward to seeing you later."

Leon kissed her. "I should be there no later than seven…seven fifteen."

"See you then."

Misty walked back to the shop grinning from ear to ear.

Her life had changed for the better since moving to Polk Island and she was determined to live for the moment. And each day with Leon brought wonderful moments and memories. They had spent the past few months exploring different festivals, dancing all night at social events, touring historic cities like Savannah and Charleston. Misty and Leon had eaten in tiny boutique restaurants and bistros. They spent a lot of time at the beach or the pool with Talei.

Occasionally, Misty had fallen asleep in his arms on the sofa in the living room. He was always the perfect gentleman. He gave her flowers and was generous with his compliments, but most important to her was the quality time spent with her and Talei.

She was grateful Leon had given their relationship a second chance. She finally had the type of man she'd always dreamed about. As far as Misty was concerned, life couldn't get any better than this.

CHAPTER THIRTY-FIVE

IT WAS THE evening before Halloween. Misty did one final check to make sure everything was perfect for the party. Leon was helping one of the employees set up two more tables. She broke into a smile. He just couldn't seem to keep himself from pitching in to help. Misty couldn't deny that it was one of the qualities she loved about him.

"I hope she likes everything," she said when Leon walked over to her.

"She's going to love it," he assured her. "Misty, I want you to relax."

"I will once the party is over," she said, "and Miss Eleanor's had the time of her life."

Leon checked his phone. "Rusty just texted me. They're on the way."

Misty announced, "Everyone, Miss Eleanor should be here in a few minutes."

She reached over and took Leon's hand, squeezing it. She was bubbling over with excitement. When Rusty came to her about the party, Misty promised she would create a well-planned memorable event to honor Eleanor. She wanted both Rusty and Eleanor to be pleased.

"Here they come," someone said.

"Oooh, the shop looks beautiful," Eleanor murmured, her eyes traveling the room. "What's the occasion?"

"We're celebrating you," Misty responded with a smile. "Happy Birthday, Miss Eleanor."

Leon embraced Eleanor. "Happy Birthday, Auntie."

She glanced over at Rusty. "Did you know about this?"

"It was my idea," he confessed. "I came to Misty with it and she graciously agreed to help me with the planning."

Eleanor kissed him. "Thank you, my sweet husband. I am truly blessed."

Rusty took her hand. "Let's greet your guests. A lot of people came to celebrate with us."

"I love seeing them together," Misty told Leon. "Such a beautiful couple."

He agreed. "They say the same thing about us."

Misty grinned. "I know."

Leon placed his arms around her. "I can't see my life without you and Talei in it. These past few months have been better than I could ever hope to be."

"I feel the same way despite the bumps along the way."

The open buffet was spectacular, Misty thought to herself. Fried chicken, macaroni and cheese, turkey, stuffing and a host of vegetables—all of Eleanor's favorites.

The laughter of the patrons, lively conversations and the music playing softly in the background pleased Misty. Rusty had entrusted her with planning the event and she worked hard to ensure that he felt his money was well spent.

"Come sit," Leon said, pulling out a chair for her at the table. "You did all this work—it's now time for you to enjoy this delicious food you prepared."

Misty couldn't remember the last time she had felt this way or had so much fun. Her senses were heightened in Leon's presence.

A server brought tall drinks to the table for them, left then returned with plates laden with food.

While Misty ate, she swayed to the music blaring through the speakers. "I love the O'Jays."

"No wonder you and Aunt Eleanor get along so well," Leon said with a chuckle. "You're both into old-school R&B."

Misty smiled. "I see you over there dancing in your chair."

"I love all types of music, but I love some

jazz. I have some friends I'd like you to meet," Leon said when a couple walked up to the table. "This is Landon and Jadin Trent. They live in Charleston. Actually, Jadin and I are related. Our great-grandmothers were cousins."

Misty smiled. "It's really nice meeting you both." Eyeing Jadin, she asked, "You look familiar. You work with the DuGrandpre Law Firm, right?"

"Yes, I do."

"My wife is a DuGrandpre," Landon stated.

"How's the family?" Leon asked. "I haven't seen Ryker in months."

"Everyone is fine," Jadin responded. "Jordin sends her love. She couldn't come because she's due any day now. My dad had knee replacement, so Mom stayed home with him."

Leon said, "Please extend my congratulations to your sister."

"We're going to have to head back to Charleston," Jadin said. "Our son is with Ryker and Garland. I'm sure with their four children, he's probably running them ragged."

Leon stood up and embraced her. "Thank you for coming."

"I wouldn't dare miss out on celebrating Eleanor's birthday. Whenever we came to the island for vacation, she always sent my parents an apple pie and she'd bake chocolate raspberry brownies for me and Jordin."

"The DuGrandpres still have a home here on the island," Leon explained.

Jadin nodded. "It belonged to my great-great-grandparents. Landon and I have been thinking about renovating it. I want to bring my son here for vacation. I have so many great memories on this island."

When they left, Misty said, "They're a cute couple."

Leon agreed. "They said the same thing about us."

When the guests began to disperse an hour later, Misty said, "I need to help the staff clean up."

"Do you want an extra set of hands?"

"No, we can take care of it."

"Any plans for later?" Leon asked. "I'd like to come by your place. There's something I want to discuss with you."

She smiled. "Meet me there in about an hour."

"See you then."

Misty rushed home to change clothes. She chose a comfortable loose maxi dress with spaghetti straps to wear. She heard a car pull up into the driveway and broke into a smile. *He's here.*

She opened the door to let him enter.

When Leon embraced her, Misty swore she could feel the heat of his light touch clear down to her toes.

He looked her in her eyes. "I love you, and I know that you love me, too. We are so much a part of one another that separate we're nothing. You're the other half of my soul and I need you in my life, Misty."

It was true. She loved him with her whole heart.

Misty felt the sting of tears.

Still holding her hands within his own, Leon placed them against his broad chest. "I want you to marry me."

Looking up into his handsome face, Misty couldn't speak for a few seconds. She thought she was dreaming, but as his words began to permeate every portion of her mind and soul, she took a step back from him. "Leon, do you really want to get married?"

He smiled, then held up a ring box. "I can't live without you. Please say that you'll be my wife." Leon opened it to reveal a stunning sapphire engagement ring. He knew it was her favorite gemstone.

Misty's heart swelled with happiness and she covered his face with kisses. "Yes, Leon. Yes, I'll marry you."

Leon's arms encircled her, one hand in the small of her back. She buried her face against his throat.

Misty relaxed, sinking into his cushioning embrace.

They reluctantly stepped apart.

"It's a nice evening," Leon said. "How about a moonlight stroll on the beach?"

"Let me grab a shawl," Misty responded.

They took a walk on the shoreline to the sounds of powerful waves crashing in the ocean.

Misty snuggled into Leon's shoulder as they walked and admired the moon reflecting on the water and the backdrop of stars sprinkled against the sky. The moonlit view was spectacular but so was the view of Leon's physique every time she stole glances at him. It was nice to be with someone who respected her choices and loved her for who she was. Leon made her feel appreciated.

Stifling a yawn, Misty reached over and took his hand in her own. "Why don't we head back to the condo," she suggested.

"You're tired," Leon said. "I know it's been a long day for you."

When they got back to her place, he suggested, "Why don't you go soak in a nice hot bath."

"You're not leaving yet?" she asked.

"I'll be here when you come out."

Leon sat down on the sofa to watch television while Misty went to her bedroom.

While the water was running, she undressed.

Humming softly, she sank down in a tub of bubbly water, scented with lavender bath salts. It had been a long day and she was exhausted. Misty trailed her fingers in the hot liquid, playing with the bubbles. Picking up the bar of soap that sat in a dish beside the tub, she bathed.

Misty got out and dried her body with a soft fluffy towel. She picked up a bottle of scented body lotion and slathered it on her skin. She slipped on a pair of lightweight sweatpants and a tank top. She pulled her hair into a high ponytail, then went to join Leon.

"You look relaxed." His gaze roved to the creamy expanse of her neck and traveled downward, then back to her face. "Did you enjoy your bath?"

Smiling, Misty nodded. "I did." She walked up to him. "I love you."

"I love you, too. More than you could possibly know."

THE NEXT MORNING, Misty woke up to the sound of clanging coming from the kitchen. She got out of bed, then padded barefoot in the bath-room to wash her face and brush her teeth.

She strolled into her kitchen to find Leon staring at the carton of eggs, sliced mushrooms and spinach. Misty burst into laughter at the ex-pression on his face.

"I love you but I'm the better cook in this re-lationship, so you sit down and relax. I'll make us some breakfast." She kissed his cheek. "I do appreciate the thought, though."

"Okay, I'll stay in my lane."

Misty quickly and adeptly prepared spinach and mushroom omelets and home fries and even had time to slice up some fresh fruit.

"What time are we picking up Talei?" Leon asked, accepting the plate of food she handed him.

"I told my mom that we'd be there at two o'clock."

"You're going to have to teach me how to make an omelet."

Misty opened a cabinet door and pulled out a black pan. "This is an omelet maker. Use this and it's super easy."

"We need one of these at the firehouse. Some-body's always trying to make an omelet, but it ends up just being a scrambled mess."

They laughed.

"I know we just got engaged," Leon began,

"but any thoughts on when you'd like to get married."

"I know that I don't want a long engagement," Misty responded. "And I don't want a huge wedding."

He released an audible sigh of relief, prompting laughter from her. "I can't tell you how happy I am to hear you say this."

"Tomorrow is the first of November, so when would you like to get married?"

"In the summer," Leon said. "I've always wanted a beach wedding at sunset. Vera and I had a church ceremony. It's what her parents wanted."

"John and I got married in a church, too. I'd prefer to do something different this time around. The beach is the perfect location."

"I can hardly wait to start my life with you."

"We can always go the same route as Miss Eleanor and Rusty," Misty suggested. "We can just have an intimate ceremony and not worry about a big fancy wedding."

"The idea is tempting," Leon said. "But I really want to say our vows at sunset against the backdrop of the ocean." He paused a moment, then asked, "How do you think Talei will take the news of us getting married?"

"She loves you, Leon. Everything will be fine."

"How do you think Elroy and Clara are going to react?" he inquired.

Misty shrugged. "Clara might eventually be okay with it, but Elroy... It's hard to call. The thing is that it really doesn't matter. This isn't about them. This is *my* life and I intend to live it *my* way."

"What do you think about hosting a huge Thanksgiving dinner?" Leon asked. "We can bring our families together and make the announcement then."

"I like that idea," Misty said with a grin. "Although it means I won't be able to wear my beautiful ring just yet."

"We don't have to wait."

"No, I really like making the announcement on Thanksgiving."

Leon pulled Misty into his embrace. "I can't wait to make you my wife."

THE MID-NOVEMBER weather was nice. The temperature was still warm and the day nice and clear. The leaves were dressed in red, yellow and burgundy hues.

"Rusty, what do you think?" Leon asked, pointing to the turkey.

"Looks good to me. I don't know if you remember, but your daddy was a beast when it comes to roasting a turkey."

"That's what everybody tells me. I wanted to make some barbecue chicken, but I'm still trying to get my barbecue sauce to taste like his. Aunt Eleanor said he guarded that recipe like it was gold."

Rusty laughed. "He added honey."

"Really? How do you know?"

"He told me," Rusty responded, slipping him a piece of paper. "He swore me to secrecy, but you're his son—this recipe belongs in your family."

Leon smiled. "Thank you."

Eleanor stepped out onto the patio. "What are you two whispering about?" She set a bowl of corn on the cob on the counter.

"Just two men bonding, Ladybug."

"Uh-huh…" Eleanor uttered. "I better check on the potatoes. I can't mess up Leon's potato salad."

"That's right, Auntie."

Leon heard the sound of tiny footsteps.

"*Oseeyo*, Eon… *Oseeyo*, Mr. Russy," Talei greeted from behind them. "You have hot dawg, pleeze?"

"It's almost ready, little one." Leon glanced over his shoulder just as Talei sat down at a nearby table.

"She sure does love herself some hot dogs," Rusty said, keeping his voice low. "I tried to give her some pizza the last time she was at the house—she wanted nothing to do with it. She just wanted a hot dog and French fries."

Leon chuckled. "One smile from her brightens my entire day. I think she stole my heart the day I took her out of that car. I love Talei as if she were my own blood."

Misty walked to the door. "Are you ready to slice the ham?"

Leon took the platter from her.

"I hungry," Talei said. "I want hot dawg and fench fries."

"The hot dog should be ready," he said. "It's in that pot over there. The fries are in the air fryer."

Misty winked at Leon before saying, "Go wash your hands, sweetie, while I fix your plate."

"Oh, yeah… I know that look very well," Rusty said. "You got that big-dog love going on. Ain't no puppy love here."

Leon shrugged. "Guilty."

He watched Misty brush a curly strand of dark hair back from the soft curve of her cheek. She was intelligent, beautiful and exquisite, Leon acknowledged.

Misty caught him staring at her. Grinning, she gave him a tiny wave.

Leon found himself looking forward to

spending time with her when the dinner was long over. In truth, he was excited about sharing the rest of his life with Misty. There was nothing he wanted more than to be her husband and a father to Talei.

CHAPTER THIRTY-SIX

MISTY BURST INTO the kitchen. "Mama, he's here," she announced. "My dad and his family just arrived."

Oma wiped her hands on her apron. "Don't worry. I'm fine."

"I just don't want this to be awkward between y'all."

"Everything is going to work out. Now go out there and greet your guests."

"Mike, thank you for coming." Misty gave him a tentative hug.

"Thank you for inviting us," he responded.

She embraced her grandmother, Jennifer and her siblings, then led them around the room as she made the introductions.

Misty held her breath when Oma walked out of the kitchen to greet Mike and his family. Her father looked uncomfortable initially, but as they talked, he visibly relaxed.

She bit back a smile. Her mother had boldly and graciously confronted the man who'd tormented her for years—a man who promised to love and cherish her. Oma was able to forgive and truly move on with no regrets. It was a beautiful scene to witness.

Leon was polite and chatted briefly with her father before moving around to greet their other guests.

Misty smiled when Jadin Trent arrived with her parents and her sister. She hadn't realized that Jadin and Jordin were twins—this was her first time seeing them together.

"Wow, you two are identical."

Jadin smiled and made the introductions. "Jordin, this is Leon's girlfriend, Misty."

"It's very nice to meet you, and congratulations. Miss Eleanor mentioned you'd had your baby three weeks ago. I have to say you look great."

"I like her," Jordin said with a smile. "Thank you, Misty. I still have some baby weight to lose. This is my third and last one, so I'm trying to get this body back in shape."

"Don't let her fool you," Jadin stated. "Her husband owns a chain of gyms. Trust me... My sister will have no problem getting her body back to pre-pregnancy size."

"She looks great for three pregnancies."

"Two," Jadin corrected. "She has a set of twins."

"I hear you have the most adorable little girl

and that she has Leon wrapped around her little finger. I can't wait to meet her."

Misty smiled. "Jordin, she can be sweet and then there are those days when she's just intent on having her own way." She glanced over her shoulder. "I'm pretty sure you'll find Talei somewhere near Leon."

The three women were talking about motherhood when another woman joined them.

"This is Garland. She's married to our cousin Ryker."

Misty embraced her.

"It's nice to meet you. I've heard great things about you, Misty. Eleanor raves about your baking skills. She also says you're a great cook, but that baking is your gift."

"You're the chair for the Children's Festival in Charleston. I remember Brittany mentioning your name. I was on the planning committee for the one we had here in August."

"I've worked with Brittany—lovely girl. I read that the festival was very successful."

"It was," Misty responded. "I really enjoyed being a part of the event."

Jadin introduced Misty to her parents.

Misty enjoyed meeting members of Leon's extended family. She was curious how Leon felt about meeting her father. She was working toward forgiving Mike and hoped that he and

Leon would be able to forge some type of relationship.

She shook off all negative thoughts. She and Leon would soon start a new life together—everything was going to work out.

When Leon gestured for her to join him, Misty slipped on her engagement ring.

"Misty and I love family and we wanted to bring all of you together," he said after everyone had gotten their plates and had settled down to eat.

He pulled Misty into his embrace, and then continued. "We wanted to share the news that we're getting married."

Everyone around them cheered and applauded.

Eleanor hugged Leon, then Misty. "I'm so happy for you both. This is what I've been praying for—that you both would find real love—one that would last a lifetime."

Talei ran up to them. "I getting married, too."

Leon bent down to her level. "Who are you marrying?"

"You."

He kissed her cheek, picked her up and said, "I have been doubly blessed. This little lady just agreed to marry me, as well."

Jordin walked over to where they were standing. "Talei, you're absolutely adorable."

"I'm so happy you, Jadin and your parents

were all able to come," Misty said. "We appreciate it."

Leon agreed.

Jadin joined them. "I spoke with my parents and they agreed to renovating the house and making it a summer retreat once again. Looks like you'll be seeing us more, especially me and Jordin. We love the beach. I've been spending time on Jekyll, but this is a family home."

"And we have so many wonderful memories on this island," Jordin interjected.

"That's great news." Leon glanced across the room. "You have to tell Aunt Eleanor. She's going to be ecstatic."

"She told me about her diagnosis. My mom took it pretty bad."

"Her mother was named after my aunt," Leon explained to Misty. "So, they're pretty close."

"Today was a great day," Misty said after everyone left and they were cleaning up. The last person had gone home an hour ago.

"It really was," Leon agreed.

"I noticed that you were a bit distant with my dad."

He looked at her. "After hearing how badly he treated you, Misty, it's going to take some time for me to warm up to him. I enjoyed your grandmother, though. She doesn't bite her tongue at all."

"No, she doesn't," Misty said. "As for my dad, we'll both take it one day at a time."

Leon kissed her cheek. "I'm willing to give him a chance. I believe everyone deserves a second chance, but I don't like the way he treated you and your mother."

"That's one of the reasons I love you so much."

EPILOGUE

Eighteen months later

LEON STARED IN awe at the two-day-old infant in his arms.

"He's beautiful, isn't he?" Misty touched her husband's arm.

He was speechless, too overcome with emotion to offer a response.

"Leon…" she prompted.

"We have a son. A very healthy little boy."

Smiling, she responded, "Yes, we do."

"I never thought I'd have another child," Leon said, fighting back tears. "I love Talei like my own—you know that. When Selena died… I just didn't think I'd ever have a family. I couldn't see it at the time. This is the one thing I've always wanted—a wife and children."

Oma entered the room with Talei. "She wanted to visit with Leo."

Leon waited until the little girl was seated in the armchair before placing the baby in her arms.

"He's so cute," Talei murmured. "I love him." She scrunched up her face, then grinned. "I love you, Dad."

Leon's heart warmed at her declaration. "I love you, too."

He enjoyed watching Talei with her baby brother. His heart was full beyond measure.

"I'm going to finish preparing dinner," Oma stated.

"Thank you," Leon said.

"Dad, it's *wado*," Talei told him.

Amused, Leon responded, "Yes, ma'am, little one."

Leon took Talei to the park to play while Misty and the baby were napping. He enjoyed being a father and looked forward to raising his children to adulthood. However, he didn't want them growing up too fast. He and Misty wanted their kids to enjoy being children—something they both missed out on.

"I have two daddies," Talei announced. "Daddy in heaven and you."

"You're a very lucky girl," Leon said. "Because we both love you dearly."

"We have a baby."

He chuckled. "Yes, we do."

"I wanna hold my brother when we get home. I won't hurt him."

"I'm not worried about that. You're a big girl and I know how much you love Leo. If he's awake, you can spend some time with him. Okay?"

Talei smiled. "Okay."

They left the park and stopped to visit with Eleanor before heading home.

"*Osiyo*, Auntie," Talei greeted. "Uncle home?"

"He's at work, sugar. How's my big girl doing?" Eleanor asked. "You just had a birthday. You're growing up on me."

"I'm four."

Leon smiled. Talei's birthday was last month, but for Eleanor, time passed differently. A touch of sadness rose up in him, but he brushed it away as quickly as it had come. She was still so full of life—he cherished every moment he had with her.

OMA HAD DINNER ready when they returned to the house.

They gathered at the dining room table to eat as a family. Leon hadn't expected Misty to join them. He'd had her mother prepare a plate and was in the process of placing it on a tray when she strolled into the kitchen.

"Sweetheart, why don't you go back to bed. You just had a baby."

"Leon, I'm a little sore, but I'm not sick. It won't hurt me to sit and have dinner with my family. I can't just lie around in bed. I need to move around."

"I wanna say the grace," Talei stated.

"Go for it, little one."

Her head bowed down, she said, "Our Father, thank you for our food we eat. Thank you for your love. We love you, too. Amen."

"Good job, sweetie."

Grinning, Talei picked up her fork and dived into the macaroni and cheese.

Leon glanced at Misty and smiled. The day that little girl had come into his life, he was forever changed.

As promised, Talei was allowed to not only hold Leo, but she was also able to feed him after her mother pumped breast milk in a bottle.

When it was time for bed, Leon tucked Talei in for the night. His eyes traveled to the framed photo of him and John on the nightstand. The other photo was of Misty.

"That's you and Daddy."

"Yes, it is," Leon said, picking up the picture. "He was a good friend."

"Do you miss him?"

He nodded. "I do. I miss John a lot."

"Me, too." Talei sat up in bed. "Sometimes

he visits me in my dreams. He told me that he was happy that you're my dad now."

Leon believed that if there was a way possible for John to visit with his daughter, he would do it. "I promised him that I'd take care of you."

Talei sat up and took his hand. "I like my baby brother, Dad. Can I have a baby sister, too? I want her for Christmas."

Leon chuckled. "I think we have to ask Mommy about that."

Oma entered the bedroom. "I promised Talei a glass of warm milk and a bedtime story."

"I'll leave you to it," he said after planting a kiss on her forehead. "Good night, little one."

Leon returned to the bedroom just as Misty had finished changing the baby. "You need anything?" he asked.

"We're fine," she responded. "Especially this little sleepyhead. He fell asleep in the middle of my changing him."

Misty repositioned the pillows behind her. "Did Talei go down without a fuss?"

"Pretty much. You mom brought her some warm milk to help her sleep," Leon said. "Oh, Talei just told me that she wants a baby sister for Christmas." He took the sleeping baby from Misty and placed him in the bassinet at the foot of their bed.

"As in seven months from now?"

He nodded. "Yes."

"Our little girl is about to experience her first Christmas disappointment," Misty said. "There's no way we can accomplish that. I'm not even willing to try."

"Maybe we can consider it in a year," Leon suggested.

Misty nodded. "I'm good with that. She'll be in school."

Leon sat down on the chaise to remove his shoes. He padded barefoot to the bathroom and took a shower.

Ten minutes later, he climbed into bed beside his wife.

"*Wado, adali'i.* You've given me such a beautiful gift."

Misty broke into a smile. "Have you been taking lessons from Mama?"

"I wanted to know how to say *wife* in Cherokee."

"What else did you learn?"

"*Gvgeyu'i.*"

Misty kissed him, then whispered, "I love you, too."

Leon was still awake long after she had fallen asleep. He slipped out of bed and went to check on Talei, who was sleeping soundly. The light in the guest room was still on, so he assumed Oma was still up, but he didn't disturb her.

He returned to his bedroom and eased back into bed, careful not to disturb Misty.

Leon had everything he wanted—a job he loved, a beautiful wife and two adorable children. The shadows across his heart were completely gone. He no longer feared losing those he loved so fiercely. Having experienced so much loss, Leon recognized how fleeting life could be, so he vowed to live and love each day as if it were his last.

"You can't sleep?"

"What are you doing awake?" Leon asked. "Leo will be wanting to nurse soon."

Misty sat up in bed. "What's going on? Why can't you sleep?"

"I think I'm just excited about what the future holds for us. We've both weathered terrible storms—we've walked through the fire and we're better for it. I was afraid to love someone again, but you and Talei changed that—you changed me."

"Your love saved me, Leon," Misty said. "I never thought I'd meet a man like you. You came into my life during a difficult time. You didn't try to rush things between us. You allowed me to grow."

Leon pulled her close to him. "From this moment forward, our life will be a blaze of love, laughter and memories to last a lifetime."

Snuggling against him, Misty whispered, "And the firefighter and his lady lived happily ever after."

* * * * *

Get 4 FREE REWARDS!

We'll send you 2 FREE Books plus 2 FREE Mystery Gifts.

Love Inspired books feature uplifting stories where faith helps guide you through life's challenges and discover the promise of a new beginning.

FREE
Value Over
$20

YES! Please send me 2 FREE Love Inspired Romance novels and my 2 FREE mystery gifts (gifts are worth about $10 retail). After receiving them, if I don't wish to receive any more books, I can return the shipping statement marked "cancel." If I don't cancel, I will receive 6 brand-new novels every month and be billed just $5.24 each for the regular-print edition or $5.99 each for the larger-print edition in the U.S., or $5.74 each for the regular-print edition or $6.24 each for the larger-print edition in Canada. That's a savings of at least 13% off the cover price. It's quite a bargain! Shipping and handling is just 50¢ per book in the U.S. and $1.25 per book in Canada.* I understand that accepting the 2 free books and gifts places me under no obligation to buy anything. I can always return a shipment and cancel at any time. The free books and gifts are mine to keep no matter what I decide.

Choose one: ☐ **Love Inspired Romance Regular-Print** (105/305 IDN GNWC) ☐ **Love Inspired Romance Larger-Print** (122/322 IDN GNWC)

Name (please print)

Address   Apt. #

City   State/Province   Zip/Postal Code

Email: Please check this box ☐ if you would like to receive newsletters and promotional emails from Harlequin Enterprises ULC and its affiliates. You can unsubscribe anytime.

Mail to the Harlequin Reader Service:
IN U.S.A.: P.O. Box 1341, Buffalo, NY 14240-8531
IN CANADA: P.O. Box 603, Fort Erie, Ontario L2A 5X3

Want to try 2 free books from another series! Call 1-800-873-8635 or visit www.ReaderService.com.

Get 4 **FREE REWARDS!**

We'll send you 2 FREE Books plus 2 FREE Mystery Gifts.

Love Inspired Suspense books showcase how courage and optimism unite in stories of faith and love in the face of danger.

HARLEQUIN SELECTS COLLECTION

19 FREE BOOKS IN ALL!

From Robyn Carr to RaeAnne Thayne to Linda Lael Miller and Sherryl Woods we promise (actually, GUARANTEE!) each author in the Harlequin Selects collection has seen their name on the *New York Times* or *USA TODAY* bestseller lists!

YES! Please send me the **Harlequin Selects Collection**. This collection begins with 3 FREE books and 2 FREE gifts in the first shipment. Along with my 3 free books, I'll also get 4 more books from the Harlequin Selects Collection, which I may either return and owe nothing or keep for the low price of $24.14 U.S./$28.82 CAN. each plus $2.99 U.S./$7.49 CAN. for shipping and handling per shipment*.If I decide to continue, I will get 6 or 7 more books (about once a month for 7 months) but will only need to pay for 4. That means 2 or 3 books in every shipment will be FREE! If I decide to keep the entire collection, I'll have paid for only 32 books because 19 were FREE! I understand that accepting the 3 free books and gifts places me under no obligation to buy anything. I can always return a shipment and cancel at any time. My free books and gifts are mine to keep no matter what I decide.

☐ 262 HCN 5576   ☐ 462 HCN 5576

Name (please print)

Address   Apt. #

City   State/Province   Zip/Postal Code

Mail to the Harlequin Reader Service:
IN U.S.A.: P.O. Box 1341, Buffalo, NY 14240-8531
IN CANADA: P.O. Box 603, Fort Erie, Ontario L2A 5X3

*Terms and prices subject to change without notice. Prices do not include sales taxes, which will be charged (if applicable) based on your state or country of residence. Canadian residents will be charged applicable taxes. Offer not valid in Quebec. All orders subject to approval. Credit or debit balances in a customer's account(s) may be offset by any other outstanding balance owed by or to the customer. Please allow 3 to 4 weeks for delivery. Offer available while quantities last. © 2020 Harlequin Enterprises ULC. ® and ™ are trademarks owned by Harlequin Enterprises ULC.

Your Privacy—Your information is being collected by Harlequin Enterprises ULC, operating as Harlequin Reader Service. To see how we collect and use this information visit https://corporate.harlequin.com/privacy-notice. From time to time we may also exchange your personal information with reputable third parties. If you wish to opt out of this sharing of your personal information, please visit www.readerservice.com/consumerschoice or call 1-800-873-8635. Notice to California Residents—Under California law, you have specific rights to control and access your data. For more information visit https://corporate.harlequin.com/california-privacy.

50BOOKHS22R

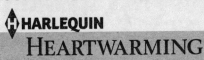
#379 CAUGHT BY THE COWBOY DAD
The Mountain Monroes • by Melinda Curtis

Holden Monroe and Bea Carlisle are hoping a road trip will give them time alone for a second chance—but it's a special Old West town they happen upon that helps them rediscover their spark!

#380 THE TEXAN'S SECRET SON
Truly Texas • by Kit Hawthorne

Single mom Nina Walker is shocked to see Marcos Ramirez again. Especially since her ex-husband has no idea he's a father to a son! Will the Texas rancher forgive her and finally claim his family?

#381 A FOURTH OF JULY PROPOSAL
Cupid's Crossing • by Kim Findlay

Former bad boy Ryker Slade came home to sell his father's house, then he'll leave. Instead he finds a connection with the pastor's daughter, Rachel Lowther. But Rachel also plans to leave town—unless Ryker gives her a reason to stay...

#382 THE MAN FROM MONTANA
Hearts of Big Sky • by Julianna Morris

Tessa Alderman has questions about her twin sister's death in a white water rafting accident, at the same time she's drawn to the man who may have the answers...Clay Carson.

Visit
ReaderService.com
Today!

As a valued member of the Harlequin Reader Service, you'll find these benefits and more at ReaderService.com:

- Try 2 free books from any series
- Access risk-free special offers
- View your account history & manage payments
- Browse the latest Bonus Bucks catalog